# THE BLACK MAGE

## First Year

### RACHEL E. CARTER

Clean Reads
www.cleanreads.com

# Where it all began...

*To Kitty & Shells,*

*You made me a writer. Before everything, there was the two of you. All the books, the music, the talks, the years of writing and dreaming... they all lead back to you.*

*Shells —There will always be Eden's Crush, Final Fantasy, and your parents' house. I can't guess the hours we spent plotting away —and it was you who always kept me going when the writing got tough. I can't wait to read your novels someday, and I am so happy to have you in my life.*

*Kitty —Who else would listen to me rave about the "poor devil" for hours on end? I might have been crazy (and a little obsessed) but you believed in me anyway. It was our stories that led me to write this book in the first place —and without you there would be no Darren. J&D 4 Eva.*

*To Christina,*

*Unlike the other two, you never had a choice. Yet you supported me always. Thank you for listening to years of stories-that-never-got-written and Savage Garden on repeat. Some day when I write about the dinosaurs, you will be the first to know. I love you and you are the best sister one could ever have (even if I don't always acknowledge that)!*

*To Darren Hayes,*

*You are my muse. Thanks for years of amazing music. And, yes, I named my favorite character after the best artist of all time. It was either that or my firstborn child, and this book came first.*

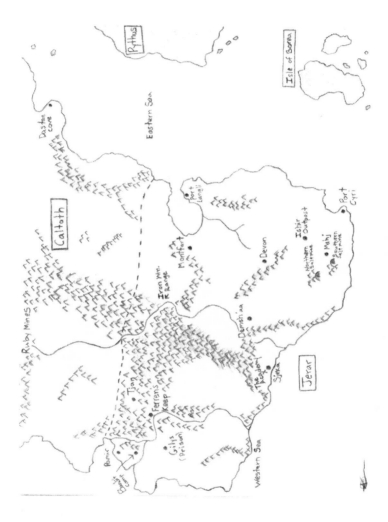

# CHAPTER ONE

"Don't look now," I said softly. *Did I sound calm?* I hoped so. It was hard to tell with the frantic beating in my chest. "But I think we are being followed."

My brother paled, hands freezing on the reins. Almost unconsciously, his head began to turn in the direction of my warning.

"Alex!" I hissed.

He jerked his head back guiltily. I hoped the movement would go unnoticed by the four riders trailing a quarter of a mile behind us. They hadn't appeared too concerned with our procession thus far, but the fact that the men were still following us after the last main road had ended left an unsettling taste in the back of my mouth.

It was getting dark fast. At the elevation we were traveling, there wouldn't be much light left for long. Already the sun had wedged itself behind one of the larger outcroppings of rock, and the rest of its rays were fading much too quickly for my liking.

I had hoped the party would stop to make camp at one of the few sites we had passed—after all, what weary traveler wouldn't prefer the comfort of a well-worn pit and nearby stream? I, for one, would have insisted as much if it hadn't been for the uncanny appearance of those behind us.

"How do you know they are 'following' us?" Alex whispered loudly. Our horses continued their steady climb into the dark hillside. "Shouldn't we be stopping soon?" he added. "I'm sure they'll continue on, and then you'll see your worry was all for nothing."

"Alex," I said through clenched teeth, "their saddlebags are far too light for a trek like this. That's not *nothing*."

"So?"

I forced myself not to let my frustration show. It wasn't Alex's fault he didn't understand my concern. His faction was Restoration. He cared about healing people, not what it looked like to harm them.

"Only fools—or bandits—would travel so empty-handed. Four grown men are not fools, Alex. Even fools would have known to take that last main road to an inn..." I swallowed. "But a bandit, they wouldn't need to bother with packs since, well, because they would be taking our own instead."

My twin slowly mulled over my words. I wondered if he would believe me. I wasn't exactly known for my easygoing temperament. I hoped he didn't think this was just another one of my "rash judgments" as our parents were wont to assume.

As I waited for Alex's response, I pretended to check the footholds, giving myself an opportunity to spy on our shadow once more. Though the men were much harder to identify without the broad light of day, there was still no mistaking the glint of steel bulging from one of the men's hips. Only a soldier or knight was allowed to bear such metal.

A chill ran through me. I doubted he was either.

"Right," Alex said abruptly.

In as much nonchalance as one could muster under the circumstances, I faced my brother stubbornly. "Alex—"

"I believe you."

*Oh.* I paused.

"What should we do, Ry?" Gone was his relaxed smile, and in its place a timid frown...and an unsure, flickering blue stare. At first I didn't recognize the expression—he looked so much younger than his fifteen years. But then I realized it was fear producing the vulnerability in my brother's eyes.

My twin, the rational, levelheaded, sane half of me, was afraid. What did that mean for the two of us? I refused to contemplate the answer. Instead, I scanned the trail ahead, trying to make out our intended route amid the lumbering pines.

Unfortunately, it was much easier to point out the problem than come up with a solution.

*We should have taken the main road,* I acknowledged belatedly. *If I hadn't been so set on the fastest route to the Academy, we would be on a nice, well-traveled path instead of a desolate mountain range, about to be robbed.*

But it was too late now.

"Ryiah?"

I bit my lip. Alex was looking to me for an answer. This was, after all, my forte. What had I told my parents before we left home? I would join Combat or die trying.

A fine choice of words. What had been meant as a melodramatic proclamation was now to be my intended irony. I could not fight our way out of this. Not against four grown, arms-holding men. Not without magic.

For the millionth time I silently questioned the gods' motive in my inability to cast. But this wasn't the time to sulk in my inadequacies. I needed to pick a plan fast.

I peered into the trees, straining to see any sort of upcoming detour. If we could find a way to circle back, lose the men in a chase, and then return to the main road... Or maybe lose them in hiding, taking cover under darkness and then move out again at first light?

Perhaps Alex was right, and the men would just carry on. We could just set up camp here and now and be none the worse.

*Yes, and pigs might fly,* I scolded myself. *You want to be a warrior mage, and yet you shirk at the first sign of danger.*

I *do not* shirk.

"When I say 'go,'" I whispered, sidling as close to Alex as my own mount could manage, "I want you to take off west. I'll head east—"

Alex opened his mouth to protest, and I hushed him.

"We have to split up. Staying together would only increase their chance of catching us."

My brother stared me down defiantly. "I am *not* leaving you, Ry."

I ignored him. "We can meet up at that tavern we passed earlier just before the fork... If...If one of us isn't there within a couple hours of daylight, then we hire the local guard to help search out the other. It might take a little longer if we are on foot." I swallowed. "Local thugs don't usually kill unless someone puts up a fight." At least that's what I'd heard.

"But what if they—"

"They won't," I said.

He shook his head stubbornly. "If they find out you're a *girl*—"

I looked my brother in the eye. "It's our best bet, Alex. If you stay with me, you will not be helping either one of us."

Alex swore. "Ryiah, I don't like this plan one bit."

I motioned for him to get ready, and leaned forward to stand in the stirrups with both hands gripped firmly to the horse's mane. Alex copied my movements, and as soon as he was in a similar stance, I nodded.

"*Now!*"

In a cloud of rising dirt and debris, my charge took off at a breathless gallop. The thundering clash of hooves and the cries of surprise from the party behind us left me with an elated sense of victory. We had managed to catch them off-guard.

As tempting as it was to check their progress, I kept my eyes glued to the forest in front of me. Dark, twisting branches struck out at my face and ripped across my skin. Harsh wind tore at my already-chapped lips. I willed myself to ignore the numbing cold and sudden, jarring cuts from above.

I hoped Alex was having better luck in his bit of the woods. I could barely see five feet in front of me and had to rely on the mare for navigation. Now that she knew our general direction, it was up to her to avoid what I could not.

The subtle whistle of steel slicing through air alerted me a second too late. One of the men's blades flew past, nicking the back of my right thigh in its course. I cried out and then immediately regretted the noise.

The wound felt shallow, but it was still sudden and biting enough for me to lose balance. I fell back against the saddle, and the mare startled at the sudden shift in weight, slowing her gallop to a canter. I hastily moved to correct the error, ignoring the added pressure on my leg as I attempted to crouch once more in the stirrups and return her to speed.

At that same moment the mare stumbled over some loose footing and sent me pitching forward. My hands, slick with sweat, lost hold of her mane, and I was sent careening to the ground. I barely registered what was happening before I hit the dirt with a sickening thud. I had only a fraction of a second to roll before hooves came clamoring past.

The mare took off into the darkness. I attempted to stand and ignore the shaking of my legs. My entire right side ached, and I had new cuts on my hands from trying to brace my fall. I wondered if the hammering in my ears was from the pulsing of blood or the approaching of bandits.

Maybe they hadn't seen me fall. Maybe they still thought I was astride. It was dark enough. I scrambled to my feet, ignoring the stabbing pains as I stumbled toward the nearest brush. I took a couple of hobbling steps until the hammering gave way to the shouts of men and the unmistakable sounds of heavy footfall.

The bandits had dismounted and were searching the area.

I ducked under the bush, ignoring the many thorns that raked across my face and arms, and prayed that the loud snapping of branches was just a quiet rustle outside my head.

Burrowing as deep as I dared, I waited. My breath was shaky and ragged, and I tried not to imagine all the horrible possibilities that could await me if I were found. I willed myself to breathe slowly, letting my racing heart ease. It was no use.

I could hear their voices. They were getting louder. A flutter of soft wind brought the rancid smell of days' old sweat and ale, and I wondered how close they were. The bush I hid under smelled oddly sweet, like some sort of forest berry. I hoped its leaves would hide me well.

*How many had followed me?* I wondered. *Where was Alex right now? Was he still riding west?* I strained to hear the approaching voices.

"...Saw the boy limping..." one was saying.

Another man cleared his throat. "He couldn't have gone far."

There were only two that I could distinguish. If there were a third man, he was staying silent. Judging from the number of footsteps, however, I was inclined to go with the former.

The crunching of pine needles a mere step away froze my heart in my throat.

One of the men was right beside the bush. I could hear the shuffling of feet against some of the outlying roots. I made a silent prayer to the gods that he would continue on.

"I reckon he went the other way, Jared," the man said. "There's nothing this way but brush."

"Naw, he's got to be this way."

The voices were now both coming from the same spot just above me. My pulse pounded so violently I was certain they could hear it. I refused to breathe as I waited for them to pass.

"Smells good out here," the first was saying.

"It's the blackberries, you dolt," the second man, Jared, replied. He shoved a hand in to grasp at a dark clumping of fruit and pulled it back back with a curse: "Fool thorns!"

The other man pushed past and reached in further, managing to catch a hand full of berries and my hair in the process. I didn't realize some of it had come loose from my braid, tangled in the thorns until the man yanked his fist back. As the hair ripped from my scalp an unwilling cry escaped my lips.

I slapped a hand over my mouth, but it was too late. They had heard me.

The next second flew past in a blur as the men yanked me from my den and tossed me roughly to the bare forest ground at their feet.

"Well, well," Jared drawled. "Seems your appetite has it uses, Erwan." He slapped the second man, a tall fellow with a big gut and muddy boots, on the back.

It was hard to see either of their faces as I struggled to push myself up off the ground. The bandits allowed me to draw myself onto my knees, making crude remarks and laughing as I fumbled once or twice before finally sitting upright.

"Now, boy," said Erwan. "Tell us where you and your little friend were headed."

I breathed a small sigh of relief. With all the blood and grime covering my brother's riding clothes they had mistaken me for a redheaded young man. The tunic was baggy, and though ripped at the arms, it still hid my form well.

I stayed silent, unwilling to answer for fear that my voice would reveal what my clothes did not.

"The man asked you a question," Jared growled. "Answer him."

Silence. And then the loud, resounding slap as Jared's palm struck my cheek. My face stung and bled in places the thorns had already opened.

"Now," Jared said. "I'll give you one more chance to answer before I start removing limbs." The bandit was holding a sword. It bore the familiar crest of the Crown's Army. But this man was no soldier. No man who pledged to defend Jerar and its people would dishonor the Code of Honor.

I wondered how the weapon had fallen into the outlaw's hands. Had his band cornered a lonely soldier on some deserted trail and robbed him blind, much like they were planning to do to my brother and me? Or had Jared killed him to prevent the soldier from seeking justice afterward?

There was an odd stain on the hilt, much like the rusty color of blood. Bile rose in my throat, and I forced myself to swallow it back down. In the gruffest voice I could manage, I coughed, "The Academy."

Jared's eyes glittered dangerously.

"Did he just say—"

"The Academy?" Jared nudged my face with his boot. "You an apprentice, boy?" He was studying my face closely.

The large man, Erwan, laughed loudly. "Some mage! Where's your magic?"

My face burned and I looked away.

"So you are one of the first-years, then," Jared surmised. His expression turned from interest to disgust. "The boy's no use. Just another village kid on his way to that blasted school. Fools, always thinking they have a gift when they should be doing real work instead."

I kept quiet, hoping the men would dismiss me as worthless and continue on in pursuit of the mare.

"Boy, did you travel with purse?"

Not much. Our parents had barely been able to afford the coin it had cost to lease the horses for the five-day journey as it was. Though the Academy was to provide a year of free room and board to each of its students, it still hadn't been enough to offset the labor Alex and I had provided in the apothecary.

I cringed, thinking of how much we would be setting the family back when one of those horses was never returned.

"The purse w-was in the saddlebags."

"Erwan, go find his horse," Jared ordered. As the stodgy outlaw began to take off in the general direction of the mare, the swallow-faced criminal kicked my stomach. "Get up, boy. You are going to help make camp until the others return. If you remain on good behavior, my companions and I will let you go once we have passed the night. If you try to run or any sort of trickery, I will not hesitate to use the sword."

I gingerly pulled myself up, trying not to let the man see how much it hurt to stand.

I refused to give him the satisfaction.

⚜

Hours later Erwan returned with my mare and a handful of logs. Shivering, I quickly obeyed Jared's orders to fetch them and build up the fire. In my condition I hadn't been able to gather more than a handful at a time, and so the flames we'd had hadn't amounted to much. It may have been a summer night, but up in the mountains encased in pine, it was hard to tell.

As I slowly arranged the wood, I strained to catch the men's conversation.

"Halseth? He still hasn't...?"

"No. Either way, he and Carl should be back within the hour."

"Do you think they caught the other?"

"I don't see why not." Jared spat at the ground, and his gaze fell to me. "You, boy, who was that friend you were traveling with?"

*No.* "J-just some boy, only met him this morn'," I croaked, attempting the same baritone as before.

"You are lying." Jared narrowed his eyes. "Tell me the truth. Is he another worthless brat like you, or does he have power?" His eyes gleamed over that last word. Power. *Magic.*

"I d-don't believe so—"

Before I could finish the lie, the man grabbed my wrist and thrust my hand into the fire. I screamed out as the flames licked my skin.

Jared let go, dropping my wrist as quickly as he had snatched it.

Blinking back tears I cradled my hand, careful not to touch the skin. It had turned a nasty, glistening red. It burned, and even though it had only been under fire for seconds, it felt as if it hadn't left.

"Well, well..."

I glanced up at the men, hate burning in my veins, and Jared shot me a secretive smile.

Panic struck my throat as I realized exactly what it meant.

*He knew.*

"Why don't you go collect us some more wood, Erwan?" Jared's eyes never left my face. "I would go myself, but someone's got to watch the boy."

Erwan shot Jared a confused look. "I just brought a whole lot of it—"

Jared snapped, "Just fetch us more wood, you dolt."

As soon as the large man had retired from sight, the bandit turned to face me, hunger playing across his malevolent gaze. Shadows from the fire leaped and danced, making the narrow chin, the long blond tresses, every inch of the swallow-faced man all the more menacing.

"Who would have thought?" he sneered. "A girl. And here I said no trickery when you were intending to play us all along."

I glanced around the site, desperate for an escape. *If I ran now, would I make it far?* I couldn't fight in the condition I was in. I'd only tussled with local children, never a full-grown man. I might be able to wrestle a boy my brother's size, but not someone a good foot taller and fifty pounds heavier.

Jared took a step closer, fingering the scabbard at his hip. "Now if you don't put up a fuss, I might be willing to forgive you."

Terror. Hate. Anger. Rage. The emotions all raced through me in a coursing panic. Bile filled my throat once more as sweat and fear drenched my skin. I tried to step back and tripped, both hands slamming the ground behind me. I cried out as the burned skin collided with hard earth, extreme pain and heat searing into my arm.

Jared leaped at me, flattening both wrists with his hands as his knees pinned my legs.

*I will not scream.*

The man bent low, breathing a foul, sour stench as he thrust his lips on mine. I threw my head forward and up, slamming it into his nose. Jared jerked back too late. There was a satisfying crunch and then the thick spray of blood.

"You insolent wench!" The man released my arm and struck my face, making me see nothing but black until my sight returned seconds later.

My face stung, but it was nothing compared to the pain in my hand as he dug his nails into the burn. Tears swarmed my vision, and I wished desperately I had found a way to access my magic. *Like Alex.*

Jared reached for the top of my tunic, and I swung my free arm as hard as it could reach. The man caught it, and I threw my weight into his hold, hoping to catch him off balance.

My act failed, and he sent me sprawling back, slapping me much harder than the last. I prepared for familiar darkness and was shocked instead when golden hues flooded my vision.

I barely registered my shock before the screaming started. I thought it was mine, but it was coming from the wrong direction.

I wondered if my hearing had been damaged.

The stifling pressure and golden glow released its hold. Nothing was keeping me down.

Scrambling in the aftershock, I attempted to pull myself from the ground, squinting uncertainly at the blinding light, trying to make sense of what had just taken place.

An immense pounding filled my head as I continued to stand and stare. The screams were like birdcalls, high and sharp. They kept going and going, and they hurt my ears. I clasped my hands to my mouth in an effort to end the noise.

But my lips were shut. The cries were coming from the shimmering thing in front of me.

All at once my vision cleared, and I saw it was Jared. He was enshrouded in flame, fire eating away at flesh and cloth in a frantic inferno. Somehow, someway he had been set entirely ablaze. And the screaming...it was his.

Without bothering to witness the outcome, I hobbled past the shrieking figure and undid my mare's lead. Her eyes were wide and afraid. I prayed she wouldn't try to bolt. She was still saddled, and all of the supplies were still in their bags.

I made swift thanks to whatever luck had led me to this moment and did my best to ignore the pain as I used my bad hand to steady my grip at the back of the saddle while my good one gripped the front. Swinging my leg up and over, I was unable to mask the groan that escaped my lips. Every inch of me smarted.

Giving the mare a reassuring pat that I hoped was more calming to her than it was to me, I nudged her forward with my knees.

"What is— Get back here, boy!"

Erwan had returned. He still sounded far enough away, however, and so I leaned down, painstakingly, and undid the other two horses' leads.

*Try to catch me now.*

As soon as my work was finished, I forced myself into a crouching posture. I dug my heels in and whooped, letting my charge take off as the other two started and scattered.

⚓

Twenty minutes later I came across another galloping party. It was too dark to see clearly, but there were only three who could possibly be roaming this road at night. And I could not wait to find out which.

Pulling at the reins sharply, I steered my horse into a hard turn, taking off in a different direction.

"Ryiah, is that you?" the other rider shouted.

This time I turned the mare with much more ease, answering my brother's call with one of my own. "Alex!" Then: "Where are the others?"

"I lost them a couple miles back by the river. They think I am following the stream south. Where are your two?"

"They don't have their horses."

It was too dark to see Alex's face, but I guessed he was grinning. "I'd like to hear *that* tale."

I swallowed, uncomfortably aware of my pain and the searing heat of my hand. My brother would faint when he saw me in the light. "Alex," I said quietly, "we have to keep going through the night. We won't be safe until we are through this pass."

"I know." He paused. "But let's take the rest of the trail at a walk. If either of us hears something, we can take off, but these horses need a break. I can barely see in this awful darkness…" He chuckled. "I don't know about you, but I have almost fallen off twice tonight and am not willing to test my luck."

I knew better than to comment. "Let's head out" was all I said.

My brother let me lead –I had a better head for directions- and the two of us quietly found our way back to the main path without further delay.

After another hour of hushed passage, we finally left the shadows of the forest behind and continued the remainder of our journey underneath the moon's soft glow and the occasional glitter of starlight.

Fortunately, we were both too exhausted for Alex to notice any abnormality in my appearance. Instead, the two of us remained silently alert, using the remainder of our energy to listen for any sounds of others approaching.

But we did not have to worry. Not once did we cross paths with the outlaws. And several hours later, just as the sun had risen, we came to a very welcome sight. Just beyond the way, a large, homely looking inn stood out among the hills like a god among men.

Alex took off with a hoot, and I launched into chase close behind, eyes glued to the vision ahead.

# CHAPTER TWO

All I wanted to do was sleep.

But that was clearly the last thing from my twin's agenda.

"How could you not tell me the moment you saw me?" Alex cried.

I should have known. He hadn't bothered to glance at me once in his gleeful approach of the inn. But as soon as he had dismounted, his enthusiasm had faded in the light of the many scratches, bruises, and blood that mottled my skin.

And then he noticed my hand. One giant, swelling blister of a palm that had only grown worse in the hours since I had last looked at it. Angry burn marks dotted my fingers like unsightly patches, and the pain was just as bad.

"It was more important to get to safety first!"

"Safety?" Alex snapped. "Don't use that *Combat* nonsense with me, Ryiah. 'Safety' would have been letting me heal you. And what happened? I thought you said—"

"I didn't say anything because I didn't want to make you upset!"

Alex made a face. "I believe I have a right to know what happened to my sister!"

"Alex, please," I begged. The last thing I needed was him raging about after he heard the tale. "Not here. Not now...tomorrow, when we are both feeling better."

19

Alex glowered. "Fine. One day of rest. And then *you will tell me what happened.*"

I put my hands on my hips. "Careful, if you keep acting like that, people will start to say *you* are the hotheaded one."

His cheeks reddened, embarrassed. "Sorry 'bout that," he mumbled. He looked anywhere but my face. "It's just, well, you *are* my sister."

The two of us entered the inn, and while I began to count our coin, Alex went ahead and found its keeper. He set to work ordering our room and a bath. Eyeing a loitering maidservant nearby, he added on a list of common salves to be brought to us at once. Then he winked.

The flustered girl scurried off, seemingly torn between confusion and intrigue. I knew what she was thinking.

Women all took to my brother the same.

While Alex and I were the same age, that was where the similarities began and ended for us. I was somewhat gangly and awkward whereas he was assured and confident.

He was also a good three inches taller, and with broad shoulders I envied. No matter how hard *I* trained, my build remained stubbornly slim. Alex, on the other hand, gained muscle at the slightest effort. He also had our parents' soft brown locks and easy blue eyes that girls, including many of my friends back home, found "handsome."

And it was those eyes that had won him many an admirer. Well, that and his humor. My eyes were blue too, but they were so light it was more common to think of them as gray than anything else. Take into account my quick temper, and it was no wonder people did not take to me the same.

In a lot of ways I was more like my younger brother Derrick than my twin.

The second Alex had finished cleansing my wounds, he gave me a wry smile. "You are not going to like this next part," he warned.

I nodded absentmindedly.

My twin pressed two fingers to my burnt palm. The added pressure stung sharply, and my pain flared. It seemed to go on for ages. I bit my tongue. A mage of Combat would not cry out and so neither would I.

The ache continued to build for another minute, almost unbearably, and then it suddenly ebbed, a trickle of coolness seeping out and enveloping my hand.

Alex kept the pressure steady until my pain had completely subsided, and then got up to grab the tray the serving maid had left behind.

My brother filled a warm glass with water and mixed it with salt. He poured the mixture over my skin. It wasn't a pleasant sensation, but more tolerable than before. He dabbed the inflamed flesh with a cold poultice a few seconds longer, and then spread a bit of honey over the top, wrapping my hand in a thin cloth when he was satisfied.

"Now I've taken the heat out of the burn," Alex said, "so you should not feel quite as much hurt."

"Thank you."

Alex shook his head. "It's a shame this couldn't have happened *after* we started the Academy. If it had, I'd be able to do a lot more than this. You are still going to have to let the rest of those cuts heal naturally."

I waved his apology away. "Just be lucky you have magic, brother. In two days' time I am going to be made the biggest fool in the history of that school when I walk in without the slightest whiff of magic."

Alex sighed at the familiar argument. "You *have* magic, Ry. You just haven't found it. Everyone knows twins always share it."

"But who is to say the Council's scrolls were talking about us?" For all we knew, they could have been referring to *identical* twins." I fingered my red locks, a sharp contrast to the muted brown of my brother.

We couldn't be more different there.

Alex gave my knee a reassuring pat. "Gods help us, Ry. Even if you *did* have magic, it isn't as if we have a *real* shot at the apprenticeships. We are just two lowborn kids without any formal training. Mark my words, this time next year we'll be applying to the Cavalry."

⚜

The next morning came much too soon. I had barely shut my eyes before Alex was back, shaking me awake with the reminder that we still had sixty miles of riding left, and two days to do it.

"And if we fall behind now, we'll miss the admission period," he joked.

I glared at my twin. "*Not* funny." I had said the very same two mornings before, which had led us to that overpass and the bandits in the first place.

He grinned in reply.

Grumbling, I dressed and walked the room, helping to gather the rest of the supplies until we were ready to leave. Alex handed me our breakfast as we exited the inn, the same stale bread as every meal before. I eyed it unhappily. If I never saw a piece of rye again, it would be too soon.

Leading the horses from their stable, I met my twin out front.

The two of us set to checking the fit of our straps and loading the saddlebags. Alex finished much sooner than me. He volunteered to assist, but I refused. Warriors dealt with pain every day, and now that the worst of mine was gone, I was determined to do the same.

Exhaling loudly, my twin mounted his charge, muttering about mule-headed sisters that were too stubborn for their own good.

I finished a couple minutes later, and then swung myself into the saddle, wincing. My body was still sore, but for the most part, a full day and night of rest had done me well. My ribs were only a little bit tender, and most of my wounds had closed. Even the burn on my hand, while still a glistening shade of pink, didn't sting.

It did itch, unfortunately. But I had enough sense not to scratch it. I'd learned that lesson plenty of times before.

"What I wouldn't give for some creamed porridge right now," Alex declared as we started out onto the main road.

My tongue salivated. "Or a honey bun."

Alex's stomach roared loudly in accord. The bread hadn't done very much to slake his hunger. "The first thing I'm going to ask the masters to teach me is how to conjure food—*good* food."

I raised a brow. We both knew the Academy only taught war casting. Even if he chose Restoration, they would never waste his lessons on something so silly.

"I look forward to hearing their response."

Alex chucked the last bit of his roll at me.

Laughing, I managed to catch it and then paused at his somber expression.

"So," he said, "are you ready to tell me what happened?"

I wasn't, but I was going to anyway.

I, at least, knew the truth. Alex had only my injuries and his wild imagination to explain them. If our roles had been reversed, I would have insisted as much.

I proceeded to tell him everything.

"That cowardly whelp," Alex snarled, "he deserved much worse than what he got!"

I cringed, remembering the strange turn of events. They still didn't make sense even now in retelling. How exactly *had* Jared caught fire? We had been scuffling close to the fire, but had he really been so senseless to roll his entire body in flame? Alex seemed to assume as much.

Or had the bandit fallen?

But that didn't make sense. He hadn't been standing.

In the heat of the moment I hadn't bothered to question it.

But now I wondered. Was there another explanation for what I'd seen? The others were well enough for Alex—he hadn't been there. I had though, and I couldn't shake the feeling that there was still something missing.

*Like magic.*

"Ryiah?"

I glanced at my brother. We had been riding in silence for the last couple of minutes. Now he was watching me curiously.

I stared at the grassy plains ahead of us, wondering if I should say the last thought aloud. It seemed too much to hope, and I would be aghast if it weren't. There had been a couple of times since Alex had found his own powers...but each time I had been wrong, and the disappointment had been crippling.

No. It was better left unsaid.

And then Alex said it anyway: "You think it was magic, don't you?"

*Am I really so obvious?* I flushed. "I know how it sounds mad..."

"But it makes more sense than the other explanations."

"It does!"

He was quiet. Then: "Are you sure about this?"

I played with the reins in my lap. "No. But the man didn't roll. Or fall. And he wasn't close enough to the pit for the flames to reach him."

"But didn't you lose sight when he hit you?" my brother asked gently. "He could have lost balance when you were unconscious."

"But I didn't the second time," I countered. "I'm not sure exactly how...but instead of darkness I saw light. *Lots of it.* I—I think it was from the fire, and then he was screaming and running around the camp in flames."

"Did anything feel different?" my brother pressed. "Were you unusually hot or lightheaded? Did you think of fire?"

"My hand burned, and just about everything hurt...I wasn't lightheaded exactly, but my head did really ache afterward." I paused. "And no, I was too angry and afraid to be thinking of anything except what was happening."

Alex frowned. "That doesn't sound like a casting, or at least what it's like for me..."

An idea hit me. "Do you think my pain released the magic?"

Alex appeared thoughtful. "Maybe...but then how is it that it only worked once? He hurt you several times before it occurred."

That was true, but then nothing about magic made sense. Maybe there was an answer, and I would find out at the Academy. Groping around in my bags, I eagerly pulled out my father's hunting knife.

"Ryiah," my brother yelped, "what are you—"

Ignoring Alex's cry of alarm, I dug the blade into the center of my good palm, reopening freshly sealed wounds as blood dripped down past my wrist.

At the same time I observed a yellowish-green mass that clung to a nearby tree. The moss looked like a perfect target, a furry patch of flammable tendrils.

Almost immediately the moss began to shrivel and smoke. As I pushed down with the blade, tiny flames sprouted forth, engulfing the plant.

"*ALEX!*"

My brother's jaw dropped as he followed my gaze.

I continued to add pressure, hardly conscious of pain in light of my new discovery. Blood continued to puddle below me. "*Alex, I have magic!*"

Breaking free from his initial shock, my twin rode over and snatched the knife away, giving me a dark look as he brandished the weapon.

The fire ceased immediately as what remained of the moss crumbled to the ground in a withered heap.

"Ryiah!" Alex scolded. "You shouldn't have to maim yourself to perform a casting!" Any joy he'd felt at my revelation had been lost in wake of my blood.

"I wasn't even sure I had it," I murmured. "But now…"

*Now that I* knew *I had magic…*

Staring determinedly at a nearby trunk, I willed my magic to take flight naturally. Without inflicting pain.

Nothing.

I squinted harder, ignoring the throbbing of my hand and the pounding in my head as I ogled the yellow-green mound. Every thought, every part of me strained as I attempted to project my magic onto the patch.

Still, it remained unchanged…

I tried, again and again. And again.

Eventually we had passed a whole forest of moss-lined trees with not so much as the slightest hint of fire or casting of any nature.

By the time we made camp for the evening, I was frustrated beyond measure.

"What is wrong with me?" I griped, tossing a handful of wood into our fire. "Why can't things ever come easy?"

Alex laughed loudly. "Because it's you, Ry. Nothing about your choices has ever been simple."

I made a frustrated sound. "It was never this hard for you!"

He gave me a wry smile. "True, but you haven't given yourself much of a chance, either. It took me two months just to get a handle on my magic, and I never did anything half as impressive as what you did to that outlaw." He reached out to take my hand. "Don't worry, Ry. I'm sure the masters will be able to show you how to use it without hurting yourself."

I hoped so. If not, I was in for a *very* rough year.

⚜

The next morning I was jolted awake by something that sounded oddly reminiscent of thunder. Jumping out of my bedroll, I found Alex awake beside me watching tremors on the ground beneath his feet.

"What is it?" I wondered at the same time that Alex said, "It sounds like a stampede."

I left my brother and walked over to the center of the road, trying to discern where the noise was coming from. It was right around the corner, whatever it was. In seconds I would be able to see—

"Ry, get off the path!" My twin knocked me back just in time as nine tall, slick black horses emerged, taking up the entire trail with their riders. The men were riding in a two-column formation with glistening livery that sparkled in the light.

Eight of the riders bore heavy chainmail with metal plates lining their arms and shoulders. *Knights.* The expression underneath their helmets was dark and unrelenting.

I felt a wave of nausea. If Alex hadn't pulled me out of the way, I would have been trampled to death in their wake.

At the center of the procession rode a young man who looked not much older than me. Unlike his guards, he wore no livery. Still, there was something formidable enough about him, and I had the overwhelming impression that he was anything but helpless.

Everything about the rider's dress unnerved me—his cloak, his pants, the boots, even his fastenings were black. What was even more unsettling, the stranger had the darkest eyes I'd ever seen. Matching his ink black, jaw-length locks, his garnet irises were the color of an endless night.

The stranger locked eyes with me as he spotted my brother and me in passing. He scowled, and I felt as if I had been kicked in the gut. I was used to the bizarre behavior of our nobles back home, but this rider's condescension was much deeper. *What sort of person carried that much hostility toward strangers?*

Still, I couldn't seem to look away.

It was only after the group of riders had completely passed from sight that I recalled what the young man had been wearing. Hanging by a thick chain round his neck, there had been a hematite stone pendant.

There was only one family in the entire kingdom that was allowed to wear a black gem of that description.

Apparently, I had just watched one of the realm's two princes pass me on horseback.

It took a moment for the shock to register.

"Do you know who that was?"

Alex nodded speechlessly.

"Do you think he's going to the Academy..." I paused. What was I saying? Of course, he wasn't.

No member of the royal family was allowed to participate. It had been that way since the school's founding, and in the ninety years the school had existed, no one had ever questioned the Council's ruling.

Alex seemed to be of the same mind: "There hasn't ever been an issue between our king and the mages. I doubt one would arise now."

I hesitated. "Well, that prince certainly looked unhappy about something."

My brother yawned. "Maybe someone spit in his morning tea. Who cares?" He pointed to our camp. "We've still got a full day of riding in any case. Now help me ready the horses."

⁕

When we finally finished our climb, the sun had set, and in its place was a rosy-golden hue. A soft glow chased what remained of our journey, and I followed its vague outline across the hillside below.

Tiny boxes dotted the landscape, little shops and houses at the center of Sjeka's seaside township. A well-trodden dirt path wove between them, slithering past the sparse pasture

until it finally came to rest at the base of an enormous structure.

The Academy.

Thick, dark slabs of grayish stone were placed upon one
another to produce a striking fortress. Three colored cloth ban-
ners hung from poles attached to each side of the edifice. One
for each faction: forest green, ember red, and raven black.

At either end was a looming tower that peaked out into
the night.

I swallowed. The castle was at least four stories high at
its lowest point, and every moment I stared, it seemed to grow.

"If this is the Academy, what do you think the king's
palace looks like?" Alex wheezed.

I had no answer.

Nudging the mare a step forward, and then another, I
began to make my descent. Alex followed softly behind, and in
what seemed like ages but was probably only minutes, we arrived at the Academy doors.

At their center, two heavy wrought steel handles awaited.

The two of us dismounted and handed off our reins to a
standing hostler.

Taking a deep breath, I reached for a handle and gingerly
pulled.

The door didn't budge.

Frowning, Alex joined me, and the two of us heaved until
it finally creaked open.

As soon as we were inside, I lost what little of my breath
remained.

Everything I had heard...it did not do justice to what
my eyes were seeing now. Of course, I had known the Academy
would be beautiful.

But I hadn't known it would be...*so much.*

Black marble covered the entire floor, making every step
we took echo disconcertingly.

In a contrast that should have been jarring but wasn't, the walls were a rough, uncut sandstone. On them metal sconces held ever-burning torches in place, but instead of the natural, golden radiance of fire, they emitted a flickering, crystalline blue flame.

At the end of the passage I could see a large room containing an enormous, spiraling stair.

As I approached the atrium, the sheer size of it seemed to multiply. The stairwell stood at its center, steadily rising and secured by thick iron railings. As it touched the second floor, the well separated into two twisting cases with a giant, many-paned window at its base. Facing due west, the window revealed the jagged rocks and sea that Sjeka was famous for.

Moonlight bathed the entire room, and I looked up to find the most riveting feature yet. The ceiling had been constructed entirely of stained glass. Thousands of twinkling red and gold glass fragments greeted my open-mouthed gaze. *Wow.*

"Looks like two more lowborns."

Startled out of my mesmerized state, I took in the rest of my surroundings. Upon entering the room, I had failed to notice the large gathering of people to my left. A hundred or so young men and women were clustered around a figure I couldn't quite make out. For the most part, they seemed to be listening attentively and had paid little heed to Alex's and my entrance, but a couple of stragglers were eyeing the two of us skeptically.

Instantly I became conscious of what we must look like. Five days of horsehair and exhaustion. Riding clothes stained from dirt and sweat and blood. My hair a shoulder-length tangled disaster. Even our arms bore a nice coating of dust since the last time we had bathed. Not to mention my injuries.

*So much for first impressions.*

I ignored the stares and followed my brother as he pushed his way through the crowd, attempting to catch a glimpse of who was commanding everyone's attention. As I squeezed past arms and elbows, I caught my foot on something hard and found myself falling forward.

Luckily, it was so packed that I just ended up colliding with the person in front of me rather than landing face down on the floor.

"I'm so—"

The tall stranger turned around.

It was *him*. The prince with the angry eyes from the trade road.

Many hours later, and it appeared his expression hadn't changed.

"—sorry," I finished lamely.

He just looked at me, irritated. I felt heat start to rise in my cheeks under his taciturn stare, but seconds later I was facing his back again.

*Well he's a charmer*, I thought dryly.

Having just annoyed one of the heirs to the kingdom of Jerar, I decided to move on to less provoking tactics. I safely navigated my way through the rest of the mass and joined Alex at the front of the room.

In a long, layered, black silk robe, a large man stood conversing with his audience. I recognized him from the insignia on his sleeve.

"Is that Master Barclae?" Alex whispered awestruck.

I nodded. Master Barclae, or as his title commanded, "Master of the Academy," was a handsome man with sharp features and a salt and pepper trimmed mustache that suited his face. He had started leading the Academy a year or two before Alex and I had been born. Many said it was because of him that Jerar's last Candidacy had had such strong contenders.

I strained to hear what he was saying.

"—first two months will be spent exploring the fundamentals and identifying the faction you will choose to commit your studies to. The remainder will be spent learning the foundation of its magic."

Someone mumbled a question.

The large man laughed coldly. "There is no such thing as 'rest.' If you want an easy career, you should have applied to one of the other schools our Crown sponsors. The School of Knighthood, perhaps, or maybe the Cavalry? The latter's retention is so high I suspect they hang gum drops from its rafters."

I glanced at my twin. There was nothing easy about either of the schools the master had mentioned.

Alex returned my anxious smile with one of his own. *Too late to turn back now.*

"Why are there *only* fifteen? Because fifteen is already *too* generous. Magic is hardly common enough to justify that number—the *only* reason we have that many is because the Crown demands at least fifteen new war mages each year to enter its company. At one point it was far higher, but it was a waste of resources and jeopardized the training of the few who deserved to be here. The Academy's expectations are demanding, and it would be idiocy to train incompetents. It is a privilege we allow fifteen as it is. Do not waste my time with such nonsense."

The students continued to pester the man with questions until he finally cleared his throat. "That is enough for tonight. It is late, and your official induction will be taking place tomorrow morning." He snorted. "Try to save such senseless queries for your other masters." Without bothering to wait for a response, the Master of the Academy exited the podium, disappearing through a corridor on my left.

Not one member of the audience moved. It was only a couple of minutes later when a frenzied manservant appeared that any of us broke free of the trance.

"Master Barclae will return in the morning," the man squeaked. "If you haven't done so already, please check in with Constable Barrius, our master staffer, in the east wing. He will assist with your placement."

Almost immediately, the crowd dispersed. Most of the students set off in the same direction as Master Barclae while my twin and I followed a handful of others at the right. As we began to make our way down another long corridor, I struck up a conversation with a friendly-looking girl at the front.

"I guess I can see why my parents didn't want me to choose the Academy."

The girl glanced at me. "My older brother tried out a couple of years ago. He said it was only as hard as you make it..." She laughed. "Then again, Jeff was one of the first to resign, so maybe I shouldn't be listening to a word my brother says."

I grinned. "I'm Ryiah.'"

"Ella," she told me with a dark hand outstretched.

"I'm here with my twin," I told her. I pointed to my brother. He was too busy to notice, flirting shamelessly with a blonde girl behind us.

*Oh Alex*, I thought. *Already?*

"You two don't look much alike," she observed.

I shrugged.

"So where are you from?"

"A couple days east. Have you heard of Demsh'aa?"

Ella nodded, ebony locks falling across her hazel eyes. "My father usually visits the apothecary there whenever he passes through. He likes the sleep sachets and swears they are better than the ones he buys from the palace mages."

"That's our family store!" I exclaimed. "Alex made those. We didn't get half as much business when it was my parents." I smiled. "He's always had a keen eye for those things. It was the biggest surprise when he said he wanted to be a healer."

"Oh," she paused, "are you planning on Restoration too then?"

"Combat."

Ella laughed. "Aren't we all."

"What about you?"

"The same." She made a flippant gesture with her hand. "My family lived at court for thirteen years before they finally gave up on me as a lady-in-waiting. I spent a year convincing them to let me try out for the School of Knighthood…but then I discovered my magic. So here I am instead."

So Ella was highborn. It explained her accent. But she was also stubborn, and that made me like her. It would be nice to have a friend in the same faction.

"What time did you arrive?"

"Not long before the two of you. But don't worry. We didn't miss much. I overheard someone say that Master Barclae was the only master to make an appearance."

I sighed. "Good. I would have been upset if we had. We made good time today, but it was still an eight hour ride."

"You do look as if you've had a long day," she observed.

I fingered my stain-covered shirt and its frayed ends. "It's been a long *week*."

"What happ—oh, look, I think we are here." Ella pointed to an opening where one of the others had just disappeared through. Following the rest of our group into the chamber, we came face-to-face with a formidable old man and the frantic-looking servant from earlier. Each one of them held a scroll with names.

"Ladies first," the old man barked.

When everyone had finished, the constable eyed us with distaste. "Well, well, young ones, welcome to our realm's own version of the Realm of the Dead. For as long as you last, this will be your new home."

No one spoke. *Is everyone here so angry?* I wondered. I had heard the staff didn't like first-years, but I had assumed Master Barclae was an exception. Now I was wondering if they hated them.

"Well, not *this* place exactly, but close to it. We keep your living quarters out behind the Academy. There are two barracks to separate each of your lots."

My jaw dropped. *Barracks?* I heard a gasp to my right and knew I wasn't the only one.

"Frederick," the old man said, jerking his thumb at the manservant beside him, "will take you there. You will carry your own bags. We don't waste castle chambers on first-years, so the barracks are where you will spend your time when you are not eating or training here in the Academy. The apprentice mages spend most of their time abroad, except for a couple months during the fall, so the layout of the Academy will be at your disposal."

"We have rules you must follow in accordance with your residency," the constable added tartly. "You are not allowed to enter the residence of the opposite sex. Curfew is ten. Classes are mandatory. No unauthorized fighting. And you may not leave the Academy grounds. There are *no* exceptions."

The man looked to the ceiling. "Any infraction of these rules and you will find yourself in my chambers. *Don't* let it happen. I have been known to send first-years home on a first offense."

⚜

The entire walk to the barracks was silent. Clearly, I wasn't the only one to expect a more amiable orientation.

When we reached the wooded buildings, I bid my twin goodnight and entered the women's residence with Ella.

The inside was much bigger than I had anticipated, even for a crowding of fifty girls, and not nearly as loathsome. Double bunks were spread out in rows with comfortable blankets and small trunks lining each of the walls for our belongings. A large fireplace stood at the furthest corner, no fire present but undoubtedly cozy in winter. There were even a couple baths in an adjoining house, and while I would probably have to spend half my night waiting to use one, at least I'd have the opportunity.

There were also two servants to contribute to the upkeep. As the constable had warned, the Academy staff didn't assist with personal needs, but they did build fires, clean sheets, and heat water for bathing. It was more than I'd had at home.

Almost immediately I could identify which girls had come from a background similar to mine, and which were highborn. The ones like me were far and few between, maybe ten amongst the fifty or so present. We tended to be the ones smiling at our luck while the others complained loudly about the "accommodations." Ella wasn't outspoken like the others, but I could sense that even she was disappointed.

Setting my bag on an unclaimed bunk, I pulled out a cotton nightshirt and my only pair of clean undergarments. Then I headed to the baths.

After an hour of waiting, I finally got my chance at a lukewarm wash and scrubbed until my skin was raw. There was no one else in line behind me, so I was able to take my time. My dirt and grime had warded off any potential bathers.

Crawling into my bunk and nestling under its soft sheets, the impact of my weeklong journey struck with staggering force. I didn't even have time to tell Ella goodnight. I had fallen asleep the second my head hit my pillow.

# CHAPTER THREE

"Ryiah, wake up! Everyone else has already left."

Groaning, I opened my eyes. Every muscle in my body felt like it had been hit by a thousand tiny hammers. It was not a pleasant sensation.

Forcing myself out of bed, I found Ella standing by impatiently.

"How much time do we have?"

"We've got about ten more minutes before breakfast ends to meet Master Barclae."

*Barclae.* Immediately, all exhaustion was forgotten, and I yanked my only clean dress over my head. I ran out after Ella, combing my fingers through my bedraggled hair and wishing I had more time.

The two of us rushed through the courtyard and into the back entrance of the Academy. We made it into the dining hall just as the platters were being taken back to the kitchens. *Wonderful.*

Ella and I took our seats at the end of a back table. I had just spotted Alex a couple seats down when Master Barclae entered looking stern and impressive in his silks.

"Well, it looks like you are all still here. I will try my best to discourage that."

I flinched. Master Barclae's mood was worse than the night before.

"What is *he* doing here?"

I turned in the direction of Ella's whisper and saw where she was looking. The prince was seated one row from Alex.

I had forgotten all about him. "Maybe he doesn't know," I whispered, knowing my explanation sounded ludicrous even to my own ears.

Master Barclae coughed loudly, and I felt my cheeks burn as I realized his scowl was fixed on Ella and me. "Have I bored you?" he drawled loudly.

We quickly shook our heads, and I lowered my own, shame-faced.

But Master Barclae wasn't done making his point. "Really, I insist, what is *so* fascinating that you needed to interrupt my lecture?"

"Nothing," I said quickly.

"Him." Ella pointed.

I quickly snuck a look at the prince and saw his garnet eyes fixated on Ella and me. The expression he wore was one of unadulterated loathing.

I swallowed uncomfortably. *Ella!*

"Ah." Master Barclae smiled sardonically. "Him. What about this *him*?"

Ella stood nervously, "The Council's Treaty states no heir of the kingdom can undertake training as a mage. T-to prevent the Crown from interfering with matters of magic."

The irritation in the young man's eyes had turned to daggers. I quickly looked away.

"True," Master Barclae admitted, "but the doctrine was alluding to first-born children who would be inheriting the throne. Prince Darren is not."

"But we've never had a prince before—"

"*You've never had one before because nobody was good enough!*" Prince Darren spat.

I winced. There was no mistaking the indignation and resentment in his tone.

Master Barclae laughed harshly. "Ah, my dears, you are so young to have already made such an unpleasant impression with a member of the royal family."

Ella bit her lip. I continued to stare at the ground. I could feel the prince's angry gaze burning us alive.

"Well, now that these two girls have finished embarrassing themselves, would anyone else like to join them?"

Silence.

"Good. Now, before I send you off to your actual lessons, I want to make a couple of things clear. Each year, students enter my school claiming to have a gift. *Please understand that having magic has never been and never will be enough.* For most of you the degree of power you possess is nothing short of insignificant."

The master grunted. "Unfortunately, it takes *months* of testing to determine. Were it weeks, there would never be such thing as a silly trial year in the first place."

Someone behind me snickered loudly. Apparently, *they* weren't worried, a sentiment I couldn't help wishing I shared.

"The constable has informed me that we have one hundred and twenty-two new faces this year. I advise you all to think long and hard on those odds. There will only be fifteen apprenticeships. Do you really want to waste an entire year under the guise of *hope*?" He eyed the audience coldly.

"Ten months of hard labor, course study, and endless repetition. *That* is what you have to look forward to if you choose to stay." Master Barclae eyed us speculatively. "Half this class will leave, of their own accord, by midwinter for that very reason—well, *that* and the realization that their magic is not nearly as powerful as they had presumed...

"In any case, we will have a weeklong trial for those that remain at the year's end. Which brings me to my final note before you begin your studies, and that is your faction.

"I know that each one of you walked into the Academy doors with a preconceived notion of which magic to train for...and for most of you that faction is Combat." He eyed his dress, smiling ironically. "The black robes of the warrior class *are* world-renowned, undoubtedly inspired by the Candidacy."

An elbow nudged me in the ribs, and I saw that Alex had made his way to where Ella and I stood. My twin gave me a crooked grin, and I shoved him back, knowing exactly what he was thinking. I already knew Combat was a long shot, but it wasn't going to stop me from trying.

"Still, I implore you to think twice. Consider perhaps the great skill of Alchemy. Or the healer's touch of Restoration. Both branches commit their service to Jerar's defense, and yet they are under-praised in light of another's glory. You have two months before you actually commence the study of your chosen faction. It would be wise to consider those odds."

The Master of the Academy cleared his throat. "That said, I will now have Frederick lead you to your first lesson. I am sure you have much to think about in the hours that follow."

⚜

Leaving the atrium behind, Alex, Ella, and I followed a winding corridor to the left. I had just finished introducing the two when I noticed the prince watching us from the corner of my eye.

"Don't look now," I said to Ella in a low voice, "but I am pretty sure if looks could kill, you and I would be dead already."

Ella's eyes shot to whom I was referring to, and then rolled her eyes. "Well, *he* can glare all he wants. I had a right to question his being here. Who cares if he's not first-born? All it takes is one accidental stabbing, and suddenly, he's the realm's first mage king."

"Would it really make that much of a difference?" Alex asked abruptly. "If anything, I think having a member of the Crown would help the mages' cause, not hurt it…"

"You say that now," Ella replied, "but you wouldn't if you actually knew him."

"You know Prince Darren personally?" I stared at her.

Ella grimaced. "Oh, yes, Darren *and* his brother. Trust me when I say not knowing is preferable."

I was instantly curious. "What did they do?"

Ella shook her head, clearly unwilling to drudge up memories of her life back in court.

Alex glanced at me, and I shrugged. Our confusion faded momentarily, however, as we entered an enormous library with the rest of our class. The three of us took our seats in a hushed silence.

Already, there was parchment and quill ready for note-taking. Beneath my chair, I discovered three heavy leather-bound books. I couldn't imagine the price they would have fetched back in Demsh'aa. Books were a privilege, a very expensive one that few nobles could even afford. Occasionally a baron or duke might have had a small collection at home, but only the king's palace in Devon and the Academy could have so many volumes as the ones I saw now.

No matter where I turned to look, shelf after shelf greeted my incredulous gaze. Thousands of books and yellowing scrolls stacked high along the walls, and at the very end of each was a ladder leading up to yet another floor of manuscripts and tables.

I hazarded a guess that the second floor was a study. There was another floor after that, but I could not make out what its contents were.

Back at ground level, there stood a raised podium with two solid oak desks at its center. At the first sat a heavy-set woman in her mid-fifties. Her brown hair was pulled back in a wavy bun, not a strand loose, and her powder was perfectly pressed. She was dressed very severely underneath a heavy blue cloak, with a high-laced collar and an emerald pendant clasped tightly around her neck. Her eyes had a severity that warned one not to fool around in her presence.

To the woman's right sat a slightly twitchy man about twenty years her junior. His vest and pants were frayed, and his hair was rather ragged. He had an untrimmed mustache that lined his chin and upper lip, but it seemed more from neglect than the careful precision of Master Barclae. In an erratic sort of way, the master stood and nervously glanced around the room. Though he seemed to be out of sorts, his eyes spoke of kindness and intelligence.

The duo introduced themselves as Masters Eloise and Isaac and wasted no time in familiarizing the class with their expectations for the year.

Magic was the very last thing on their agenda.

"There is no point in learning to cast if you haven't a clue what you're doing," Master Eloise sniffed. "What you need is basics. I don't care how much tutelage you have had, one can never know too much."

"Yes," Master Isaac added quickly, "'tis far more important to know the 'why' than the 'how' in casting. The basics will give you that knowledge."

The "basics," it turned out, were history, science, mathematics, and geography. No weapons, medicines, or "anything of interest" as Ella had grumbled. I couldn't help agreeing.

It would be two months before we would actually commence the study of our factions. "This way," Master Eloise had noted, "I can be assured you have a *proper* foundation."

✦

Four long hours later, mind reeling and stomach growling voraciously, I pushed my way past the slow mob of students and practically collapsed into the dining hall. Ella found me just as I was piling my plate high with salted pork, spiced cheddar, and a variety of colorful vegetables.

"Hungry much?" she observed.

"You have no idea," I said through a mouthful of toast. I could feel other first-years' eyes on me as I ravaged a second roll, and I made an effort to eat a little more slowly.

"For the five days it took us to get here, all we've eaten is rye and one too many handfuls of dried fruit," Alex added, snatching an apple off Ella's plate as he joined us at the table.

Ella snatched her fruit back from my brother. "I guess that explains why you looked like a ruffian last night."

Alex reddened and I snorted, drink spraying across the table. It had been a long time since I'd met a girl who was immune to my brother's charm. It was a refreshing, and amusing, change of pace.

Ella turned back to me. "Ryiah, *you* look wonderful today. Your hair is such an interesting shade. I've never seen one like it before. I bet all the boys back home loved you."

I choked into my glass. "Hardly."

Alex snickered. "Ry was too tough for the boys in Demsh'aa. She was too busy fighting them to notice."

I kicked his foot. "We were training, not fighting, brother." I glanced at Ella. "What about you, Ella? You've only been here a day, and you already have a shadow—that boy from the library."

She laughed loudly. "Oh, James? He is hardly my type. I need a man's man, like that Master Barclae."

Alex cringed. "But he's so old!"

"And mean," I added. "He was mean to us."

Ella scoffed. "He doesn't look it. Besides, he knows how to carry himself. I don't need any of the young men here. Most of them are younger than us. Have you noticed that?"

"The nobility," Alex offered, "they all took advantage of the early admission at twelve and thirteen, I'd bet."

"I don't see why." Ella frowned. "I *am* highborn, and it always seemed more of an advantage to wait until the cut off at seventeen. A better chance to build up your powers, especially since they don't even start to emerge until adolescence…" She laughed lightly. "But I guess the three of us didn't wait that long either. I suppose it's hard to wait once you discover your magic."

"Prince Darren is older," I observed, "and so are some of the others too."

"He's one of the smart ones," Ella admitted. "He's had his powers for awhile. Thankfully most of the students rushed admission, like us."

I reflected on our first lesson. "It certainly didn't seem that way in the library."

"All that extra tutoring," she assured me. "Not that I should resent them for it. My parents would have done the same if they hadn't been so set on a convent."

"Still, they knew so much more than me," I sighed. "In Demsh'aa Alex and I were one of the few kids who knew how to read and write, but that was only because our parents were merchants! I didn't even realize it would be a part of our studies!"

"Well, it makes sense, doesn't it?"

I just groaned and put my head in my hands. "And all the work they gave us? It's the first day, and they already expect us to read through four chapters and do fifteen sets of those horrid math equations?"

"We can start on them now. We've got a half hour until our next session," she suggested lightly.

I frowned. "I would, but if I take in any more 'learning' right now, I think my head will implode."

Ella chuckled.

"I'll study with you, Ella," Alex said a little too quickly. He flashed her a winning smile.

Ella turned to me, ignoring my twin. "It's not going to get better. Remember my brother. There's a reason people leave early on."

I shook my head. "I'll meet you guys at the armory before our next session."

"Okay," Ella said shrugging. "Just don't be late."

‎⚜︎

As I emptied my tray and started down the Academy's long corridor, I spent the walk fantasizing about the goose-down pillows that were awaiting me back in the barracks. I was only four hours into my year, and I was already longing for sleep. It couldn't be a good sign.

*First couple weeks are always the hardest...*

I sighed. *Or maybe that's just a saying, and it really is horrible all year long.*

I had just turned the corner when I suddenly collided with someone coming from the opposite direction.

"I'm so..." I began, and then froze.

Seriously? *Not again.* Why was fate so determined to make me continuously cross paths with the one person who so clearly wished he'd never met me?

The prince tightened his lips and bent down to pick up the pieces of parchment he'd dropped. I reached down to help him, but he snatched them up before I could offer a hand.

Straightening, Darren made way as if to pass, but I stood my ground. I had to apologize about earlier. Even if Ella were right about him—and she probably was, judging from our encounters thus far—I still owed him an apology. If someone had questioned my being here, I probably would have reacted in much the same way.

"Your grace," I began anew, "I want to apologize for earlier—" Darren glared at me, but I continued on hastily: "It wasn't right. You deserve a chance just as much as anyone else, especially since you are not the heir—"

"Thanks," the non-heir cut me off sharply, "but I don't need some backcountry peasant asserting what I can or can't do."

My whole face burned in indignation. "I didn't mean—"

"Look," Darren began, with as much irritation-free politeness as he could muster. It wasn't much. "I didn't come here to socialize with commoners and learn about their feelings. I came here to be a mage. So, if you don't mind, I have more pressing affairs than listening to you apologize for your own incompetence."

Darren pushed past me as I stood, dumbfounded. Any initial guilt I had felt earlier was gone. I wasn't sure exactly how I had expected the apology to transpire, but certainly not the way it had. Even the highborn children back home hadn't treated me with as much hostility.

There was nothing modest about this prince, this *non-heir*. Ella was right: there was no way I would want someone like that on the throne wearing a crown *and* a mage's robes. What had compelled the masters to make such a blatant exception?

*You've never had one before because nobody was good enough!* That's what Darren had yelled at Ella and me. Was that why Master Barclae had decided to make the distinction between an heir and someone who was second-in-line to the throne? Because Darren had shown exceptional talent?

*If he chooses Combat, I'll wipe that arrogant sneer off his face the first chance I get,* I decided. *How exceptional can a non-heir be, really? He wasn't even good enough to be first-born and get a throne.* It was a cruel thought, one that didn't even play out logically, but I welcomed it all the same. *I hope you lose out on an apprenticeship to many, many commoners.*

Arriving at the large wood-paneled building that served as the Academy's armory, I found Alex and Ella at the back of a crowd facing its doors. The two of them were chummier than before, and I began to wonder if introducing my brother to Ella had been a mistake. If she fell for him, I would lose the one friend I had gained since coming here. I'd certainly lost enough back home.

Joining the two, I noticed that Ella seemed to be more entertained than enamored. I held onto the hope it would last.

"Welcome first-years," a booming voice roared.

Immediately everyone stopped talking and looked to the entryway of the armory.

Out stepped the most intimidating man I had ever seen. Extremely tall with bulging muscle, the man seemed to crunch the ground with each step that he took. His hair was cut short, and his eyes were an almost disconcerting green. His dark skin was glistening, and he had several white scar lines that reached down across his arms.

The man wore the livery of a knight, not a mage.

*Was there some sort of mistake?*

"No, I am not one of your masters here," the man boomed, registering the crowd's shock.

"But don't you be getting any ideas. I will still be involved in *every* step of your development this year. I served on the King's Regiment for twenty years, and the last ten I have spent training young mages here alongside Master Cedric." I noticed a thin, wiry man in red robes that had stepped out behind him. "I am Sir Piers, and I will be leading you in the physical conditioning needed for your factions."

"*I thought we were to be sorcerers, not pages!*" someone hissed behind me.

A chortle of quiet voices voiced the same irritation.

Sir Piers heard them and glowered. Instantaneous silence.

"Many of you might wonder what use I am to your precious studies. Can I have a volunteer please?" No one moved. "I have my pick then," he announced almost gleefully, dragging forward one of the boys that had been whispering behind me. The boy was shaking, and I really couldn't blame him. Sir Piers was a big man and clearly enjoyed scaring his charges.

"Now, what is your name?"

"Ralph."

"Well, Ralph, it's your lucky day. Which faction do you want to end up in?"

"Combat," Ralph squeaked.

"Yes, *always* with you first-years." The man laughed.

"Now," Piers continued. "Show me what you can do."

"It's n-not much," Ralph stammered, snatching a twig off the ground. He began to stare at it intensely, and I knew almost instantly what he was going to do. Seconds later, the familiar sprout of tiny flames encompassed his stick.

*Great*, I thought darkly. Ralph didn't even need to hurt himself to get it burning. A twelve-year-old showed more promise than me.

"Now," Piers said after the twig had turned to ash, "I want you to run a mile—the course of the stadium's circumference."

Ralph's face fell.

"What are you waiting for?" Piers barked.

Ralph took off like a jackrabbit, but about two minutes in to the run, his pace slowed. I could sense his discomfort. None of us had dressed with a strenuous workout in mind. I was still wearing my dress.

For the next seven minutes, poor Ralph ran around the track huffing and puffing as the rest of the class watched, careful to avoid meeting eyes with Piers and becoming his next "volunteer" victim.

Eventually, a sweaty, shaking Ralph returned to take his spot in front of Piers.

"Light fire to another stick," Piers ordered him.

"I—" Ralph choked, "—need...a moment..."

"NOW!"

Ralph scrambled to find another branch and tried to repeat the same casting, to no avail. He was too busy taking deep gulps of air to concentrate.

"You just gave the enemy an opening, boy. You are now dead on the battlefield. Take your seat." Piers eyed the boy unhappily and looked around. "Do I have another volunteer? Someone with more prowess in mind?"

Everyone looked to the ground quickly, except for the non-heir who seemed unperturbed as he met Piers's eyes dead on.

"Alright, princeling, have at it."

Darren stepped forward and picked up a twig. I breathed out a sigh of relief. He *was* normal like the rest of us. It would have killed me if he put on some sort of supernatural display.

Darren clenched one end in his palm, eyeing a nearby tree.

*You've got to be—*

The entire trunk exploded in a blaze. Branches with crackling leaves crashed to the ground as the tree became a charred black torch.

The non-heir cracked the twig in his palm.

The fire instantly abated.

Dead tree limbs scattered the grass. Darren looked to Piers for instructions.

I glanced at Sir Piers as well to gauge his reaction. Both the commander and the wiry Master Cedric had approving smiles on their faces.

"Well done," Piers boomed. "Now, do the same to that tree—there."

We all looked to see where he was pointing. A similar oak stood half a mile off at the other end of the stadium.

I braced myself, knowing better than to hope the prince would fail miserably.

Darren reached down to grab one of the small charred branches from the first tree he had lit fire to. Part of the stick still looked red-hot beneath its gray exterior, and I wondered if it burned. Still, Darren showed no sign of pain as he rolled it back and forth between his palms, keeping his stormy gaze on the target.

Moments later the tree caught fire. *Not as dramatic as the first, but still impressive,* I noted dryly. The fire quickly died out on the trunk, but continued on in most of the higher branches.

"You may take a seat now," Piers told the non-heir in a much friendlier tone than he had addressed the previous boy.

Darren nodded curtly and then made his way over to the bench where Ralph sat.

Piers addressed the rest of us. "What did those two have in common?"

*Nothing.*

"The dynamics of war," Piers continued when none of us spoke up, "show us what may not be openly obvious to you magic folk. You think you can blast your enemy with sheer force, and maybe you can. But the further you are from your opponent, the less power you are able to exert. We can't waste all this time training you to be powerful mages and have you faint at the first sign of battle. Not one of you will be sitting in an ivory tower pointing your finger and making your enemies crumble. You will need to be close to your enemies to do damage, but you need to be able to maneuver in and out of battle to safely engage.

"By building up your physical reserves, we will be increasing your tolerance to pain and your fortitude. By strengthening your prowess, you will be more capable of focusing during moments that test your will.

"Early on, the Council learned that they were losing too many mages' lives on the battlefield. In response, we developed a training program that incorporates the physical conditioning we put the pages in the School of Knighthood through. While none of you will be as successful as a full-fledged knight, this program will better prepare you for the realities of battle. It gives you more endurance, whether you are a Restoration mage going from one wounded to the next, or an Alchemist helping with dangerous flasks. For the faction of Combat, it is a little easier to picture the battlefield, but even if you were to never participate in a single war, endurance and fortitude can only help, not hurt.

"So for the rest of the day I will be gauging your physical competence. When you walk away today, I will have a thorough understanding of how badly out of shape you are, and then from tomorrow on, we will be attempting to fix that.

"*Oh*," Sir Piers added, almost gleefully, "and if you are wondering when we will train with any of the fun weapons you may have seen a knight handle, keep in mind you have to get through two months of my class first...

"Now, we have a change of clothes for the lads and ladies in the building behind me. Those will be your attire for the rest of your time here at the Academy. After today you will no longer be wearing personal garments or insignia. You will notice the garb is old, ill-fitting, and not particularly attractive. That is to be expected. Year one is not a cause for celebration, and so the masters do not waste coin financing your personal fashions. We will go ahead and let the ladies go first. Lads, while you are waiting your turn, I advise you to start stretching. It's going to be a long two hours."

Two hours into the pain and agony that was Sir Piers's idea of *light* conditioning, I found myself dry-heaving at one of the wooden benches on the side of the field. I heard Alex off to my right making similar noises. All over the stadium, first-years were dropping one by one.

Piers had decided we would run five miles. Five miles, he had added, interspersed with twenty lunges and presses each time we completed a lap. That would have been fine, hard -but fine, if that were all he had asked of us. But it had only been a warm-up.

Once we had completed his first demand, Sir Piers had barked new orders for everyone to line up across from one another. When we did that, he had heaved heavy wooden staffs at us and instructed us to "proceed."

Since most of the girls and a couple of the lowborn boys had never held a weapon in their life, Piers then had to show us how to hold the poles, where to stand, and which way to lean our weight. We spent just as much time rapping each other's knuckles as we did the staffs.

When one girl had dared to quietly ponder the usefulness of the drill to her partner, Piers snapped: "You think you'll never need to use a weapon, girl? What happens when you have used the last of your magic and you are stranded in the middle of a battlefield? When a mage is powerful enough to send daggers cutting through the air, do you think he randomly decides their course? *No*, he studies and practices *exactly* which cutting blows are needed to hit those precious arteries. *Nothing* I teach you here will be pointless!"

For the remainder of our lesson, no one dared to brave a single complaint. Even when he decided to introduce a new routine involving the many flights of stairs surrounding the field.

But that still didn't stop our bodies from reacting to the horrible circus of exercises Piers was putting us through.

Taking a deep breath, I told myself that it couldn't get any worse.

We were on a fifteen-minute break before our session with Master Cedric, but for most of us, the fifteen minutes was spent trying to crawl or limp our way to a display of water pitchers on the other side of the stadium. Refreshments had been brought courtesy of Constable Barius's staff, all of which had decided to take a late afternoon break.

I think the water was just an excuse for their entertainment.

Still, entertainment or not, water was what I wanted. As luck would have it by the time I reached it there was almost none left.

Greedily, I downed what remained and then scanned the bench for any unattended glasses I could finish off. None. Had I really expected anything different? Deciding I had only a minute or so left, I sat down to observe the rest of the student body from my resting place.

Ella stood a little way off, red in the face and a little clammy, but somehow still charming in her disheveled state. She was talking to my brother as he attempted to stretch his calves. The two of them were chuckling at a joke he had just made. I winced. I couldn't even imagine laughing. My lungs were still burning from those stairs.

Shifting my gaze to the left side of the field, I spotted a group of five that appeared much better off than the rest of the class. At their center was the newfound bane of my existence. Admittedly, the non-heir wasn't that hard of a poison to swallow when he was far away. He looked so casual, leaning against the fence post, surrounded by laughing companions.

Whether or not he was a prince, Darren had clearly spent a large part of his lifetime in the sun and immersed in some sort of physical engagement. Far from being out of breath and drenched in sweat, the prince made Piers's drills appear as if they actually were an intended warm-up.

Even his hair seemed unaffected. While most of us, myself included, had hair sticking to all sides of our face, Darren's had somehow maintained its natural, slightly tussled state. Short, choppy, side-swept bangs and jaw-length locks that could trick a girl into thinking he was attractive.

That is, if you could get over his charming personality. Because no matter how alluring he might seem from afar, up close Darren's hostile eyes would undoubtedly tell a different story.

Still, as I watched him now, I was not seeing anything remotely unreceptive in them. Possibly, *very likely*, because of the beautiful girl on his right: Priscilla.

Ah, yes. The one young woman who had out-distanced, out-lunged, and out-pressed the rest of my gender. How someone from such high lineage was able to best those of us who had had to actually forage and hunt for our food, I will never know. With her long, silky brown hair, violet eyes, and sinewy curves, I could understand Darren's interest but not her status. Priscilla looked the part of a highborn lady, and I wondered why she was here at the Academy. Usually, girls like that went to convents. They didn't bother with magic or knighthood. They had no need.

Priscilla was older than most nobility in attendance too, and I vaguely wondered if it had anything to do with Darren since he seemed to be around the same age. Maybe she had followed him.

The rest of the non-heir's group consisted of the two burly-looking brothers and a young girl whose skin was so pale it seemed translucent. The girl was so tiny and fragile, I wondered how she had made it into their little following. She didn't talk much, and she seemed more interested in something on the ground than her companions.

"Alright children, let's gather round!" Sir Piers barked.

We all came together slowly, regretfully acknowledging the end of our break.

"Well, well, that wasn't so bad, was it?"

None of us dared to contradict him.

Sir Piers chuckled at his own joke, knowing very well what our silence really meant. "Well, you always have tomorrow. I will go ahead and leave you in Master Cedric's capable hands." With that, Sir Piers left the field, and we found ourselves waiting anxiously for Master Cedric to begin his own introduction.

Master Cedric nodded to his audience and spoke with a much softer inflection to his tone. "Well then, for the next two hours I am going to be leading some basic exercises that are conducive to all factions."

I glanced at Alex and Ella excitedly. *Finally, actual magic.*

"This first month will be spent emphasizing magic's most important foundation: focus. Without the proper application, you will not be successful in your chosen practice."

My enthusiasm died. *Focus.* So we wouldn't be learning how to heal a dying knight or cast a lightning storm. Not today. I had to say I'd had enough "meditation" practice during my time on the road. Two hours of coarse physical activity might actually beat the boredom induced from focusing on a blade of grass for the same length of time.

I heard someone groan to my right.

"You might have great potential," Cedric interjected loudly over his disgruntled audience, an incredible feat for such a timid-looking man. "But if you can't concentrate long enough to will the magic you wish to enact, you will never find yourself beyond the basics. The more advanced castings require a greater dedication that cannot come from acts of whimsy.

"Mages die quickly on the battlefield when they can't summon proper focus. As Sir Piers said, you will not be hidden away in a tower. You will be immersed in an atmosphere full of distractions waiting to tear your concentration apart.

"You will also not be performing simple steps. If you go into Restoration, you will be expected to understand the anatomy of an individual when you are caring for a deep flesh wound. Collapsing a tower in Combat would require you to understand its structure and materials. It's important to know where to make your magic touch count. You could blindly devote your magic to the entire attack you want to enact, or you could learn to focus your magic on specific components so that your castings are precise and don't exert any needless energy.

"Now, let's not waste any more time and begin your first exercise."

I grudgingly joined the rest of the class in forming a giant sitting circle that spread out across the grass at Master Cedric's instruction. From this angle we could see not only the master and his four assisting mages, but everyone else in our group as well.

*At least I'll finally stand out*, I told myself. I may not have had practice fighting with staffs or learning the names of Jerar's eastern seaports, but at least meditation was something I was good at. Years of failed magical attempts could attest to that.

The next two hours seemed set aside to prove me wrong. I wasn't horrible, but I was at best a little better than the norm.

Master Cedric and his assistants walked around our giant group, each carrying a heavy satchel filled with small, white pebbles that they distributed each time one of us failed the exercise.

For the first half hour we had simply been instructed to close our eyes and keep still. We were to maintain an "air of calm" and to focus on a moment of peace and tranquility. That was easy enough.

But then I realized the role the instructor and his assistants were playing in our meditation—pouring hail one second, thousands of angry bird cries the next. I tried not to flinch when I felt the slimy, wiggling body of a snake against my skin, but I could not suppress the tiny whimper that escaped my lips when I felt thousands of tiny, bug-like wings on my face. I opened my eyes just in time to see one of the assistants set two stones by my feet.

Luckily, most students had a small pile forming next to them as well. Unfortunately, there were still those without a white rock to bear.

For the second part of our exercise Master Cedric had the class keep their eyes open while continuing to practice the same meditative state. Of course, sight only made our practice harder.

It was *not* easy to remain calm when you realized a hoard of angry rodents was headed in your direction.

Whenever I made a mistake, I'd take a quick peek to see how everyone else was faring. Most had as many as I, but there was still a small portion of our class that hadn't collected any stones yet—Darren and his group of four, plus seven others.

As minutes ticked by, the exercise got increasingly difficult. The small piles began to resemble mountains. My forehead pounded, my muscles ached, and sweat stung the corners of my eyes. I was trying hard not to give in to the distractions Master Cedric and his assistants were casting, but fear and surprise were not easy reactions to ignore. When a small stampede of spiders took over the field and proceeded to climb up several students' arms, mine included, I lost it, screaming and shaking the vile insects off.

A lifetime of fear could not be erased in two hours.

Eventually, the session ended. We all looked at one another and greedily eyed each other's failures. No one was stoneless, not even Darren and his cohorts. The pale, blonde-haired girl had only two, and Darren and a couple others had no more than five a piece.

I had twenty. Alex had even more. Ella, fifteen. We were all failures in comparison to the prince and his following.

Everyone waited to be dismissed.

"How many of you have changed your minds about the uselessness of meditation now?" Cedric rasped.

Several of us cast our eyes down, shame-faced.

"As you have just witnessed, we are too often allowing sight to dictate our actions. That's fine in day-to-day living, but it will not get you very far in your magical studies.

"Most of you were sufficient in the initial stages of your mediation—that is, until you opened your eyes and saw what types of horrors my assistants had cast. Sight is *not* an understandable reason to lose focus. Sight cannot harm you, and it should not be a cause to waiver in your meditation. Sight can only invoke fear, not pain.

"Physical pain is an understandable reason to lose focus. Sight is not. The precious seconds between seeing the snake—a harmless act—and its venomous bite could make all the difference in a casting. Focus cannot be rushed—that is true—but in magic, every second counts.

"If you want to succeed here, you had best master your fears early on because sight is the least of your worries. There are two much more uncontrollable detractors of focus, pain and emotion, which will require much more effort to control."

Master Cedric cleared his throat: "As I see it, there are many of you who will fail. The Academy is not meant for everyone. Today's exercise is usually a strong indicator of how the year will end. Thus, if you did not perform well today, keep in mind you will most likely continue to struggle throughout the rest of your study."

⊰⊱

As I trailed off to the dining hall with the others, I bitterly acknowledged the reason so many resigned early on. *Why waste a year when it was so blatantly obvious how behind I was?*

There was no doubt who the most promising first-years were. Not one member of Darren's highborn following had been below the top quarter of our class for any of the masters' lessons. Of course, I shouldn't have expected anything less. The prince's contemptuous comments earlier on had made it clear that he would only associate with the best.

Now, his group of five had expanded to include seven more. Four of the newcomers were *not* of noble standing from what I could tell either. But all of them had done well, extremely well, in comparison to the rest of our class.

Apparently, the non-heir would make exceptions to be around "commoners." But I, like most of the lowborn students present, was not promising enough to be worthy of his time.

Glancing around the dining commons, I saw more evidence of changes taking place. At the morning meal, students had sat next to friends or others of similar background. Now more emphasis was spent on sitting with those that had performed at one's own level during training.

At the far end of the hall, where I had previously sat, were the rejects of our year: those that had not performed well in the first day's sessions. Toward the front of the room were those that had.

At the very head of the dining hall was Darren's table. While the prince had yet to arrive, a small cluster of loud highborns sat waiting for him. Their dreams were shattered moments later when Darren and his company of eleven appeared. One sharp look from the non-heir sent the disgruntled nobles retreating to a less prestigious table. They spent the rest of their meal eyeing the four commoners of the prince's new crowd jealously.

Rather than trying to negotiate a spot based on skill, I sat down in the only available open seating, the far end of the reject table. I was pleased to notice Alex and Ella followed. It would have been difficult if my brother and friend had decided they were too proud to sit beside me. It had been a rough first day.

I spent the entire course of dinner listening to a lively exchange between the two while I pushed gravy-soaked peas across my plate. Alex and Ella seemed to be the only ones that found our entire situation humorous. While everyone else was strategizing or complaining, my brother and friend were more concerned with making me laugh. I felt grateful for their company. I needed more positivity, and while many of their jokes were at the expense of our own mishaps, it was nice to laugh them off.

"Did you see me during our drills with Sir Piers?" Alex was asking.

Ella snorted. "I was too busy breathing to notice anyone besides myself."

"Well, while you girls were busy attempting to keep up with us men—"

"Hey!" Ella and I both interrupted. We had both done better than Alex in conditioning. My brother might have brawn, but he had spent the majority of his life indoors.

"—*I* was trying to romance a lady that was actually performing well during the drill," Alex continued on, grinning.

"And how did that go?" I interjected.

"Well—"

"And which damsel in distress would she be?" Ella taunted. "I saw you entertain several before class had even started." It looked like my dark-skinned friend was not enamored after all.

"Hardly," Alex chuckled. "What you may allude to as flirtation, I call harmless conversation."

Ella and I exchanged amused looks.

"So I tried to strike up a conversation with that lovely lady," he finished, pointing his orange to Priscilla from Darren's entourage. It was at just that moment the girl raised her eyes to catch the three of us staring. I saw her frown and turn to the rest of her table to whisper something, shooting a disgusted glance in our direction.

"Seems like a fan," I remarked casually.

"Sure it went well, lover boy? That looks more like disdain than admiration," Ella added.

Alex tore off a bit of rind from his orange and threw it at us.

"Well, it started off well enough. I'd caught her eyeing me a couple of times during practice—"

"Probably in an attempt to avoid you," Ella laughed.

"—So I figured I'd try my chance at some conversation. I'd just managed to catch up to her when my foot caught on one of those lovely stairs Piers had us climbing.

"So, of course, I did what anyone does when they are falling. I grabbed on to the nearest support which just happened to be the lady in question. She left in a hurry after that little incident. Shot me the look of death, that one did. Now all I can think is that not only did the girl outrun me, she also thinks I'm a complete chump."

"You poor thing, most of the class can outrun you," Ella sympathized, patting his shoulder and laughing at the same time. "Can't believe you thought you had a chance with Priscilla."

Alex guffawed but then continued stubbornly, "But why not? I thought status wasn't supposed to matter here."

I choked on my roast, and Ella just rolled her eyes. "It will always matter to some," I finally managed to say through a mouthful of spinach. Darren's angry eyes flashed in my mind.

"Especially," Ella added, "to those who plan on joining the royal family." She jerked her head in Priscilla's direction.

"Are you sure?" Alex asked reluctantly.

"I grew up with her," she replied. "Believe me, *that* girl has eyes for one thing and one thing only."

"So, she's here for Prince Darren," Alex surmised.

"Most definitely." Ella twisted the water glass in her palm. "Her parents are *very* well-known courtiers. Social climbers like Priscilla's family dedicate their lives to building close relations with the Crown. Priscilla is a very pretty girl, and her family has enough standing to make her a very eligible wife. Everyone knows that, as future king, Prince Blayne's hands are tied with a political marriage, but Darren's are not. Every power hungry family in court who has a daughter around his age has been after that title since the day he was born."

As I listened to Ella, I found myself watching Priscilla interact with those closest to her. Ella could say she was power hungry, but the girl had still performed very strongly in all of our lessons today.

"I don't think she's just here for the prince," I remarked, causing both Alex and Ella to start. I continued, "Priscilla's much too prepared. She might want to secure an engagement, but I think she came here for a robe."

Ella just shook her head. "If she wasn't good, she wouldn't have a chance at the throne to begin with."

"Why?"

"Because magic is all that prince cares about," Ella explained dryly. "I thought he'd grow out of it, but since he's here, I'm quite certain he hasn't. Priscilla and her parents were undoubtedly smart enough to figure that out. I'm sure as soon as they realized how serious he was about the Academy, they got her the best tutor money could buy."

I looked back to the end of the table where Priscilla and Darren and the rest of their following were seated. I'd already started to hear rumors that the prince and his entourage were going to make the apprenticeship.

*Really.* On day one. To already have that kind of reputation.

*It isn't fair.*

Alex noted my stare. "I heard some people have already decided to change their faction."

"Huh?"

"After practice today, some of the others were saying they didn't want to be second best. Two people said there was no point in hoping for Combat when the odds were so set against them."

Master Barclae's predictions were already coming true. I couldn't believe it.

"They might say that now and change their mind later." Ella pointed out. "Jeff changed his mind three times before the end of his first month."

"I can see why," I remarked slowly, "when you are competing with someone who even Master Cedric and the others are impressed with. They have seen hundreds of first-years. To impress them at this point means you really stand out."

Ella folded her arms. "Well, future apprentice or not, no one is going to sway me but *me.*"

Once we had finished off our dinner, Alex, Ella, and I headed to the library's upper study to begin the day's assignments. Most of the class had gone off to the barracks to wash. Though the three of us were smelly and not particularly attractive at the moment, we knew we would fare better studying without the echo that a hundred or so lowered voices would bring if we cleaned up first like everyone else.

Entering the room, it was immediately evident that we were not alone. There were a couple other small groups already inside, but they were few in number. They seemed friendly enough so I didn't mind much. I recognized one girl, Winifred, as someone from back home. Alex recognized another, Clayton, his friend from a nearby village. Before long, we had amassed a small group of our own: Alex, Ella and I, Winifred, Clayton, another boy named Jordan, a girl named Ruth, and Ella's admirer from the library, shy James.

It was nice to study in the company of so many. We all had something to contribute to someone else's work. While Winifred spent most of her time lecturing us on the mathematical equations we were trying to break down, Alex and I helped with the sections on herb lore. Having parents who owned an apothecary was an advantage.

Ruth and Clayton were able to assist with geography, and Ella, shockingly enough, with history, especially the battles. As she explained to our speechless group, Ella used to follow her father around while he drilled the village soldiers and then practiced later in private. No wonder the girl wanted Combat. She had a warrior mindset I envied. It also explained why she had fared better than most of us in Piers's conditioning. Ella had been second only to Priscilla and a couple of the boys.

Even if none of us knew the answer to a problem, eight of us searching different volumes provided much quicker results than trying to do so independently. By the time the rest of our class had arrived, most of the assignments were finished.

Packing up my work, I felt a lot more confident than hours before. I still had problems to complete, but they were significantly fewer in number. The only thing that detracted from my mood was Ella—or rather, her insistent whispering and pointing as we turned the corner to exit.

Darren and his entourage had arrived, and in the short time they had done so, they had already taken over the most comfortable lounge in the library. This had left the rest of the ninety students trying to squeeze into the smaller aisles on the second floor. No one looked happy.

"Injustice at its finest!" Ella hissed when we shut the door behind us. "Treating the Academy like it is just another court back home!"

Alex glanced at our friend, eyebrow cocked. "You really don't like the prince, do you?"

"No!"

"Why?"

Several heads turned to glance at Ella, myself included. True, I was no fan of the angry-eyed prince, but Ella had never told me what it was Darren had done to make her hate him so venomously. I had my own reasons for not liking the prince, but Ella's hatred seemed much more impassioned. Maybe now I would hear the reason behind this loathing.

Ella set her mouth in a hard line. "It's none of your concern, Alex."

My brother looked disappointed. "I was hoping for a good story."

I had to admit, so was I.

"Well, there's nothing to tell," she replied tightly. Her lively brown eyes were unreadable in the candlelight.

Alex laughed uncomfortably. "Just wanted to know what the poor guy did, so I didn't repeat his same mistake. I'd hate to have the hatred of such a beautiful lady."

Ella smiled slightly, and the tension in the hall left the air. "You are much too charming to make the same mistake," she told him lightly. Then, she leaned forward to kiss him on the cheek. She had to stand on the tips of her toes to reach his sun-tanned face, and by the time she finished, his skin had a deep red tint to it.

Ella continued down the hall while Alex stood frozen in place, eyes trailing after as the girl turned another corner and disappeared.

"Don't you even think about it," I warned him.

"I don't...she..." His face grew redder, and conscious of the amused expressions of our group, he shook his head to clear away the confusion, sandy brown locks flailing wildly in his attempt. "I have to go."

Alex took off in the same direction as Ella, though he was headed toward the boy's housing.

Clayton snickered. "I think Ella is going to give your brother a run for his reputation."

"She's only interested in older men like Master Barclae," I replied without thinking.

"People say a lot of things. That doesn't mean they are always true," James piped up, a little too eagerly.

We all laughed at the truth of his statement and parted ways to our barracks. I spent most of the time making small talk with Ruth and Winifred until we had finished bathing. By the time I entered our sleeping quarters, the rest of the girls had arrived with large piles of parchment, books scattered across the floor in every which direction.

Out of the corner of my eye I saw Priscilla directing a scrawny girl where to set her load. Meanwhile, Priscilla sat idly brushing her long locks and complaining loudly about how much harder it was going to be for her to rest surrounded by "this lowborn mess." Somehow, from Priscilla's tone, I didn't think she was referring to the books.

"I think she and the prince will do nicely together," I remarked quietly to Ella as she sat down on the bunk next to mine. "They are easily the nastiest people here."

Ella smiled.

"Do you still have work left?" I asked her.

"No, I finished most of mine earlier during the break at lunch."

I looked longingly at my pillows. I still had at least an hour of assignments left.

"I still have a couple problems too," Ruth offered from a couple bunks down.

"What time do they check the lights?" Winifred wondered.

"I think the constable said eleven, which should be any minute now," another girl next to Winifred remarked.

"Do we have any candles or matches?" I needed to finish my work somehow.

"I don't think so, but I can conjure light," Ruth offered quickly. "Do you want to try and finish your work with me after the constable has finished his rounds?"

I nodded, grateful for her offer and jealous she had a skill I didn't at the same time.

We decided to go to the bathing corridor so as not to keep the others up with our studying. Unfortunately, about ten minutes after we thought the constable had finished his rounds, his servant Frederick pounded on the door and demanded we go to bed at once. Fearing the reprimands Barrius had promised, we quickly heeded Frederick's order. I was a little nervous that I had not finished, but at that point there was nothing I could do until morning came.

"Please wake me when you are up," I whispered to Ella as I crawled into my bunk. "I still need to finish my work."

"Mmm-hmm." I hoped she would remember in the morning.

I wrapped myself in my blankets and shut my eyes. In a matter of moments I had forgotten the day's events and was fast asleep.

# Chapter Four

The cruel, harsh light of day was not there to wake me that following morning. Instead, the horrible toll of bells sounded from somewhere outside the Academy and continued to ring across every inch of its campus.

I groaned and rubbed my eyes. The sun had barely risen, and every muscle in my body was tight in protest.

"I know. It's a wonder you were able to sleep through it yesterday," Ella remarked as she stood up.

"How much time do we have until breakfast?" I asked.

"Not much, they expect us to start right away."

I had thought I would have some time to study. *Lovely.*

"Ugh, they brought us more of that delightful training garb," a sarcastic voice said to my left.

I glanced around. At the front of the room was a large crate of shapeless brown breeches and forest green tunics, equally plain. Next to it was a pile of old leather belts and high boots splattered with mud and dark red stains that looked suspiciously like blood. As Piers had promised, the clothes were worn and frayed. It was obvious they were hand-me-downs that had been passed on year after year to the incoming class.

I was appreciative for the new wardrobe, if only for the fact that it would help lessen the stigma of class that ran rampant in the halls. *Some* of us could certainly use the reminder that we were all supposed to be equals here.

Smiling inwardly at the groans coming from the side of the room that had been unofficially designated upper class, I quickly dressed and headed down to the dining commons. I was tired but anxious to finish at least a problem or two of mathematics over steaming porridge and a hot mug of tea.

When I arrived, Alex was already seated in our normal spot.

"How many problems do you have left?"

I sighed. "Too many."

"Me too," he contributed cheerfully. "What do you think will happen?"

I stared at the equations on my paper, willing them to make sense. "I hope we aren't the only ones" was the only reply I could think of.

Unfortunately, as my brother and I learned, we were indeed the *only ones* to not complete the first day's assignment. The rest of the class had either copied each other's answers, or they had all better managed their time. Even Ruth, whom I thought had a couple equations left, managed to turn in a complete paper.

As punishment for our negligence, Alex and I were expected to spend two hours after supper assisting Constable Barrius's staff with the mucking of the stables.

"But we didn't have enough time to finish last night's work! How am I supposed to finish today's *and* clean the stables?"

"Miss Ryiah," Master Eloise began slowly, squinting down at me, "if you can't meet the Academy's demands, then perhaps your time would be spent better elsewhere."

Behind me I heard several students snicker.

My face burned. "Just because I didn't ch—"

Alex kicked my shin, and I paused to glare at my brother. His eyes narrowed and I swallowed. His expression was clear. I was only making it harder on the both of us: *Did I really want to drag him down with me?*

"My apologies," I mumbled to Master Eloise. "It will not happen again."

"See that it doesn't."

I followed Alex to our seats, avoiding the gaze of those I passed. When we had reached our desks and the masters had begun their lecture, I turned to him.

"Why did you stop me? You knew half the class cheated!"

"Do you really want to make enemies on your second day?" he countered.

"No..." I stared at my hands, frustrated.

"Besides," Ella pointed out, joining our hushed conversation, "arguing with the masters will only strengthen their opinion that you should not be here in the first place. It's your job to prove them wrong."

"But how can I if I don't have enough time to do what they ask in the first place?"

Ella raised a brow. "I think the only ones who know the answer to that are the ones that already have an apprenticeship." She tapped her books with her quill, "Now pay attention, you two. I can't have my only friends leaving me to fend for myself."

⁜

After four hours in the library and the shortest lunch imaginable, Alex, Ella, and I headed for what was sure to be the worst part of our day: two hours with Sir Piers.

Expectations did not disappoint.

After another five-mile run, which was much worse now that everyone was sore from the day before, Sir Piers had us practice again with the staffs. Somehow he expected us to have significantly improved.

Instead, our exhaustion just led to more mistakes than the last session.

When I got down the line to Alex, he and I spent our five-minute drill barely moving in order to catch a quick break. When it was Ella's turn, she spent the entire time trying to helpfully contribute tips that I neither wanted to hear nor heed.

Sir Piers spent the whole exercise shouting. I was convinced someone had told him the louder he yelled, the harder we'd try. It didn't work.

Half the class was at the point of collapse by the time the second hour had finished. It was all I could do to walk my staff back to the armory.

"Just where do you lot think you are going?" Piers barked.

The crowd of students froze, and I turned back to see Sir Piers and Master Cedric scowling at us.

"Gods, *no*," Alex said in a hushed voice.

"We are not finished," Sir Piers bellowed. "I need all of you to return with your staffs. Master Cedric and I have a new exercise for you."

My stomach fell. My legs were weak as jelly, and my arms felt like lead weights.

The assisting mages from yesterday returned, passing out small strips of cloth to each student they passed. Alex, Ella, and I each took one, exchanging dubious expressions as we lined back up in the two-columned formation we had been practicing in.

Master Cedric cleared his throat. "As all of you now have your cloth, I'd like you to place it over your eyes and form a blindfold. Today's exercise is going to expose the problem with the majority of your performances yesterday. Of course, some of you already have an understanding for what today's task is about to explicate, but I feel it is my duty to educate the rest of the masses."

As I tied the rag across my eyes, I wondered briefly what it was we were about to learn. Considering yesterday's experience, I was prepared for something equally offsetting. I felt silly standing there, unable to see anything, hands clutching the staff that Piers had insisted we bring back.

"Now that you are all lined up and ready, please assume the traditional stance with the person on the left defending while the right leads the assault."

Really? Staff fighting *while* blindfolded? This was only going to make me a million times worse.

Grudgingly, I began the engage with the gangly girl who had been standing across from me. As the attacker, it was much more difficult than I had imagined. My sense of orientation was completely thrown off from blindness. The echo of a hundred wooden staffs clashing was deafening.

I spent most of my time swiping the wind or accidentally knocking my staff into the person on my right's shoulder.

"Change positions!"

I had thought blindly hitting someone was hard, but it was much worse when I was trying to guess where my offender was coming from. My shoulders ached from being continuously whacked. I concentrated hard on trying to hear the slight whistle of rushing air when the staff was coming down, but I couldn't hear anything above the clamor. My best bet was to try and focus on the crunching of the grass whenever my partner shifted stance, or the stink of sweat when he raised his arm.

After a couple more five-minute drills, I was sore but better off than when I had started. I had been able to defend myself about half of the time, and I was a little more secure in my footing after I had grown accustomed to the darkness.

"You may now take a seat and remove your blindfolds," Master Cedric announced.

Relieved, I tossed the sweat-stained rag aside and took a place beside my latest staffing partner. We both looked to Cedric for the speech we knew was coming, the reason we had just spent thirty minutes hitting sticks blindly.

"Forgot about the other senses before today, didn't you?" Piers asked us wickedly.

Master Cedric expanded: "The reason I had you blindfolded was so that each of you could properly identify the other senses that are so often forgotten in one's general conduct. You've spent two days drilling with staffs, but it has been my observation that most of you have only been using sight to tell you where to block, where to strike, how to proceed.

"The truth is that every action requires more than vision for a performance to be completely vested. The best soldiers and mages alike embrace their senses. Just now, all of you were forced to recognize other ways of predicting an opponent's actions when you couldn't use your sight to answer the question for you. Heightened listening, body heat, smell, and an increased understanding to the different points of pressure in a blow should have all helped contribute to your knowledge of staff fighting.

"If you were to engage in a casting, these types of observations would increase the potency of your magic. Your spells are derivatives of the information, experience, and desire you put forth. I'm sure all of you have desire—it's why you are here—but the amount of information and experience you put into your castings will be important indicators as well. You may want more than anything to produce an effective sleeping draught, but if you can't build up the proper projection within your mind, it will not be very effective. You need to consider all aspects, not just the image or obvious sense of the action or thing you are trying to create."

I strained to listen, but the pounding in my head was so much that his words were coming out as an endless drone.

"The irony of your training here at the Academy is that while we require you to ignore your physical senses in meditation and acute focus, we ask you to embrace them in your mental casting. You are not allowed to feel what is physically going on around you during the moment of your spell, but you are expected to cast an image evocative of all those physical senses in your mind. I admit that the practice of these two things is not easy. It is not something you can master in a day, or even years. All I can advise is that the more you practice, the more you dedicate yourself to exploring these two states, the better your chances will be at succeeding within your own magical faction."

The end of Master Cedric's lecture was spent in silence. Most of us were still trying to take in everything as we followed him out to the field to continue yesterday's meditative exercise. I hoped it would make sense after a long night's rest.

At the end of our session, we were informed that this would be the pattern for the rest of the month—half of the class practicing a heightened awareness to the senses, the others learning to block them out. Supposedly with enough practice we would be able to transfer easily between the two states.

Of course, to be "competent" we'd have to continue the practice on our own during any "free time" we were lucky enough to acquire. Knowing how much free time I actually had at my disposal, it was obvious that the highborn students had a huge advantage.

Those that had grown up with a mage tutor advising them didn't have to be worried about the lack of free time they had now. The non-heir's group wouldn't falter under our intense workload. I, on the other hand, would be struggling for any free moment I could find in order to try and catch up.

It was unfair that I would be working doubly hard, but it was an inevitable reality as long as I remained. If I didn't try, I'd only be widening that gap in the months to come.

By the time dinner had ended, I was in a very irritable state. I said little to Alex as we forked piles of manure out of the straw. I continued my silence on our walk back to the castle as well, unable to let go of my growing resentment of the privileged class. Statistically speaking, those that had the extra learning would have no problem finishing each night's assignments. Which meant it would always be people like Alex and me mucking out the stables.

Granted, I had known all along we would have a disadvantage, but I had hoped the masters would help the underprivileged instead of capitalizing on their weakness. Why take away free time from the ones that needed it most? Why punish us for incomplete assignments using mundane tasks that had nothing to do with the practice of magic? It was only going to make it harder for us to succeed, not easier.

By the time I had reached the barracks to grab my books, I had only an hour left before I was expected to return. I looked for Alex as I entered the crowded library, but he was nowhere to be seen.

Grumbling, I shoved my way past a horde of students and made my way to the back of the room. I could see why Ella had been so irritated the day before. With Darren's group hogging the largest, most comfortable lounge, there was little space left for the rest of us. There was crowding down every aisle on either floor, and the chatter was loud enough to set my teeth on edge. There was no way I'd be able to concentrate.

Spotting a ladder at the end of the room, I decided to leave the masses and see what the third floor could offer. When I reached it, I could see why no one had bothered. There was no torchlight, no books, and no seating.

This "floor" was nothing more than a cramped alcove with spider webs hanging from empty shelves. At a corner on the left was a makeshift bench composed from wooden crates. The place had probably been used as a study at some point, but it had been long since abandoned.

Avoiding the darkest part of the room, which I suspected was crowded with unfriendly spiders, I made my way to the only source of light. Dragging one of the crates to sit beneath a dirty paned window, I quickly commenced my study. The alcove wasn't very comfortable, but it was quiet and remote.

My time passed quickly. It had been productive, but I was nowhere near done when I heard Constable Barrius ordering the first-years to return to their quarters. I was in the midst of grabbing my belongings when I began to contemplate my situation. If I left now, I would never finish the day's work.

*But,* I thought as I listened to the pounding of busy feet, *I could stay up here, and no one would know.* It was risky, I knew, to stay out past curfew. If the constable spotted me, I could be expelled on the spot...but if it worked, I would never have to worry about chores again.

I was careful not to make a sound as I leaned over the edge of the rail to watch everyone exit the library. I held my breath as Barrius and his assistant made their final inspection of the studies.

Finally, after much pausing and condescending chatter, the two left, leaving me alone in a situation I hoped very much not to regret. I had no idea how I would make it to the girl's barracks unnoticed, but I saved the thought for later. I contemplated going down to the lounge where there was more light and comfortable seating, but I knew it was too risky. Who knew how often Barrius would check the library? I had best stay where I was and make the most of it.

I had only been studying for twenty minutes when there was a slight creaking sound from the doors below.

Carefully setting down my belongings, I tiptoed to the railing's edge and peered down into the dark study beneath. Sure enough, it wasn't my imagination. In the darkness I could see a hooded figure quietly shutting the door as it clutched a handful of books and parchment much like my own.

Seconds later I heard a familiar nasal voice coming from the hall.

I watched as the figure ducked behind a bookcase to the right not a moment too soon. All at once torchlight illuminated the library, and I watched as the constable chastised Frederick for his imagination.

"But I thought I heard someone—"

"You think you hear a lot of things," Barrius cut Frederick off. "But once again, you've managed to waste my time."

"But shouldn't we still search?"

"Really, Frederick, who would sneak off to the library of all places?"

"I don't—"

"Out!" Barrius snarled.

"Yes, sir."

After the echo of footsteps faded, the figure chuckled. I watched as it settled comfortably upon the couch below. Moments later a small fiery glow appeared. It wasn't very bright, just enough to give out light to read, and see the face of my fellow rule-breaker.

The hood had fallen away to reveal black bangs and the dark eyes I had since become accustomed to loathing. *Darren.*

The non-heir sat below poring over the same books as me.

My jaw dropped. The very thought that he and I had shared the same idea was distressing in more ways than one. *I* had come here to make up for lost time, but Darren, who already had such an advantage in his training...*he* had come here to study *anyway*. Someone who didn't even *need* to, someone who was *already* at the top of our class...

And I bet he had come here the night before too.

I refused to consider what it meant.

Turning back to my studies, I tried to focus my mind and block out anything other than the problems on the page in front of me. I bit my lip resolutely. *Do* not *let this opportunity go wasted, especially with* him *down there.*

Minutes slowly trickled by as I read questions once, twice, three times before attempting to solve. *You can do this.* I stifled a yawn and kept at my work.

An hour and a half later I finally finished the assignments.

I could have left at that point but, seeing as how Darren was still working below, I decided to stay. My conscience could not allow a condescending prince to work harder than me. Especially one that had insinuated I was here to "socialize."

So I stayed. Math and Crown law were beyond comprehension at that point, as was geography with all of its confusing maps, so I chose a history scroll instead. It was the right choice. Almost like a storybook in narration, the long and detailed accounts of Jerar's fighting mages helped retain my focus into the late hours of the night.

Our last war had been ninety years ago, but the book's breakdown of battle strategy made me feel as though I was a part of it now. There were so many things I had never considered, aspects of battle that I had thought were reserved only for the knights of our kingdom. I'd had no idea how involved the planning was behind our army's attacks. *Silly me*, I had always assumed victory just came down to how much power a nation's mages had.

I had just started reading about a particularly bloody battle when I heard a stifled yawn downstairs. Taking that as my cue, I packed up my work and stood by the rail to watch for Darren's departure. As soon as he left I would follow.

I had barely shifted the books in my arms when my quill dropped. It echoed unsettlingly down the stairs, and Darren jerked his head upward in my direction. He didn't ask who was there, but he did get up to investigate. Rather than waiting for him to find me, I gave up my hiding place and started down the ladder.

Settling onto the first floor, I turned to find Darren standing with a palm full of light in one hand and a stunned expression on his face.

"You?" he rasped.

"You're not the only one who wants to get ahead," I told him curtly. Then, because I couldn't help it, I added: "You know, us *commoners*, not all of us are just here to 'socialize and talk about feelings.'"

Darren's eyes flashed dangerously. For a moment it looked like shame had crossed those cold, fathomless features, but it was gone just as quickly as it had appeared. Then it was just the two of us staring for an uncomfortable moment: me, aware of my ragged, manure-tinged appearance, and Darren, looking as inscrutable as ever.

Sighing, I broke his gaze and squeezed my way past.

I was almost to the door when he cleared his throat loudly.

"Wait—"

I paused and looked to the non-heir: *What could he possibly want now?*

"Don't take the right hall," Darren said abruptly. "Barrius had Frederick patrolling there last night."

"A-alright." The confusion must have shown on my face because a second later Darren's eyes narrowed in their familiar condescension.

"The last thing I need is for you to get caught and make it harder for me to come here at night."

The abrupt change of tone cut like a knife. Of course, *this* was the person I had been expecting all along. "My furthest intention," I assured the prince dryly.

He just stared, eyes dark and unreadable, and I hurried out the door in the direction of the women's barracks. As I was crossing the field, I saw a hooded figure stealthily approaching the men's, and I knew Darren had retired for the night as well.

Lucky for him, however, the non-heir's routine did not have him taking a freezing bath at such an ungodly hour. I tried to be careful not to make any noise as I scrubbed the stable stench from my hair and skin, but it was impossible to keep completely quiet with the water sloshing around.

Still, it appeared I was undiscovered as I crawled into my bed. The bell had long since tolled an hour past midnight, and once again I was asleep within seconds of hitting my pillow.

# CHAPTER FIVE

The next two weeks flew past in a blur. No sooner had I crawled out of bed I was rushed to the dining hall with Ella in hopes of catching the last couple of minutes of the morning meal. Even then, I was too tired to do much else besides stare lifelessly ahead. The extra hours I was losing had started to take their toll, and it was all I could do to stay awake.

The only thing that made the experience worthwhile was catching sight of Darren across the hall. There was something gratifying about seeing the non-heir gripping a steaming mug with the same blood-shot eyes as me. He may have been better at hiding behind a steely composure, but there was no denying the fact he was just as miserable.

Alex and Ella at first wondered why I stayed behind studying each night, but it hadn't been hard to convince them I needed the extra time to myself. Both of them knew how slow I was at learning some of the assignments. No one in the girl's quarters even mentioned my absence. I think Ella was the only one who had noticed, but she kept it to herself.

Each day was filled with the same tedious coursework as the last. The bright side, of course, was that I was no longer behind. My assignments were always turned in complete, and I could tell from Master Eloise and Isaac's approving remarks that I was no longer a disappointment. Mathematics was still a time-consuming ordeal, but with the extra two to three hours each night, I was easily gaining traction in the basics and moving on to more complex issues that dealt with warfare and Crown law instead.

It was a strange schedule, and a tiring one, but it seemed to be working. Still, I was beginning to wonder how much longer I'd be able to hold out. I was doing well in the first half of my day, but three weeks of sleep deprivation had weakened my performance in the remainder. I was lagging through Sir Piers's drills and Master Cedric's lessons, and while everyone else had started to improve, I was still as clumsy as the day I had started. To make matters worse, *everyone* had noticed.

The worst embarrassment had come today.

"What is wrong with you?"

I froze, cheeks burning as I tore off my blindfold. The entire class was silently staring. Priscilla of Langli stood in front of me, one large, red welt plastering the left side of her face. She was furious.

"Didn't you hear me give the command to halt?" Sir Piers barked.

"I m-must have missed it." I had been so exhausted I hadn't heard anything other than the pounding in my head.

Priscilla dropped her staff and stormed off in the direction of the armory.

Sir Piers eyed me distastefully. "If you can't stay awake long enough to hear your commander give you an order, you shouldn't be at this Academy—or anywhere near a weapon—in the first place."

I nodded, eyes watering, and went to return my staff, avoiding my brother's sympathetic gaze. It was harder to miss some of the comments of the others, however. Several of Priscilla's friends were loudly telling anyone that would listen that my blunder had been an "attack of jealousy" since Priscilla was clearly the "leading female of our year."

I met people's stares with a glare of my own. Both Alex and Ella tried to talk to me after class, but I was too upset to listen to anything they had to say.

It seemed that no matter what I tried, it would never be enough. I didn't have enough time to do everything the masters asked of me, and when I tried to make time, my work only suffered somewhere else.

＊

My evening became progressively worse when I ran into Darren as he was leaving the dining commons. As soon as he spotted me, a grin spread across the non-heir's face. He'd become less icy since we had started our late night studies, but it didn't mean he had become any kinder.

"What?"

"Do you always attack the blind?" Darren asked, dark eyes filled with humor.

Several students nearby snickered, and my cheeks flushed.

"There's a first time for everything," I snapped. "Maybe I'll try a prince next."

"Ryiah!" Alex grabbed my wrist just before I could throw my tray at the arrogant halfwit. Darren laughed and sauntered off to join his table of admirers while I was left brimming with rage.

"*What has gotten into you?*" my brother hissed.

"It's not fair!" I growled, "I am going to fail this place—"

"Then let's have you try something new, not challenge the royal family to a duel." My twin dragged me back to the table with Ella and the rest of our study group.

"Did you just threaten a prince?" Ruth asked incredulously.

I stabbed at a cherry tomato on my plate. "Wouldn't matter if I did. I can't keep up with Piers's drills to save my life. Darren would have disarmed me in a second."

Alex glanced at Ella. "Anything you can do to help her, beautiful?"

My friend scowled. "Am I or am I not the daughter of a knight?"

"Does that mean yes?" I asked wearily.

Ella smiled wide. "For the girl that challenges princes, it is most definitely a yes."

⁕

An hour later I met up with Ella at the armory for our first lesson. She was practicing some sort of complicated footwork when I arrived, much more advanced than what we had gone over in class.

"Thanks again," I said as she stopped her routine to toss me a weighted staff.

Ella shrugged. "I should be doing this anyway. I need it after watching Piers sing that prince and his minions praises all week long."

I laughed and matched Ella's starting stance. "It's pretty obvious, isn't it?"

"It's downright depressing," she griped. "I grew up around weapons, and I've trained with them almost as often. At no point should people who grew up reciting their family trees be besting me at those drills...Hold that pose, Ryiah."

My sore muscles protested as she adjusted my form. "Don't I need a blindfold?"

The girl snorted. "Let's not test your luck just yet."

We began the drill again only to have her stop me again.

"What now?" I was unable to keep the exasperation from my tone.

"Stop being so tense!" she ordered. "If you don't loosen up those muscles, you are going to strain something. You need to be relaxed and fluid when you block, like you are dancing."

"I've never danced."

"Well, like you are water then," she said quickly. We began our practice again. "Really though, no dancing?"

"You wouldn't have either if you saw what Demsh'aa had to offer." I attempted a block and overcompensated, swinging wildly to my right.

Ella chuckled. "You'll be doing this dance every day now."

"I hope it works."

We were practicing in the shade of the armory building, but the air was still thick with humidity. Flies swarmed about. I was almost tempted to use them for my target. At least then I'd get some satisfaction out of our endless drilling. I was so exhausted from parrying blow after blow. And after so many endless deflections, it didn't matter that Ella was holding back. I could have been facing the great Sir Piers himself.

I took my turn leading the assault. "Will I really get better?"

"I know it doesn't seem that way now," Ella replied easily as she blocked, her voice a relaxed lull in contrast to my heavy gasps for air. "But all this—the soreness, even the fatigue—if you keep at it, it won't come any easier, but you will improve."

The burning ache in my side challenged her claim.

I swung a more concentrated pass, and for the first time it met its mark with a resounding smack. Ella actually faltered for a second, more from surprise than the weight of my blow. *Still*, it was an improvement.

"Pain is a sign you are working your body to its limits," Ella continued as we kept on. "My dad always said that is why lowborns usually outperform nobility in battle." She paused and remarked somewhat ironically, "Though you wouldn't guess it here." Ella lowered her staff and glanced up at the darkening sky, "Well, I guess that does it for today."

I followed my friend to the armory to dispose of our weapons. My entire body ached, but for once I was comforted by the prospect.

"We've got about an hour left until they make us go back to our quarters," I observed.

"Definitely not enough time to wash up if we want to catch up with the rest of our group."

I eyed my friend skeptically. While she was certainly not sweet-smelling of peonies and fresh linen, her clothes were not nearly as sweat-stained as mine, and the light tint of perspiration on her forearms only highlighted her complexion. I looked like a sunburned rat dripping with sweat.

"Yes," I said, fingering my tangled locks and trying not to breathe too deeply into my own stink, "that'll certainly be a shame for some of us."

⚜

That evening I spent hours poring over my assignments, fighting fatigue and dreaming of my family back in Demsh'aa. I missed my old life. I missed my little brother's jokes and my parents' patience. I missed their support. It was nice to have Alex here, but I missed the easygoing life I had left behind. One where I was not a fumbling mishap among a crowd of prodigies.

When I saw the familiar flicker of light emerge from Darren's first floor study, it only fueled my determination.

*I am no fool.* I was not as incompetent as he and the rest of the school imagined.

I read about war mages that had fought tens of knights with a simple sweep of their staff, mages who had learned archery only to invoke a rain of razor sharp blades upon their rivals, mages who had studied the foundations of architecture and then sent their enemies' castles crumbling to the ground.

It was time to train. Hard.

I had a robe to wear after all.

⚜

"*Come on*, Ryiah, pay attention!"

"I am!" I groaned and deflected another blow, scrambling to get my defense up in time.

I barely managed.

"Again," Ella shouted.

I made another mad attempt to defend myself.

And then another.

And then I cried out as my friend's staff came into contact with my ribs, and I dropped my pole. I'd guessed wrong again.

"Once more, where am I coming from?" She held her stance, willing me to try and see what it was I had missed the first time.

I watched my friend closely, trying to figure out where her next strike would be. All signs pointed to a low upswing from the left, but I had made that mistake before, and my ribs were paying dearly for it now.

I frowned. Her shoulders were deceptively loose with her eyes drifting ever so slightly to my right, and her hands gripped the staff at a crooked angle. I had seen it all before. What was I missing? *Pay attention...*but to what?

Ella had spent enough time reminding me not to be too sure of myself. Any good opponent will try to trick you, she'd said. Anyone that practiced close range fighting would know the importance of deceit. Let your enemy think they've got you figured out, make it look like they can see where you're coming—not too obvious, just enough so that they get cocky. If someone thinks they know your next move, they are more likely to let their guard down.

"Look at me, Ryiah," Ella said again. "Where is my staff going to land?"

I tried to see the impossible. Sweat stung my eyes as my gaze traveled up and down my friend's build, searching desperately for a sign.

Then I saw it.

Her knees were lightly bent, feet apart, with the right heel slightly off the ground. It was easy to miss—her dark boots were bulky and obscured sight easily—but there was a slight indent in the leathers on the right front of the foot that betrayed where she had shifted her weight.

"You're going to come from the right with a top-swing," I announced confidently.

Ella relaxed her form. "You *are* learning," she said happily. A little too enthusiastically for someone that had constantly assured me I was doing well. I briefly wondered if she really had believed that, and then buried the thought at once.

"It's funny," I noted, as we retired our weapons for the evening. "Each day Piers and Cedric ask me to practice in a blindfold, and then you make me watch whenever we train out here."

"Well four days with me is not an eternity," Ella replied. "And for you, I really think you need a better grasp of the basics. It's a little ambitious what they are putting us through. I think the masters are so used to highborns coming from private tutelage that they forget what it's like for the rest. My background at least came in handy, but for you it's a matter of tireless diligence."

I groaned.

⁎⫿⁎

For the rest of that week and the next, Ella and I continued our daily practices. It was an endless cycle of madness, but fortunately I did not fall any further behind.

In the meantime, two straight weeks with Ella correcting my form and watching my every move had paid off. I was still as sore as that first day I had arrived, but I could tell my breathing was much less labored in the drills Piers put us though. Even my arms felt stronger. The wooden staff no longer felt like a foreign extension of my arm.

Piers had since stopped criticizing my technique and moved on to some of the other, less fortunate first-years that were still grappling with the concept of a proper guard.

I had to hold back a small smile when I heard Piers inform Priscilla she could learn from my approach after she complained about the "unnecessary repetition."

The commander pointed his chin in my direction. "That one may not have your skill, my dear, but at least she's willing to learn."

"The ones that *need* to learn this are the ones that shouldn't be here," the girl retorted hotly, refusing to cower under the knight's scowl. "Highborn children learn to fight with staffs in their sleep."

Several students gave loud hoots of agreement. It didn't take a mastermind to figure out which lineage they came from.

"You would think that," Sir Piers replied idly, "and, most of the time, you'd be right. But each year I've been here, there's been one or two lowborns who shame all that extra coin your families put to use. It's the ones that *need* to learn you should be worried about."

Priscilla flinched and immediately stopped her protest.

"The worst thing wealth does is give those that have it a false sense of security," Piers concluded loudly, addressing the entire group as he motioned for us to dismiss. "You stop trying as hard, and there's always another that will gladly take your place."

⚔

Later that evening my newfound glee was still in full swing when Ella and I retired from the armory. It seemed that Piers's speech had instilled a newfound sense of urgency to some of the more confident first-years. We were now one of six small groups that practiced near the building after our evening meal.

Most of the students, I noticed, were practicing much more advanced moves than Ella and I, but it was a compliment that they had shown up just the same. Maybe they

didn't view me as a serious contender but now they were at
least willing to consider the possibility.

Ella turned to me as we entered the library. "Feels good,
doesn't it?"

I just smiled brazenly.

"You smell terrible," Alex greeted us.. The library was
packed as usual, which unfortunately did very little to allevi-
ate the telltale odor of my clothes.

Ella gave him a look.

"Ella, my flower, my sweet, that comment was for my
dear sister alone. You smell as enchanting as—"

"Save your prose, pretty boy," Ella cut Alex off, laughing. "We've got enough to worry about without your attempts
at romance tonight."

Our study session came and went without much ado. We
were mostly silent because the night was our last review of the
fundamentals. Starting the next day, we'd be focusing on one
faction a week, beginning with Restoration. And orientation
meant casting.

We were all nervous. The tension in the air was thick as
we poured over our volumes, each silently hoping that we had
learned enough to not humiliate ourselves in the weeks that
mattered.

The second and third months were when we would lose
the most students, according to Master Barclae's ominous admission that evening at dinner. "*You can't fake it for long here,*"
he'd warned. "*Beginning tomorrow we will see what you can do
instead of what you know. Many start to resign because they see
what kind of magical prowess they are actually going up against.
That, and they can't keep up.*"

In any case, the entire library was much more quiet than
usual. When Barrius came round for his usual dismissal, it took
twice the time it usually did for him to clear the first two
floors. Everyone was reluctant to leave. Unfortunately, that
also made it impossible for me to escape to the alcove unnoticed.

Irritated, I retreated with the rest of the crowd to my barracks, resolving to sneak my way back at the earliest opportunity.

After the constable's final round, I hastily pushed my blankets away and reached for my books in the darkness.

"Still at it?" Ella whispered from her bunk nearby.

I should have known better than to expect everyone to have already fallen asleep.

I clutched my materials and squeezed my way past the scattered belongings strewn across the floor.

"I'll see you in the morning," I told her quietly as I passed her bunk.

"Don't be up too late," she reminded gently. "We've got our work cut out tomorrow."

"I know," I replied grimacing. "I'll try not—"

"*Would you two keep it down?*" an irritated voice shot out from across the room. It belonged to my biggest fan, Priscilla.

I hastily crossed the room to the door while Ella told Priscilla where she could stick her complaints.

Upon exiting the building, I made a mad rush for the backdoors of the Academy. They were only a couple hundred feet away, but the pathway was completely exposed without a tree for cover. Barrius's staff would be patrolling since it was still early on, and the last thing I wanted was to be discovered.

I had just made it across and quietly shut the doors behind when I heard a slight squeaking a couple paces to my left.

I froze. It was too dark to see. Holding my breath, I waited, praying whoever was there hadn't heard me.

Silence.

I waited a couple moments longer, but there was no further sound.

Suddenly, a chamber door slammed and I heard two servants' excited voices. They were far enough away that they hadn't spotted me yet in the shadows, but I knew it was only a matter of time.

To make matters worse, there was a bright light coming from the furthest end of the hall. The servants' torch was quickly eating away the shadows and casting an unflattering light across the walls it touched.

Panic filled my gut. Who knew how far Barrius would go if he found me breaking curfew? I couldn't get caught.

I felt my way along the rough sandstone wall, inching towards the light, trying to remember if I'd seen a passageway this close to the back entry of the Academy. Surely the servants had some quarters nearby. I was in the constable's corridor after all.

The voices were drawing nearer, as was the light, and I knew I had only a minute or so left before I was spotted. I continued my blind fumbling, ignoring the pain in my hand as I shoved it against the wall's uncut surface, desperately seeking a handle or crevice that would indicate a room behind.

My hand caught on a smooth, hard panel, and I knew I had found a door. I felt around for the knob and had only just opened it a crack when an arm shot out and yanked me inside. The door slammed shut just as a hand covered my mouth to muffle my cry.

It took a second for my fear to subside as I realized who had pulled me back. There was the slightest bit of light coming through the cracks in the wooden frame, and it was enough for me to recognize the face of my so-called captor. Darren quickly let go and motioned for me to stay still.

I could hear the two servants just outside our door.

"—Know I heard something this time," the first was saying. "I'm sure of it."

"Well, come on then. Help me open this door," the second drawled, "I bet you there's a first-year hiding on the other side. The constable will have a field day when we show him!"

I swallowed and looked wildly to Darren who stood closest to the door. The two of us were crammed in some sort of storage closet. Giant sacks of flour and wheat lined the shelves, and there was nowhere to hide. We barely had enough room to stand, let alone disappear.

Darren didn't look too worried, however. Instead, he put a finger to his lips and then shut his eyes, leaning against the nearest shelf.

*Meditation isn't going to do much good when they catch us,* I thought crossly.

The knob rattled. I held my breath and prepared for the inevitable result.

Nothing happened. The rattling continued, but the door stayed shut.

"That's strange...This door doesn't even have a lock."

"Let me have a go at it."

The metal knob continued to shake, but it was no closer to opening.

I looked to Darren in the shadows, suspicious and relieved. The door had opened easily enough for me. It was clear he was doing more than just meditating.

"It's not letting up."

"Well, let's check the gardens, maybe whoever we heard made it outside."

"Must have," the second agreed. "Nobody could have opened this door."

The rattling stopped, and the servants' steps retreated. After a couple of minutes I willed myself to breathe more easily, taking slow gulps of air.

"They're gone now. Come on." Darren seemed impatient as he held the door, stealing nervous glances down the hall.

I stared at him. "How did you do that with the door?"

Darren ignored my question. "Are you coming or not?"

I sighed and joined him in the hall.

Darren shut the door behind us, softly, and turned to face me.

"Don't make any sudden noises," he instructed. "There's still bound to be a few more servants up at this hour."

He started off, heading towards the west corridor, and I called out after him, "Where are you going?"

The non-heir turned and gave me an odd look, or what I was convinced was one. I couldn't be too sure since it was dark again without the servant's light in the passage.

"The library. Where else?"

I felt like a fool.

"That's where you're headed, right?"

"Yes." I raced after Darren as he started down the hall.

"Try not to get us caught this time," he said.

I didn't reply, deciding silence was better than the retort I had half a mind to say. He *had* saved us after all, even if he was being conceited about it.

We made it the rest of the way without any trouble. It seemed the two we had first encountered were the only servants concerned with patrolling the east wing of the castle, and we didn't run into anyone in the west passage leading up to the library either.

Entering the giant study, I watched as Darren shut the doors behind us and conjured a bit of light in hand. There was just enough to clear up the shadows between us and cast a dim glow on our surroundings.

I cleared my throat. "Thank you...for helping me back there." The words were hard to say.

The prince scoffed. "I didn't do it for you."

"Just take my thanks," I told him exasperatedly. Whatever his motives were, they had helped me twice now.

Darren looked amused. "Your thanks?" His expression seemed to imply that they didn't amount to much.

I balked. "Well, don't read too much into it. You've been nasty enough that I guess fate was bound to have you do one decent thing for me."

The prince recoiled. "And I suppose you think you've done nothing wrong?" he demanded. "In case you failed to remember, you and that girl you always go around with tried to get me thrown out of here."

"Well, you *are* a prince," I shot back. "You have to admit it isn't exactly fair."

"I will not apologize for my birthright," Darren said stiffly. He narrowed his eyes and added callously, "I am tired of trying to explain myself to everyone that questions my right to be here. *Especially* people like you."

I glared right back. "I may not be as well-off, but even if I was, I wouldn't use bloodlines as a means to demean everyone else."

"I wasn't referring to your trivial heritage." He looked at me contemptuously. "I care little enough whether you grew up in the fields or a damned palace." He took a step closer and looked down at me, speaking the next few words slowly. "When I say 'people like you' I am referring to the ones that so clearly *have no* real *magic or potential of any kind.*"

I clenched my fists until I could no longer feel, fire burning in my veins. Prince or not, I had never come to this close to hitting someone.

"You..." I couldn't even come up with the rest. I was livid.

Darren continued, unaware of how dangerously he was treading. "Really, it's unthinkable that the masters could even consider the possibility of denying *me* in favor of someone like you who plainly has no purpose attempting the robes in the first place."

My nails dug into my palm, and I was vaguely aware of the warm trickle of blood filling my fist. Heat clouded my vision, and Darren's smug face filled my mind. *When I say people like you.* His words were like fire, singeing my skin every place they hit.

"What are you—*stop*! STOP!"

My vision cleared, and I saw Darren madly shaking the sleeves of his tunic, flames spouting from its edges. The flames were getting bigger every second and perilously close to his arms.

"Don't just stand there!" he shouted. "Make it stop!"

I looked down at my hands, which had since unclasped. There was no more pressure or pain. The fire should have snuffed out on its own like it had that time with the moss

Only it hadn't. Just like that other time, with the bandit. *What was wrong with me?*

"I can't," I exclaimed, panicked.

"Well, I can't get it to either!" he shot back. "My magic isn't—" He cut off mid-sentence and swore as a flame nicked his skin.

"*RYIAH!*"

I raced over and bit back a cry of pain as I helped hold his sleeves while he pulled his arms out one by one. As soon as he finished, I hurriedly lifted the tunic off and tossed it to the floor, stomping out the remaining flames against the black marble.

"You fool!" Darren declared as soon as the fire was extinguished. The sleeves of his thin undershirt were scorched in several places, revealing painful red swells on both wrists and part of his forearm.

"I didn't mean to—"

"Of course, you didn't mean to!" the prince snapped. "You have no control over your own magic!"

I winced. "Is there anything I can do?"

Darren lifted one arm at a time, testing the extent of his injury.

"Do you want me to help you back to your quarters?" He needed to soak those burns before they started to blister. I didn't have to be my brother to understand that much.

Darren laughed hoarsely. "I'm staying right where I am. I didn't come all this way just to turn back."

I gaped at him. "You can't be serious. Your arms..."

"I've experienced far worse than this." The prince picked up his books and paper and carried them over to his usual chaise. He noticed my stare and added wryly, "You don't become the best if you aren't willing to stick your hand in the fire."

"I always thought that was an expression."

The corner of his lip twitched, and for a moment I thought Darren was about to smile. "I think it was...until tonight."

⚡⚡

For the rest of the evening I remained on the first floor of the library with the newly-injured non-heir. I could have retired to my alcove, but there was a certain amount of guilt—and curiosity—that prevented me from leaving. Whatever I thought of Darren, he was never what I expected.

I wondered what he had meant by experiencing "far worse than this." Darren was a prince. How much suffering could a child of the Crown have had? I bit my lip. He must have been jesting, trying to appear valiant, though he was wasting his efforts on me. I was hardly the one he needed to impress.

Still, he hadn't sounded like a braggart or appeared remotely interested in my reaction. If anything, there had been an edge of bitterness to his tone. It was unsettling.

*What did a* prince *have to be bitter about?*

"Are you done staring?"

Dropping my quill in surprise, I flushed and met Darren's amused gaze.

"I-I didn't realize I was," I mumbled.

He fingered his burnt tunic. "You know, I was wrong about you earlier."

I gaped at him. *Was Darren apologizing?*

"But I hope you understand why I wasn't wrong to assume it."

I bristled. "What are you talking about?"

Darren pointed to the book in my lap. "We've been down here for thirty minutes, and you have yet to turn the page. For someone so bent on Combat, you sure are making a lot of mistakes."

"How did you know I was going to pick Comb—"

"Please." Darren rolled his eyes. "I've seen you in the practice yards. No one spends that much time trying to impress Sir Piers for his charm. It would be admirable, if you actually knew what you were doing."

"Pray, enlighten me," I growled.

He cocked his head to the side. "Hard work doesn't mean anything here if you don't have the castings to back it."

I glared at the prince. "I have magic. You saw it." *And you just admitted that.*

Darren raised a brow. "I know. But you aren't trying to develop it."

"I am trying!" I resisted slamming the book in hand.

Darren shot me an incredulous look. "You spend all your time in those books and drilling with your friends."

"What does that even mean?" I demanded.

Darren smiled wolfishly. "If you really want an apprenticeship, I am sure you'll figure it out."

⚜

The next morning I awoke with a sense of dread. My stomach was in knots, and Darren's mocking counsel had done nothing to assuage them. The best first-year in the school had insinuated I was making a huge mistake. And instead of telling me how to fix it, he had left me to fend for myself.

*You spend all your time in those books and drilling with your friends.* What was wrong with that? I devoted more time than any other student, with the exception of his highness himself, to my studies. Wasn't that what I was supposed to be doing?

And what did Darren mean when he said he had been right to assume I was one of "them," the ones with no *real* magic or potential? We hadn't even started casting yet. How could he even discern who the ones with potential were without seeing them cast beforehand?

He *had* to be alluding to Master Cedric's lessons. His were the only ones I continued to struggle with. But it was meditation. Who hadn't fallen asleep during it?

And, sure, I hadn't exactly tried to improve my standing there. But I only had so much time. I couldn't do well in everything. What more could Darren expect of me? Surely learning to fight and Master Eloise and Isaac's lessons were more important than focusing on a blade of grass for two hours?

And why did it matter anyway? Why was I so upset over something the non-heir had said? He wasn't a master. He was a first-year, a very, *very* opinionated first-year.

I shoved my blankets off my cot and stood resolutely. Darren didn't know what he was talking about. He was just trying to unnerve me. Maybe my potential scared him. I wouldn't put it past the prince to try and intimidate me into leaving.

Determined not to give Darren's words another thought, I hurried to the dining commons to join my friends.

"Ready for a change?" Ella greeted me.

I smiled weakly. "Would it make a difference either way?"

Alex chuckled.

Ella elbowed my brother. "Well, ready or not, you two, we are about to embrace the magical realm of blood and bandages."

I groaned. "Lucky us."

It was bound to be a long, arduous week.

# CHAPTER SIX

The first day of Restoration did not want to end. If I had ever complained of lack of time before today, I regretted it now.

Four hours were spent staring at complicated diagrams of human anatomy. Thousands of foreign sounding names for the parts of the vessel and the various rules one was expected to understand in order to mend. We learned about the most common complaints during a knight's service, and I was surprised to see how much time was spent going over natural maladies. Battle wounds were, apparently, too advanced for the week's orientation. Instead, we were to focus on the most common inflictions: jungle rot, frostbite, burns, and dehydration.

Alex and I had an advantage thanks to our years in the family apothecary. Unfortunately, most of that knowledge was lost to some frazzled recess in the corners of my mind. Darren's warning from the night before kept invading my thoughts, destroying any semblance of concentration I had.

The next few hours were even more disheartening. Piers had kept our regular conditioning, with its various laps and lunging and stretching between, but he had traded our staffs for heavy, weighted sacks of grain.

We were instructed to carry, lift, and drag them up and down the field. Repeatedly.

"Those are your patients," he barked. "Don't think you'll always be able to treat a victim in the middle of a battle-field. If there's still a fight going on, you'll need to get them to safety first. So pick up the pace, children!"

By the end of the exercise my arms were too weak to even reach up and adjust my hair.

Master Cedric's exercise wasn't any better. I had thought our first week of actual casting would change things, but it didn't. At least not in the way I had hoped.

With the help of the his assistants, Cedric had us divide into several small groups and take turns healing one another from the maladies we had studied earlier while the rest of the group watched. We were given two tasks, name the remedy and then cast out your magic using the projection of that cure to heal your patient. If you failed, the next person in your group would start his or her own attempt.

I did well enough during the first half of the lesson. Both Alex's and my background in the family apothecary helped with remedy. But when it came time to cast the cures for our patients, I was useless.

"What do you think you are doing, first-year?"

I whirled around to find Master Cedric frowning. I glanced at the small hand knife in my palm. It was my turn to cast.

"She can't cast without injury, sir," my twin quickly said. "She's tried, but for some reason—"

"Is this true?" Master Cedric stared hard at me.

I reddened. "Yes."

"Perhaps next time you will think twice before falling asleep in my class." The master walked away without a second glance while Alex and Ella gawked after him.

"Did he really just say that?"

"He's not even going to *try* to help you!"

I tossed the blade to the ground, furious. What good was my magic here if the masters refused to help me?

"Don't let him get to you, Ryiah," Alex said softly, aware of the attention Master Cedric's presence had brought to our circle.

I stared at the girl across from me. Master Cedric's assistant had given her the slightest bit of frostbite. She was waiting for me to heal her.

I tried to remember what Master Cedric has said at the beginning of class.

*Use all your senses. Shut out everything. Focus solely on the projection in your mind...Once you have a strong hold of what you need to do, project your will onto it, and if you have done so correctly, your magic should come through.* I kept repeating the instructions over and over, willing my magic to take effect.

But it never did.

At one point I caught Darren watching me from the corner of his eye. When I whirled around to catch him, he gave me a wink before casting a healing of his own.

I felt like screaming.

"Maybe next time." Alex gave my shoulder an awkward pat.

The assistant returned to heal my partner, and I looked down to avoid any more sympathetic glances from the rest of our group. No one else had failed this exercise.

"I'm sure once Master Cedric sees how hard you are trying, he will change his mind," Ella offered. Like Alex, she had no idea why my magic wasn't casting. None of her suggestions had worked either.

I sighed. Judging from the mild-mannered master's response, my month of dozing off in his class was irreparable.

Alex, on the other hand, did even better than expected. He grasped Master Cedric's lesson almost immediately. Even though I'd only seen him cast the most basic of spells back home, he was very apt at putting the new castings to work. When it was his turn, it took only minutes for my brother to heal his patient of sunburn.

It was hard to contain my jealousy.

I tried to tell myself that it was just Restoration, that my castings didn't matter here, but it was hard to evade the truth. *If I couldn't cast now, how would my week of Combat be any different?*

⚜

That evening after dinner, Ella did not come with me to the field to continue our nightly conditioning. She needed to spend the extra time studying now that we had moved on from the basics. The rest of our group went with her, including Alex.

When I arrived at the armory, I could see I was not alone. Granted, there were less students now that we had started the first faction's orientation, but there were still no fewer than twenty first-years drilling when I arrived.

Someone had brought out a pile of staffs and blunt training swords. Glancing at the two weapons, I considered trying the blade. It would be the perfect distraction to my dismal day thus far, but without Ella for proper instruction, I knew the best thing to do would be continue working on my practiced routine with the pole instead.

Whimsy, however, got the best of me.

"Do you even know what you are doing?" a familiar voice jeered.

I jumped and then turned to find myself face-to-face with Priscilla. She was watching me awkwardly clutch the sword handle while Darren and the rest of his following stood only a couple feet away.

She had picked the wrong day to bully me.

"Don't you tire of playing the witch?" I shot back.

One of the two husky brothers snickered, and I was almost certain I saw Darren smile.

Priscilla, however, was less than amused.

"Go on all you like, lowborn. It will not save you from your pathetic casting. The only good use for that sword is if it ends your own paltry existence."

"Oh no," I snapped, "I think it would do wonders for your own. Besides," I added shortly, "like Sir Piers said, it's the ones that *need to learn* you should be worrying about."

"The only thing I worry about is being stuck in the same quarters as a common wench!" she cried.

"What in the name of the gods are you talking about?"

Priscilla looked me up and down. "Tell me where you sneak off to every night. Explain *why* Sir Piers had suddenly started to take an *interest* in the same halfwit he was so keen on condemning a week ago? Seems to me you must have found a way to earn his praise through your skirts—"

All I saw was red. I felt that same rage from the night before crackling and sputtering its way to the surface. "I would never!"

"Then tell me where you go," she countered. Behind her, the rest of our audience had fallen silent. There was a malicious smile on her lips, and it took all my self-control to stop from lunging.

"Unless you've got something to hide," she added with a smirk.

I took a deep breath. *Ignore her*, I commanded.

I loosened my grip on the sword's hilt and cast a glance at Darren. The non-heir had an amused expression on his face and did not appear the least bit interested in defending me. Apparently, he was perfectly content to let Priscilla think the worst of me, so long as it didn't sully *his* reputation.

*We'll see about that.*

"You can say what you like, Priscilla," I said finally, eyes locked on Darren as I spoke. "But there are some things wealth will never afford. And before you go around soiling my good name, you might go and ask your precious prince where it is he goes each night as well."

Priscilla blanched and immediately turned on Darren. "What did she mean by that?"

Darren kept his face perfectly still. "That lowborn doesn't know what she's saying, Priscilla," he said smoothly.

"Then why did she—"

"Because she has nothing better to do." Darren glanced at me, dark eyes flashing. "The girl is trying to upset you, and you are letting her. Honestly Priscilla, I expect more from you."

"He's lying," I told her.

Darren glared, and I ignored him.

Priscilla glanced from me to Darren and back again, unsure whom to believe: the girl she hated or the boy she loved. "Well, I should tell the constable she's sneaking out—"

"No!" both Darren and I began at the same time.

"What I mean, Priscilla, is that you shouldn't waste your time on someone as insignificant as her," Darren amended quickly. His eyes dared me to disagree.

I reluctantly kept silent, knowing better than to say anything foolish again.

"Come, let's practice closer to the field," Darren told the girl, gently leading Priscilla away from where I stood.

As soon as his following had left, I took a deep breath.

"What was that about?"

I glanced up and saw Ella walking toward me.

"How much did you see?" I asked her.

"Enough." She picked up the sword I had dropped and snatched a second for herself. "It seems I'm not the only one who has a bone to pick with the prince. I was just coming down to check on you when I saw what was taking place. Sword?"

I shook my head at the offered hilt. "I don't know how to hold it," I told her.

"Well, it's a good thing I've joined you," she replied easily.

"Are you done with the assignments already?"

Ella shrugged. "No...but I figured you needed some cheering up." She gave me a kind smile. "This week is only Restoration. I'll manage."

An hour later, Ella and I made our way back to the library for the last leg of our study.

"The prince must really dislike you," she said as we turned the steps of the corridor. "He usually goes out of his way to ignore people."

I laughed loudly.

"So what did you do?" she asked, pausing to glance at me curiously.

"I think my very existence offends him."

She cocked her head to one side.

"Well, you've made a nice enemy out of Priscilla. If I were you, I'd avoid the both of them."

I sighed uncomfortably. "What has changed?"

She paused, and I almost crashed into her. Ella had a strange look in her eyes.

"Just be careful," she said softly. "When people like them notice you, that's when you should be worried."

I stared at my friend, trying to understand the odd intensity to her warning. "What happened when you lived at court?" There was something she wasn't telling me. "Why did your parents choose to leave?"

Ella stared at the walls behind us. "Just don't trust them." She looked anywhere but my face. "Don't trust them, and you can't get hurt."

When Darren arrived at the library later that evening, I was waiting for him.

"What are you—" He set down his books.

I cut him off: "You can *not* let Priscilla say those things about me. I don't care if it gets us both expelled. If you do not defend me next time, I'll tell everyone the truth. I swear it!"

He didn't blink. "What was I supposed to do, Ryiah? Defending you would have only made her hate you more. And you aren't innocent in all of this. You baited her with all those cheeky retorts and then practically insinuated you were laying with me instead!"

I blushed. "I didn't mean for her to interpret it *that* way."

"Well, everyone that was out there with us formed the same impression, so I hope you keep in mind that you have only yourself to thank for your tarnished reputation."

"I'm sure they didn't—"

"Oh, but they did!" He exhaled loudly. "I corrected them, but if the rumor had reached the constable or Master Barclae, you'd have the both of us tossed out of here for misconduct!"

I stared at the floor. "I had no idea."

Darren's tone fell flat. "Clearly."

Neither of us spoke for a minute. Then I remembered what I had been waiting to ask him.

"What did you mean when you told me I was training the wrong way last night?"

"Huh?" The non-heir looked at me, thrown by the abrupt change in subject.

"I've tried following Master Cedric's lessons," I began again, "but nothing he says makes any sense, and he won't show me what I'm doing wrong!"

"You've fallen asleep in his class. Twice." Darren's expression was unsympathetic. "What did you expect?"

"I don't know." I bit my lip. "But is that really enough to condemn me? I'm trying. You more than anyone can see that!"

Darren did not reply.

"No one else can help me," I pleaded. "Even my twin brother doesn't know why I can't cast normally. But you do. I *know* you do. It's why you told me I was training wrong."

"Even if I did know, why would I help you?"

"Because it's the right thing to do."

He snorted. "Well, good luck with that."

"You can't just give someone advice and then not show them how to use it!" I seethed. "It's not advice if it doesn't help them!"

Darren balked. "Well, I certainly wouldn't give it to the girl that has tried to get me tossed out of this place not once but twice now—oh, and let's not forget your most inglorious moment, when you tried to light me on fire!"

"I've made some mistakes." I met the prince's eyes defiantly. "But you have made just as many, and you wouldn't have given me advice if you hadn't been feeling guilty about them in the first place."

Darren regarded me grimly. In that moment I was aware of how near we were standing. This close, I could smell some sort of wooded musk emitting from his clothes, a mixture of pine and cloves that reminded me of home.

Hair had fallen across his forehead and into his eyes, but instead of being distracting, it highlighted the dark garnet-brown of his irises, which oddly didn't seem quite as opaque as I'd initially assumed, enclosed in those dark, dark lashes. They seemed much less hostile this close, more like liquid shadows playing across flame than embittered stone.

And right now those shadows were doing strange, flippy things to my insides. I felt as if someone had wrenched the ground right out from under me. I was uncomfortably conscious of how much I was staring, yet I could do nothing to pull away.

"Are you done berating me?"

The trance was broken, and I stepped back quickly, flushing. His sudden presence had caught me off guard, and I hoped he hadn't noticed.

"I—" I faltered. Darren was looking at me as though I was mad. "See here," I began again, flustered at my inability to speak.

"You want my help," he prompted.

I reddened. "Yes." It seemed one-syllable sentences were all I was capable of. I'd had no trouble scolding the prince moments before, but apparently I was no better than a fumbling oaf when he stood close. *For the love of the gods, he isn't even that good-looking!*

*…Okay, maybe a little,* I conceded, *but certainly not enough to make you an inept convent girl! Pull yourself together!*

I straightened and regarded Darren coolly. "I know you have no reason to," I conceded, "but if you were to show me how to call on my magic, I swear I would never bother you again."

He raised one brow. "Well, as tempting as your offer is, I do not have time to help every girl that bats her eyes at me."

"I was not!" My speech impairment was gone as fast as it had come. "And if you spent a little less time disparaging me every time we crossed paths, you'd realize how abundant your precious time actually was! If you were really so secure in your own standing here, you wouldn't think twice about helping someone you believed might constitute a threat."

"You really think the way to charm me into helping you is by insult?" Darren was no longer frowning, and I had the distinct impression he was enjoying the debate.

I glared. "Would you prefer me to lie like every one of your blindsided subjects?"

He didn't bother to hide his grin. "It would be a nice change."

"Fine." I put my hands on my hips and said in my most sickly sweet impression of Priscilla: "O, valiant Darren, brave ruler among men, please help this humble first-year learn…"

Darren raised a brow when I had finished. "I was wrong. Humility does not suit you."

I glowered. "Does this mean you'll help?"

"I will—if only so I can start realizing 'the abundance of my precious time.'"

A couple of minutes later we had cleared a space in the center of the study, and Darren was facing me, a skeptical expression on his face.

"Do you know how to light a fire...without magic?"

"Of course."

"Have you ever done it with flint?"

I raised a brow. *Who hadn't?*

"Well, we are going to use it as a metaphor for how to cast. Master Cedric has been saying the same sort of thing for weeks, but evidently your naps were more important."

I cringed.

"When you cast your magic out, you need to be picturing what you want to create in your mind. The stronger the idea, the better your casting will be. All the lessons we've been learning should have shown you how important the senses are. When you cast, you need to be using those to build the projection. You can't expect to use your magic to create something real if you don't even understand what that thing you are trying to cast is...What is something you can describe well?"

"Fire." I felt like a fool for not coming up with anything else. But I couldn't help it. Fire was the one thing I'd been able to successfully conjure repeatedly. At least now I could see what would happen if I tried without self-mutilation. It would be a nice change.

"How inspired. Now describe it to me."

"Um, well, it's hot...It doesn't really have a taste. When things get burned, there's a charred flavor...It's chalky and bitter. It's soft like a moth's wings but scalding at the same time. It looks like—" I froze as a thought crossed my mind: *like your eyes.*

I looked away from Darren. "It looks like the fragmented tips of a red and yellow kite billowing in the wind."

"You are missing two senses," Darren said, unperturbed by my haphazard ramblings. "What does it sound like? What do you smell?"

"It sounds like low clapping. It smells repugnant. Sickly-sweet like spun sugar but tinged with smoke."

"Now, what do you want to do with the fire?" he asked. "What type of casting do you want to perform? Keep in mind it should be simple."

"What about holding it in my hand? I've seen people—"

"Do you want to burn yourself?"

I shook my head.

"Then don't try to do what you've seen others do, their castings are more complicated than they appear. Try lighting a candle instead."

"Do I actually need a candle?"

"You are a beginner, so yes." He tossed me a taper.

"How...?" I paused, fully aware that there had been no candle in his hand a second ago.

"Yes, well, I am not a beginner." Darren exhaled. "Now think back to how you would light a fire naturally. This image you are describing is the flint. You need to focus on its details in your mind. Block out everything except the image you want to cast out. The steel that you strike this 'flint' with is your will. That's the easy part because it is rare for someone to cast something they do not want. If you have desire, you have will.

"It all comes down to those two things: steel and flint. The resulting spark is the physical manifestation of your magic. If you have potential, it should be effortless. If you are struggling, it's a safe bet you are wasting your time trying to practice magic in the first place."

I glared at him. "Maybe I struggle because I didn't have a lifetime of mage tutors like you."

Darren stared at me. "I never even considered becoming a mage until four years ago. I hardly consider that a 'lifetime' of training. The only reason my father relented was because the palace mages insisted he would be a fool to overlook my powers. It wasn't privilege that got me the training. It was my *potential*." Darren narrowed his eyes at me. "You can't tell me your family wouldn't have tried harder to get you a tutor if you'd shown a great aptitude for magic."

I took a deep breath and told myself what Darren had to teach me was more important than mauling the non-heir to death.

Darren was watching me closely and seemed to recognize that I was not going to respond. "Well, it appears you have self-control after all."

I stayed silent.

The non-heir gestured to the candle. "Now, light the taper."

This was it. I rolled the candle in my palm, letting its smooth, waxy surface calm my racing nerves. I felt self-conscious with Darren watching me, but I hastily blocked out those thoughts, letting them trickle away until all that remained was a vision of fire. I felt its searing heat in my mind. I saw the sputtering flames. It smelled adversely sweet, and my tongue recoiled at the taste of scalded flesh. I reached further into my mind and heard the sharp sound of crackling flames against wood.

I stared at the candle's wick with the image of fire concrete in my mind. I imagined the cotton string being embraced by its flames, all of the senses engulfing the candle's end, a tiny flame sputtering that would carry all of my fire's features.

*Please!*

The sting of scalding wax hit me all at once, and I shrieked excitedly. The candle in my hand had a flame protruding from its tip. Wax was spilling over onto my palm, but I couldn't care less.

"I did it!" I looked to Darren, eyes alight with exhilaration.

"Yes," he agreed, stepping forward to close the distance between us.

My breath caught.

The prince leaned closer, and I froze, heart beating wildly in my chest.

And then Darren blew out the flame and took a step back. "Now do it again."

"What did you do that for?" I sputtered.

"That was too easy. I want to see you do it under duress. It's much harder to concentrate when you have distractions."

"Like what?" I was instantly suspicious.

A slow smile spread across his face. "How about I repay your favor from last night?"

*What favor?*

Darren snapped his finger. I glanced around frantically but did not see any changes to the room. "What did you—" The words caught in my throat as I noticed a long shadow quickly making its way across the dark marble floor. As it trailed closer, I cried out involuntarily.

The shadow was a herd of very large, very hairy brown spiders that were very quickly coming toward me.

*How did he know?* My legs went numb with fear.

"I'll stop them the moment you light that candle," Darren said, eyes dancing wickedly.

I swallowed as I looked to the incoming mob. "Can't you try something else?"

"Stop making excuses" was his only reply.

My eyes shot to the extinguished candle in my hand. The tip was tinged with black from the previous flame, and I willed it to light once again. *Please.*

I tried to visualize a fire using my senses, but it was much harder to actualize with the loud pounding in my ears and the fear of spiders just inches away.

*Why did he have to choose them?* The anxiety had my blood racing, and I kept losing focus to peek down at the ground.

"Ignore the spiders, Ryiah!"

I bit my lip, and inadvertently my gaze slid down to the insects again. They had just reached my boots and were beginning to climb. My insides froze.

"RYIAH!"

I shut my eyes and tried to picture a fire. The image came swimming back. I took a deep breath and tried to drown out the desire to run screaming and shaking the creatures off my legs. I recalled the taper and opened my eyes, practically throwing my impression at it.

Instantly the candle's wick caught fire, but it was fast diminished as a mountain of wax spilled out over my hands. There was nothing left of the candle. I glanced down at my tunic and saw the spiders were gone.

*Thank the gods.* I glared at the prince, hands on my hips. "You didn't have to use spiders."

"How will you get better," the prince countered, "if you are not willing to face your fears? I did you a favor. Maybe now you'll stop napping during Cedric's lessons."

I peeled the wax off my hands, wincing at the swollen flesh beneath. "I haven't done that in weeks," I told the non-heir.

"Well, I have done my part." Darren waived a dismissing hand and sat down in his chaise with a wry smile. "So where is that promised solitude?"

"Can you just answer one more thing?"

Darren groaned. "What is it now?"

"How did you know I was training wrong?" I bit my lip. "You seemed to know something was wrong before you'd even seen me cast."

Darren gave me a tired look. "I didn't, not really. But when you attacked me with that fire it was pretty obvious you didn't know what you were doing. Since I had never seen you practice your casting, there was no way you could have depleted your stamina." Darren coughed. "I *had*, otherwise I would have been able to put out the flames myself. It wasn't hard to figure out the rest."

"How come no one knew how to help me?"

Darren narrowed his eyes. "You really know nothing about magic, do you?" He didn't wait for a response. "The fact that you can cast using pain is unusual. Most people can't, which means that your magic operates at a different level. You can't expect the same rules to apply to us."

"Us?" My voice squeaked.

Darren studied his fingers. "For the weak, castings come easily, but people like you and I have to work harder to project them. Our magic requires better focus because it is *more*. You will always have to work harder to cast, but when you do, it will be better, stronger too." He laughed coldly. "*Powerful* magic requires those concentrated projections Master Cedric was alluding to, not acts of whimsy."

I frowned. "But then why is it so easy with pain? I don't have to build up a projection at all."

"Spilling blood is the exception, not the rule." He gave me a hard look. "It's not a reliable form of casting. The powers you exert will be unpredictable and much harder to control. Your flames didn't stop last night, did they?"

I sighed. "No."

"Exactly. The masters here don't even teach that method to first-years. It's dangerous, and you should be grateful you haven't lost a limb trying it."

I winced.

Darren's eyes danced. "Of course, if that's your intention, it would be very amusing to watch."

I threw my quill at his head, and he caught it with a grin. *He has a nice smile.* I quickly averted my gaze. That was the *last* thing I needed.

⸸

The next two weeks of Restoration and Alchemy's orientation were spent trying to learn as much as I could about casting. Thanks to the reluctant help of the school's resident non-heir, I finally understood what Master Cedric had been saying.

I was also painfully aware of the warning we'd received on that second day of training: that the skill would not be something I could master "in a day, or even years." It was a

very ominous thought, and it plagued my every waking moment. I became consumed with practicing the meditation exercises whenever I could. It didn't matter what time of day or
where I was. I channeled visualization during walks to the armory, meals, and even once or twice during lessons when I had
deemed the material irrelevant.

Unfortunately though, as I had learned from my time
thus far, every choice had a consequence, and it was clear as
night and day that my newfound hobby had put an unavoida-
ble cramp in the rest of my routine. I no longer participated in
any of the lectures, and I had started to copy Ella's answers to
most of the math. It wasn't ideal, but it was either that or
muck out the stables each night.

"Whatever it is you think are doing," Master Isaac had
said to me when I handed him the latest assignment, "I'd re-
think the decision carefully. Ignorance will not save you at the
end-of-year trials." My response had been a blank stare of in-
nocence.

The master's crinkled frown did little to assuage my guilt.
I was not fooling anyone.

It was even worse with Master Cedric, who had yet to see
me succeed in a single one of his sessions. I fumbled through
the two weeks of Restoration and Alchemy with the grace of a
stupefied pigeon. It was true that I could finally cast, but since
I had not devoted any time to the study of human malady and
combustive potion-making, I had no way of casting a successful projection to invoke my magic in the first place. You had to
know what it was you wanted to cast, and I hadn't the slightest idea.

I wanted desperately to show my masters I *was* trying,
just not in those first two factions.

Fortunately, there was one individual I did not have to
worry about disappointing.

Since anything Sir Piers taught was applicable to Combat, I had made it a point to keep up my devotion to his les-

sons, and I used them as the training ground for the visualization techniques I had been learning thus far.

I began to notice every little detail during our drills, whether we were heaving large sacks of grain or hurling heavy jugs filled with sand at targets impossibly far off: "For those pesky inferno flasks you Alchemy mages are so fond of," Piers had noted. I made it a point to study the way the actions affected my senses. I scrutinized what others were doing that made them throw further, pull faster.

As soon as I had formed a good impression in my mind, I began to cast out my magic and use it to magnify my own attempts.

Often, I was too exhausted in the midst of performing to actually utilize my powers. But there was once or twice when I was tossing a flask, and it worked, making my vial land farther than my throw alone.

The best practice, of course, was my self-imposed training after the evening meal. Alex stayed behind with the study group, but Ella had made a habit of joining me since she too had little need to take in all the "useless material of the other factions." Granted, it wasn't useless, but it certainly seemed to us given the time we had available.

During those practices I told her about Darren and how I had finally learned to cast. Ella couldn't believe the non-heir had helped me, and to be honest, neither could I. I rationalized that it must have been a stroke of madness, or extreme confidence that I was too weak to constitute a threat.

Though she tried as any friend might, Ella couldn't argue with the latter. We both knew the two of us were leagues behind Darren in terms of magic.

In any case it was in no small part due to Ella that I picked up the basics of fencing a lot faster than the staff. By the end of our second week's orientation, I was confident enough to try my hand at casting with the sword during our evening practice.

The first time I was in the midst of holding guard when I missed an obvious indicator for Ella's next swing. My shoulder should have been red and smarting all evening, but as I realized my mistake I cast out a projection for the correct defense. Her blade hit a second sword hovering just above my arm, the familiar zing of metal on metal ringing in both our ears.

After that, I used the move every chance I got. It was as if I had a blade in both hands, and while I was not savvy by any means, I was certainly gaining momentum. Ella had even started using her own magic, figuring if I was brazen enough to cast and parry without a true grasp of swordplay I deserved any injuries I got.

My magic didn't always work, especially if I were exhausted or had cast out too much in one day. Still, it was a clear improvement. I just hoped it would continue to grow.

It was one thing to have magic, but it was another to have so little to start. I was no longer at the very bottom of our class in terms of casting, but I was also nowhere near the top, or even the middle. Though I had only completed orientation for Restoration and Alchemy, I had seen enough successful castings in the past two weeks to make me worried. Tomorrow we'd be beginning Combat, and given that it was the most popular faction, I had no doubt there would be even more competition to contend with.

Thinking back to that first day with Piers and Cedric, I saw the magical spectrum I'd be chasing for the next eight months. At one end, whimpering Ralph clutching a twig that struggled to burn. At the other, Darren, and the two imploding trees far out in the distance.

It was bound to be a very long trek.

# CHAPTER SEVEN

"*Faster!*" Piers roared, his booming voice carrying across the stadium. "This is what all of you consider trying? You are pathetic excuses for mages. I've seen war horses with more spirit than you!"

*He is trying to kill us.*

I swallowed back a mouthful of bile and continued heaving my way down the long track. I might as well have been a limping fowl chased by a pack of rabid wolves, only instead of the many haired beasts of the forest, I had Piers's insults tearing me limb from limb. My legs burned, my arms ached, and my entire chest felt as if it were on fire. I could barely breathe.

I had fifty more minutes. Fifty minutes of sprints, *endless* sprints, and the horrible obstacle course we were required to complete at the end of each mile's lap.

Today's drill, Piers had promised, would make it clear whether we were "cut out for the hard life of Combat, or the cushy life of the other two factions." None of us had wanted to disappoint him with that kind of introduction. Unfortunately, his new routine was proving quickly how difficult that would be.

I ran my fastest mile ever—seven minutes exactly—only to lose the momentum I had been building during the second portion of the sequence. Running, it turned out, was the easy part.

The obstacle course was Piers's worst invention yet. Somehow he, his assistants, and the constable's staff had created a breeding ground of pain and misery. Now we had giant sacks of barley to haul, a rope to climb, a tightrope to cross, flying arrows to dodge in the pathways between each station, and, last but not least, a quick three-minute joust with one member of the constable's staff.

All ten of the constable's men just happened to have some experience wielding a pole. They weren't very apt, but after twenty minutes of trying to complete Piers's course, it didn't seem to matter much.

*"I am not joking. Pick up the pace first-years!"*

I kept running, trying to block out the scattered curses around me.

My feet were in pain. Raw, excruciating pain. A couple slivers of glass had somehow made their way through the supple leather of my boots, and it was all I could do not to sit down and pull them out. I'd managed to avoid any flying arsenal, but I was afraid of the three more laps I was still expected to complete. As Piers had pointed out at the beginning of class, we had healing mages on staff to treat us once we completed his program, but unless we were near the point of immediate death, we had "better run fast."

"Master Barclae informed me today that no one has left yet!" Piers bellowed. "That, apparently, *I* haven't been hard enough. I don't agree. I told him you were just a resilient batch. But if the Master of the Academy has declared my course too easy, then it is too easy." He continued to pace the field and eye us all challengingly. "I promised him that I would break at least five of you by the end of this week. The fact that you are all still here brings a bad stink to my name. I can't have people thinking I've gone soft, now can I? So it's time to sink or swim, my children, sink or swim."

I was halfway into my second lap when I started to notice a change.

When we had started the trek, it had been hot and sweltering without a cloud in the sky, but somewhere in the last ten minutes the temperatures had plunged dramatically. Now, I could hear the soft rumble of thunder, and the sky was drenched in a purple haze.

"D-doesn't...look...good," Alex panted beside me. "Not... natural..."

I had a feeling my brother was right. Five minutes later, as I was dragging a weighted sack to its designated location, I felt the first drop. Seconds later the entire class was being pelted with rain and small pellets of hail.

Lightning flashed, and I scrambled to make it to the next destination: the climbing rope. My arms were still weak from my last attempt. Luckily, there were three people ahead, so I had a couple minutes to recuperate before the next ordeal.

Grimacing, I bent down and slowly, *carefully*, pulled out a protruding shard from my boot.

"No more sheltered training!" Sir Piers roared over the thunder. "All of you want Combat—no, don't you dare shake your head at me, Karl! Anybody who says they came here for anything else is a lying coward. You want a black robe, then prove it! I don't want to see a single one of you stopping unless every bone in your body is broken! If you are waiting in line, you had better be jogging in place, or giving me crunches!"

The class groaned, and I hastily jumped up to begin running in place. This was insanity. I had no idea how I would complete the course two more times.

When I finished climbing the rope, my hands were raw, and my arms were shaking. While the rain felt good on my sweltering skin, it had made the climb especially slippery, and now I had a hefty rope burn to show for the effort.

I made my way over to the next station: the tightrope. The hail was getting bigger, and it felt as though someone were pelting me with tiny rocks. The ground was turning to slush, and my clothes were soaked through.

The rope's length wasn't a far distance to cross really, maybe ten feet at most, and no more than a foot or two above the ground. But I wasn't exactly known for my balance, and now with the rainstorm and my slippery boots, I was especially wary.

"Hurry up," Jake, one of the two stocky brothers from the prince's following, growled at me. He shoved me closer, and I swallowed.

Taking a deep breath, I forced myself to take one solid step at a time.

At first everything was fine. I was gingerly making my way across, inching one foot in front of the other slowly. Then the wind picked up and I instantly lost balance. My foot started to slide. I twisted my body awkwardly to accommodate the lost footing.

Somehow, I managed to keep my position on the rope.

I quickly crossed the remaining distance and then hopped to the ground.

The first-years after me charged the rope. As I was walking away I could hear the boy who had shoved me struggling to balance. A second later Jake yelped. *Ha.*

My glee was short-lived. I had barely taken a step forward when the sound of whipping air alerted me to a danger at my left.

I ducked, only just in time to avoid one of the assisting mage's magically-steered throwing knives. It was as if someone had read my thoughts. I guiltily made my way to the final station, resolving not to rejoice at any more of my fellow students' misery.

I picked up a staff and turned to face a swallow-faced manservant. This one looked very thin and wispy, and he clutched his weapon awkwardly. But, like my previous sparring partner, his lack of skill was well-matched for my fatigue.

I made the first move. Feigning a downward swoop and attacking from the left instead, I caught my partner off-guard and managed to place a satisfying hit.

My partner glared at me, no doubt angry at his new bruise, and he lunged at me with vengeance. I hastily put up a defense and deflected his oncoming blows. It was a short three minutes, but it was tiring just the same.

By the time I had started my final sparring session I was at the point of collapse. I was panting so heavily that I was unable to keep my staff level, let alone lead the attack.

As luck would have it, I ended up partnered with the same disgruntled servant as the last two rounds. He had grown confident in my increasingly weak defense, and he seemed determined to take it out once and for all. I had a feeling most of constable's team was doing the same—seizing the opportunity to take vengeance on all the first-years who had made their lives difficult, even if our only crime was inhabiting the Academy.

"What's the matter, first-year?" my opponent crooned. He was spinning the staff in his hands as he circled me, looking for an opening.

I refused to respond and focused all of my senses on the pole in his hand.

"Too good for me, are you?" The man lunged left.

My arms shook from the impact and I gritted my teeth. *Two more minutes, Ryiah,* I promised, *two minutes, and then this is all over.*

Smack!

My ribcage stung with the sudden impact. I doubled over, cursing my stupidity. I'd stopped paying attention for a second, and the manservant had delivered an especially hard blow to my ribs.

"Don't know why you first-years bother," the small man taunted. "It's the same every year, and yet you still come here thinking you are different." He positioned himself to strike left again, and I braced myself, too tired to read into the telltale signs that he was feigning the movement.

*Wait...*

Too late I saw where he intended his staff to land. With all the strength I could muster,I cast out an image of the block I was too slow to carry out. It was the same technique I had been practicing with Ella, but I had never tried it in class.

The loud clap of wood-on-wood resounded in my ears. I gave way to a small sigh of relief. It had worked.

The man turned to our commander a couple paces away. "She cheated!"

Sir Piers shrugged. "She used her magic, just as any soldier would use what skills he possessed in battle."

"Very good," Master Cedric said, coming to stand beside Piers. "It would seem you pay attention after all."

I flushed.

"Thank you, master." I bowed my head and then hurried to set down my staff and join the group of first-years who had already finished across the field.

When I got to the benches I eagerly grabbed a flagon of water and then sat down to watch the rest of the class complete the drill.

In five short minutes the ordeal was over. As soon as everyone had finished, Piers commanded his audience to spend the final hour drilling with the staffs at a more "relaxed" pace.

Only the most injured were allowed to be seen by a healing mage. Apparently, our cuts and bruises built character. We needed to build up our tolerance to pain, not succumb to it. Piers emphasized that unless we had a deep flesh wound or a broken bone, we were not to be treated.

Only two of us fit that category. A chubby girl with auburn curls had a horrible gash on her lower calf. She'd been victim to one of the throwing knives. Seeing how the girl had only finished a couple minutes after me, I was deeply impressed.

The only other to receive medical attention was Darren's friend Jake, the burly boy who had rushed me at the tightrope. Apparently, he'd twisted his ankle while falling and broken the bone in a clumsy attempt to avoid hitting glass.

"Glad I'm not that chap right now," Alex remarked cheerfully behind me.

I turned to look at my brother. He looked in far better spirits than the rest of us, despite the fact he'd been wheezing just moments before. I wondered if he had healed himself, though he'd be a fool to try in front of Piers.

"Oh pipe down, you big oaf," Ella told him, stepping in beside us. "That boy could have been any of us."

I followed the two of them as we discarded our training staffs and waited for Master Cedric to return and begin the next lesson.

"I wonder what Cedric planned for the Combat castings?" Ella mused.

I bit my lip. *Whatever it was, it wasn't going to be easy.*

⚜

The next two hours stole every ounce of will from my body until all that remained was the empty shell of a corpse. I honestly have no idea how I carried on from the two hours with Piers prior, but by the time I had finished Cedric's session, there was nothing left. No strength, no magic, no resolve.

While Piers's time had revolved around breaking our physical reserves, Cedric's made sure to tear down our magic's limits. He started us off with simple castings against one of the various trees surrounding the field. We were to experiment casting various inflictions, whatever magic we so desired as long as it contributed to the practice of Combat.

"Show me what you know! Test your limits, challenge your castings! This is your chance to figure out what you know and what spells you need to improve. If you don't get the desired effect cast again. Keep casting those ailments until the tree can no longer stand. Don't worry about the field. My assistants are plenty experienced repairing your messes!"

By the end of the first hour, the pine Ella and I had been practicing on was a crackling tower of flame. I was ridiculously proud, until I saw the giant fissure Darren and his friends had created. Ten pines lay crumbled in its center.

Afterwards, Master Cedric had us drill similarly to how Ella and I had practiced during the previous weeks. Each of us lined up against an opponent, one of us clutching a staff, the other weaponless. While Ella and I had been able to rely on our prowess first, magic second, Master Cedric's exercise forced one person to depend entirely on their magic to block their opponent's attack. I was tolerable at first, but after twenty minutes my blocks were so weak that my opponent's staff kept falling straight through the wavering defense.

During the last thirty minutes the training master had us casting individually with the heavy barley sacks from Piers's drill. We were expected to blast our targets from afar, by whatever means necessary. Within the first five minutes I had exhausted any left over magic. I could barely budge a sack, let alone cast enough force to knock it backward.

A third of the way into our final drill half the class had run out of magic. Of course, we were still expected to try. But without a magical reserve they, like me, spent the remaining time pretending as they watched the few still casting with unabashed envy.

The non-heir appeared self-assured as he sent the giant sacks flying backward across the field. The castings relied on huge gusts of magical exertion. I couldn't imagine the power it took to throw fifty pounds with the mind. I couldn't even do that with my hands, and I'd had those all my life.

Darren was not alone either, though he did look the most at ease during the procession. Some of the remaining first-years were even smiling. The non-heir had the most blatant grin of all. From the looks the victors exchanged, it was clear they considered the practice nothing more than a game.

They took turns trying to out-distance one another. Darren was the clear victor, but the blonde girl stood out the most. Darren had cast the most most magic but two of Eve's castings had gone at least a quarter of a mile further than anyone else's reach, including the his.

I had a vague suspicion the girl was holding out. I wasn't sure exactly why but I had a feeling that I would find out at the end-of-year trials. Darren was hard to beat, but something told me I'd be a fool to think he had no rivals here. I suspected Eve was one of them—and hopefully me, if I were to ever catch up.

When the lesson had ended that last impression stayed with me long after I had finished the evening meal.

⁕

By the time I had retired to the library's third floor for the evening I was fighting sleep with every page I turned. My eyelids kept involuntarily falling closed. At some point during the first hour I must have fallen asleep because it was only during the toll of the Academy's midnight bell that my reverie was broken, and I realized how late it had actually become.

Sluggishly, I gathered my belongings and descended to the first floor study.

"In case you have ever wondered, you snore like a drunken sailor."

I finished stepping off the ladder's frame and turned to face Darren. He looked pretty worn out himself, but not so much that I couldn't catch the wicked humor in his eyes.

I had no energy left for witty banter. "Not that it's any of your concern," I said, trying to stifle a yawn, "but I wasn't asleep the entire time."

I made my way to the door and was startled to see the non-heir had joined me, books in hand. Usually he snuck out a minute or so after I left, whether as a cautionary measure or to avoid conversation, it was anyone's guess.

Darren noticed my stare and shrugged. "It's been almost two months, if you were foolish enough to get caught, it would have happened by now."

I attempted a frown, but I was too tired to give anything more than a slight grimace. "Thanks for the vote of confidence."

He twisted slightly to look at me, the air of mockery gone and replaced with a much more candid light. "I guess I never expected you to last this long," he admitted, "but you aren't nearly as hapless as I expected you to be."

"Am I supposed to take that as a compliment?" I asked, affronted.

He smiled wolfishly. "Interpret it however you like."

I rolled my eyes as we turned the corner of the hall.

I watched the prince reach for the door. "I wonder if you have ever given someone a compliment that wasn't a backhanded insult."

Darren's grasp on the handle stilled, and he glanced back at me, eyes dancing amidst the surrounding shadows. "I prefer not to. It gives people an unsettling impression of self-importance."

"Me?" I scoffed. "Self-important? Have you checked a mirror?"

He didn't look away. "You will thank me one day for not filling your head with false compliments. Adversity teaches one more than flattery ever will."

"A compliment never hurt anyone."

He snorted. "If I had listened to everything the courtiers sang, I never would have gotten to where I am today. The people that tell you what you want to hear are the most dangerous enemies you'll ever meet."

I stared at him. "You must have had a dark childhood if you mistrusted anyone who was ever kind to you."

Darren tilted his head and gave me a wicked smile. "You'd rather I tell you what you want to hear?" The prince took a step closer, effectively closing the gap between us. "What do you want me to tell you, Ryiah?" His hand was still on the doorknob, leaving me pressed against the wooden frame as he leaned closer, his face only inches from my own.

My breath caught in my throat. I could feel tingling from the top of my spine to the tips of my toes, and my skin was unnaturally warm. My heart rate slowed. I felt light-headed, thrown off by the dark, bottomless eyes boring into my own.

*What are you doing, Ryiah?* Some part of me, conscious of the disaster that was about to unfold, pleaded to return to sanity. But all my senses were in chaos.

I didn't like how Darren was able to turn my body against me. He had stolen reason and made me no better than a swooning convent girl whose only purpose was to marry and waste her life away bearing spoiled palace brats. Like the one in front of me now.

"You should never trust a wolf in sheep's clothing," Darren said faintly. His eyes burned, scalding my flesh as if he had torched me with flame. "Because the only thing the wolf will ever want to do is break you." He reached down to catch a strand of my hair that had somehow fallen loose, twirling it with his finger and watching me the way a hunter regarded its prey. "Is that what you want me to do?" he murmured. "Do you want me to break you?"

Yes.

Wait...

*What was wrong with me?* I snapped free of the tempered fantasy to glare up at the manipulative young man in front of me. "I don't know what lines you feed the ladies at court," I told him angrily, "but they won't work on me."

He laughed softly. "Are you sure?"

I opened my mouth to protest, and Darren stepped aside. "Rest assured you are not one of my conquests, Ryiah."

I choked indignantly. "I would never!"

The non-heir raised a brow. "You have a long road ahead of you, my dear. If you want to join the victor's circle, you are going to have to stop taking offense to everything I say."

"If I want to join your 'victor's circle?'" I shot him an incredulous look.

The dark-haired prince opened the door and waved me forward. "I wasn't lying when I said you might have potential."

"Well, as long as it's been decided," I said sarcastically.

"That," he said slowly, "is a decision I have yet to make."

✢

I woke the next morning feeling as if I had downed an entire bottle of my parents' precious wine stores. My head spun, my limbs ached, and my dreams had been alarming to say the least.

*If you want to join the victor's circle.*

Frustrated, I heaved my pillow at the wall. *I don't want or need your help, you self-inflated peacock.*

*Do you want me to break you?*

I felt bile rise in my throat as I recalled my weak-willed reaction during the prince's attempts to disarm me.

*No. I want you to leave me alone.* I tore off the bed sheets and hastily pulled on my breeches and tunic.

"Bad dream?" Ella inquired from the bunk beside. She looked groggy as well, and I could tell from the way she stretched, flinchingly, that I wasn't the only one who would be suffering during today's lessons.

"You have no idea."

"Well, it's a new day," she remarked. "I'm sure another session with Piers and Cedric will leave your nightmare far behind."

*Not far enough though,* I grumbled.

# CHAPTER EIGHT

On the last day of Combat's orientation, no one had resigned, and Piers came into practice with a raging fervor.

"I told Barclae I'd cut this flock by five!" he roared. "And yet you have all remained to spite me... Apparently your lot has a backbone. I intend to break it. *No one* leaves my class today until I have five."

I exchanged nervous glances with Alex and Ella. We had all known this was coming. Piers had been growing increasingly upset as the week progressed, and today would be the accumulation of his wrath.

We were not mistaken.

Piers had teamed up with Master Cedric and his team of assisting mages to create the four most intensive hours of our time thus far. Instead of the traditional obstacle run around the stadium we were led out to the mountainous terrain just east of the Academy and the Western Sea.

Today there was only one rule: don't ask for help. There would be no healers. The only way we would receive treatment was if we withdrew. We'd had almost two months of training: "At this point you either have what it takes—or you resign."

The course had been designed for Combat, but we were still expected to participate even if it wasn't our intended faction. Endurance and stamina were prerequisites for all lines of

magic. Any student that chose to leave would never have made
it far anyway.

Now we were supposed to race up and down a treacher-
ous trail dodging a random assault of castings. The constable's
team had been invited to participate too, only unlike the last
six days they now lurked throughout the entire mountain,
awaiting unsuspecting first-years to engage.

We were to reach a ravine that was only accessible by a
long climb and descent a good hour or two in each direction.
And, of course, somewhere in the middle of that narrow valley
was a chest filled with a hundred copper tokens.

There were one hundred and twenty-two of us.

"You have not completed my course until you hand me
your token," Piers warned. He didn't tell us what would happen if we didn't, but it was clear that those without would be
subject to some sort of horrific test, the kind that wouldn't end
until he had gotten his five deserters "by whatever means necessary."

There was no direct path to our destination, and it
seemed that whichever way I turned, a new obstacle was waiting.

The first route I tried seemed simple enough, until giant
bolts of crackling lightning appeared out of nowhere. They
struck the ground with frightening intensity, spawning a huge
grass fire that rapidly spread.

There were large barrels of sand nearby. I realized they
were probably reminiscent of the barley sacks we'd been required to push and conjure the previous week, an aid to those
that could exert the casting necessary to reap their benefits.
Unfortunately I knew from past experience it would be a futile
effort. The bags were easily twice if not three times the weight
of the sacks we'd used earlier on, and I'd been less than successful with those.

I had no way of cutting a path across the flames.

Ahead of me some of the first-years, including the prince,
were conjuring up two of the barrels. They spilled a trail of

sand across the fire. The flames nearest the group were imme-diately extinguished.

I considered running after, but I held back.

My choice was justified a minute later when a desperate boy shoved his way past in an attempt to utilize their opening. I stopped what I was doing to watch the chain of events un-fold. One of the first-years pointed. Eve whirled around and sent the surrounding sand flying so that Ralph was encased in a circle of hungry flames. The boy was trapped. Like me, Ralph did not have the magic necessary to conjure an escape.

I turned away and started off after a group of first-years to my left.

A minute later I heard Ralph cry out for Piers.

One down, four to go. Maybe we wouldn't have to worry about those tokens after all.

First-years were starting to act merciless. It did not sur-prise me in the least that Darren's friends had been the first to lead the charge.

The new path I took was more challenging than the last, and it was the one more traveled. I was following a horde of scrambling first-years up the rocky side of a cliff. Many mem-bers of the constable's staff hid out behind boulders. I had to be doubly careful. The assisting mages were casting arrows as well.

Eventually our group reached a dead end. Before us was a raging stream, easily twenty feet across. Its waters were white, dangerous, and not particularly appealing. There was no other way to get around. It was immediately evident that if we were to continue our trek, we would have to cross the slippery logs and moss-covered stones to the other side.

Like the fire and its barrels of sand, I recognized this challenge as another of Piers's makeshift obstacles. Only in-stead of a tightrope and shattered glass, we were now expected to cross a river. The commander and Master Cedric had stuck us in the middle of a real-life obstacle course.

Cautiously, I started my way across, following the crowd of first-years in front. Seconds into my progress a girl in front of me lost balance. She cast out her magic just in time, a long pole stuck out from the river to hold her in place. As I approached the same slippery rock, I reached out to grab her stake for extra support. It vanished.

The girl laughed loudly. She was one of Priscilla's friends. I should have known better.

I barely kept my balance, and I would have fallen if Alex hadn't caught my sleeve at just the right moment. Apparently, he'd been forced to take a deviation from his original route as well.

"Thanks," I told my twin.

His eyes were locked on the shore ahead. "Thank me when it's over."

By the time we had crossed the stream, we were even further behind than when we had started. Another group of first-years had passed, having used their combined magic to secure a long climbing rope atop an extremely tall pine in the distance.

"Ry, behind you!"

I spun just in time to conjure a defense against the downward swing of my attacker. It was the same servant I had faced during that first day of Combat.

Our staffs collided with a loud smack. The man rushed off, having lost any advantage now that the element of surprise was gone.

"That was close," I breathed as Alex grabbed my arm, dragging me forward.

"Come on," he panted. "We've got to get to the chest before all the tokens are gone."

I rushed after him, breathing heavily as we climbed the increasingly steep face of the bluff. We had just reached a level break when I caught sight of its clearing.

Just beyond reach, a cluster of first-years was engaged in a full-on assault with Darren and his friends. The non-heir's group was fewer in number, but it didn't seem to matter.

I could see Darren throwing out blasts of howling wind, knocking his opponents to the ground with the sweep of a hand. In a matter of seconds he had disarmed a large group and given his team an opening.

Meanwhile, Jake and his burly brother William were conjuring daggers mid-air. The blades were quickly embedding themselves in the remaining rivals' limbs.

It was a blood bath.

Alex and I didn't move, waiting instead for the prince's friends to finish their attack and pass. I watched from a distance as they ended the skirmish and took inventory of their surroundings. They had just begun to move out when Darren turned around.

His eyes met mine, and a shadow of a smile played out across his face.

Moments later the dirt-packed earth Alex and I were standing on began to quake. I jumped back, pulling my brother with me as the ground before us split open.

In the place we had just been standing was a deep fissure, too wide to jump and too deep to climb. It effectively cut us off from the trail we needed to follow. When I looked back to Darren he was gone.

"That pompous jerk just destroyed our chances!" Alex burst out.

I bit back a scream of frustration. The non-heir had gone out of his way to do this. I had the distinct impression that if it had just been Alex it would not have happened.

"We can still make it," I said finally. "We just need a running start."

"And break both legs in the process?" Alex grabbed my arm. "It's not worth it, Ry." He motioned for us to turn around.

I refused to budge.

"What is it?"

I stared at the gap, envisioning a thick fallen pine covering the hole. It would be bigger than anything I had ever attempted, but that didn't mean it couldn't work.

"I'm going to get us across," I told him. "Just make sure no one interrupts me."

Alex opened his mouth to protest and then thought better of it. He knew just as well as I how much time we would lose if we were forced to turn around again. He reached down to grab a jagged piece of loose granite and took a few steps down the path to keep watch for anyone who might pose a threat.

I set to work, concentrating on my breathing until it became a slow, even pace. I willed myself to lose focus of the distractions around me: the buzzing of summer insects, the humidity of the sun's ever present rays, the dull and aching sensation of my limbs.

Slowly the distractions trickled away until all that was left was the image of a sturdy robust pine, a mixture of textured amber and darkened wood. I breathed in the intoxicating scent of its sharp, resinous odor. I tasted the tang of its bitter needles.

I heard the trunk land, thudding against the dense clay earth. I imagined it spreading across the length of our hole.

Gingerly, I opened my eyes and saw the log that now covered the gap in front of us. Alex emitted a low whistle, returning to stand next to me.

"You've been holding out, Ry," he remarked.

I shook my head. "I didn't even know I could."

Alex took a step forward, but I quickly cut him off. "I don't want you to break your neck if this doesn't work."

Hesitantly I put one foot forward, and then another, until both feet were firmly planted on the tree. I was still on the part that covered the ground. Now came the hard part.

I took another step, testing my weight. The trunk felt stable enough, and the coarse bark seemed to hold me well enough in place.

I quickly crossed the rest of the distance. An immense headache started to set in as I watched Alex follow suit.

He was about three-quarters across when the casting gave out. Without warning, the dull ache in my forehead became a mad pounding. The trunk vanished.

Alex fell forward, grasping at air. Crying out, I only just managed to catch my brother's hand before he was plunged into the shadowy abyss.

I helped him off the ledge.

"C-close call," my brother gasped.

As the two of us stood I apologized. "I don't know what happened!" My head felt like it was on fire. My stomach was reeling.

"I've seen things like that before," Alex gasped, "when someone tries to cast above their means!"

The two of us hurried down the path. I tried to continue, ignoring the pain until it finally became too much.

Ducking behind a bush, I spilled the contents of my stomach until there was nothing left. A sour odor filled my nose. I wiped my mouth against my sleeve, the headache instantly gone.

Alex was waiting for me when I returned. He didn't ask, and I was grateful.

We didn't encounter another first-year for a while, but eventually we did make out another group in the distance. Ella was with them, descending the steep switchbacks below. I hadn't noticed her at first because she was so far ahead, but now I did, her black bangs and bronze skin glistening in the sun.

I didn't see Darren's group below, so I could only assume they had taken another approach. A second later I realized my mistake. There was a cluster of telltale green racing down the ravine much further on. I could see Darren leading his troop along a winding stream, gesturing to what was undoubtedly a large wooden chest at the edge of the river's fork. It was almost directly beneath the rocky ledge we stood now.

Our best bet was to take the same path as everyone else, using the gradual round descent instead of a risky climb. With only two groups ahead Alex and I still had a chance.

I blinked and then swore as I noticed another company of students emerging from a hidden alcove at the bottom of the trail. They must have found a way to go around the overpass. There were about twelve or so in Darren's group, and this new hoard easily accounted for thirty. Add Ella's large group of sixty, and that left a shortage of tokens.

Somewhere behind us were bound to be fifteen or so stragglers, but it was not enough. Alex and I needed to get ahead of the first-years in Ella's group. Not all of them, but at least ten to be safe. I couldn't be too certain of the numbers ahead.

"We are in trouble."

I pointed to a steep slope to our left. "We'll never catch up if we take the same route as everyone else." We were certain to catch up if we avoided the switchback and used the drop to cut straight down the mountainside instead.

"You can't be serious." Alex stared at the ledge. "That's easily two hundred feet of granite!"

I shook my head, vehemently. "I used to climb rocks all the time in Demsh'aa. You know that." I began to lower myself into the first foothold.

"I can't follow you, Ry." My brother had a crippling fear of heights.

"Don't worry," I told him. "We only need one of us to reach that chest in time." I braced myself against the cliff's face. "We can meet back at the first river crossing on return. If either of us gets a token, we can grab an extra for the other."

✢✢

For the next thirty minutes I scaled the side of the cliff as if it were no more than a large boulder back home.

My hands were cracked and bleeding from the constant friction of rapid flesh against the sharp edges of rock, but I didn't have time for a slow climb. I had no way of measuring my progress against the rest of the class—the stone wall blocked my view of the trail—and I could only hope I had made the right choice.

In what seemed like forever, I finally reached its base. Sprinting over the scattered brush, I raced in the direction of a babbling stream.

No more than a quarter mile out I could see a crowd of first-years rushing back. Flashes of red and orange—telltale copper coins the size of my palm—glittered from tightly clenched fists.

I shoved my way past the group, not caring to apologize as I made my way toward the chest. I ran the two minutes it took to reach its wooden coffer and snagged two medallions. There was still a large handful left.

"Well, well, the lowborn is a thief."

My elation broke as I came face-to-face with Priscilla. She had been missing from Darren's party earlier, I realized dimly. Judging from the gathering of others behind her, Priscilla must have been leading the large mass from the switchbacks.

I quickly closed my hand around the two coins I had taken. I started to push past but Priscilla shoved me forward.

"There's enough for both of us!" I hissed, not wanting to draw attention. People would not take kindly to the fact that I had taken more than my share.

Priscilla grabbed my wrist, and I jerked it away.

"She grabbed two!" Priscilla shrieked.

Angry faces filled my vision.

"It's for my brother!"

"Does anyone think it is fair that she is trying to sabotage us?" Priscilla demanded.

"No—I wasn't..." I paled, nervously inching backward, only to find myself surrounded by the hoard. *Where was Ella? Alex? Any of my friends from the study group?*

Anxiously I scanned the crowd, but I could find no friendly faces. My friends had either already grabbed a token or were too far away to be of any help.

"Give us your tokens, Ryiah."

I glowered at Priscilla, angry that she was playing the part of the people's savior even though we both knew it was her furthest intention. Her only loyalty was to the prince. She was just using the students here in her personal vendetta against me. Our last encounter was coming back to slap me in the face.

I should never have baited her.

Out of the corner of my eye I spotted Ruth and Jordan at the edge of the mob, but they both sadly shook their heads. There were too many others for them to come to my aid.

The last thing anyone wanted to do was find themselves in the same position I was.

I had no way out. If it had just been Priscilla I would have tried to escape. She was more powerful than me, but I might have stood a chance were it one-on-one.

Twenty-on-one was a whole other story.

*I'm sorry Alex.* I tossed my brother's token to Priscilla.

"I said both coins."

"But I—"

"You should have thought about that before you got greedy!" The dark-haired beauty scanned the crowd, smiling maliciously. "Does everyone agree Ryiah should pay the price for her crime?"

A unison of nods.

"This is ridiculous!" I argued. "I have earned my—"

"You steal, you suffer the consequences. Give us the other coin, Ryiah."

Glaring, I hurled the second copper at her.

"Now, does anyone want to help me make sure she doesn't get her hands on anymore?"

Several hands shot up, and I froze.

"Wait," I argued, "I gave you what you wanted—"

She smirked. "Really, Ryiah. You act as if we are doing this out of spite. Please understand we are only doing what we think is fair." She stepped forward and snapped her fingers.

Instantly, my hands were bound, and a thick cloth strip muffled my cries. Priscilla took another step forward and leaned in close so that only I could hear her next words: *"Darren told me the truth about where the two of you go each night. You might try to play coy, but I know your end game. If you ever come near my prince again, I'll make it my personal promise you don't last the year."* She glanced back at her volunteers. "Now who wants to help me move her?"

⚔

I was tied up and bound to the base of a towering oak, a mere fifteen paces from the wooden chest and its now empty contents.

After Priscilla and her entourage left, there'd only been five medallions left, but in a matter of minutes another grouping of first-years had appeared, snatching the last of the tokens.

I tried to cast myself free, figuring a couple of flames were all I needed to weaken the ropes, but there was no magic left. I had drained my powers crossing Darren's fissure.

So there I was, tied to a tree with a giant piece of parchment above my head that read "hoarder." Thanks to the label none of the passing first-years had bothered to help, no doubt deciding it was not worth their time to try and help a girl who had enough enemies to tie her to a tree in the first place.

After ten more minutes passed I spotted Ella and my brother. Unable to draw their attention through anything but muffled shouts, I waited for them to notice me. Ella was the first, interrupting Alex to point in my direction.

They both came running to my aid.

As soon as Alex read the sign above my head, he ran a hand through his messy locks, hanging his head.

I pointed to the empty chest.

Alex swore. Ella angrily hurled her dagger at the ground.

"We've got to...head back," I coughed between huge gasps of air. "Our only chance...Piers said he and Cedric...would keep everyone...that didn't have a coin...until he had his five." I stopped and pointed to the tunnel everyone had been using to return.

"There's only been one person to come through here since the chest emptied," I finished, "which means there's still some others left. If we get back first, before the others without a token, maybe Piers will go easier on us?"

"Well, it's better than hiking back up that mountain," Ella said, somewhat reluctantly.

The three of us started towards the dark passageway. As we walked I explained how I had ended up bound to a tree.

"Priscilla really does hate you," Ella observed. "That's the second time she's gone out of her way to torment you."

I winced as I tripped over a small rock, grabbing onto my friend's arm to keep from falling. "She thinks I am after Darren."

Ella snorted, and my brother laughed loudly.

"My thoughts exactly."

After an hour of darkness we finally reached the tunnel's end.

"Now that's more like it." Alex raised his hands to the sky, bathing in the warm glow.

Ella pointed to a sloping hill in the distance. "We've still got to get up that thing and whatever else is out there."

She was right.

Ten minutes later a barrage of arrows came flying from our right.

"You just had to say it," Alex complained.

The three of us ducked and dodged, racing up the grassy slope.

Eventually, we made it past the missiles' range and continued, cautiously, down the other side of the hill. I could see a large crowd at its base. Instinctively, the three of us picked up speed.

Sir Piers and Master Cedric stood waiting with the rest of the class. There was an ominous expression on their faces. A heavy burlap sack sat between them, glimmering with the copper tokens we had tried so hard to obtain.

Piers twirled a coin in his hand, watching it spin and then falter, falling flat in his palm. He did this two more times and then glanced up at the class.

"The rest of you are dismissed." Almost immediately, a flurry of students began to retreat.

"Not you, boy." Piers snatched the shoulder of a first-year that had tried to escape unnoticed. He eyed Alex, Ella, and I. "Don't even try," he warned.

Master Cedric cleared his throat. "Shall I?"

Piers smiled, white teeth flashing. "I insist."

Cedric reached out to touch Piers's throat, leaning on tiptoe to reach the height of our brawny commander. "Go ahead," he told Piers.

Piers cleared his throat, "Attention all remaining first-years!" His words screeched across the landscape.

Several departing first-years turned around to see what was happening.

"Anyone who has not handed me a token shall report to the starting point now. You have five minutes. Then your final test will begin. I've got four more spots to fill, so you had better pray to your gods that one of them is not you."

Cedric released his grip on Piers, and the commander turned to face the four of us that were already present. "Rest up children," he said. "You might be here all night."

In the shortest five minutes known to man, the remaining first-years made their appearance. Each one looked worse for wear than the last, and I was sorry to note Winifred among them.

Once the final student arrived, Piers turned to Master Cedric. "Is Ascillia ready?"

One of the assisting mages stepped forward, a short blonde woman with twinkling violet eyes. "I am." In her hands she held a flask the size of her palm.

Ella gripped my arm. "Whatever happens, don't let me be one of the four."

"Alright, children, gather round." Piers barked.

We came forward, and Master Cedric motioned for us to take a seat in the same circle we had assumed so many times before.

"Is anyone familiar with the basics of hallucinogens?"

Several of us looked around but no one dared to speak.

Ascillia laughed and held her bottle high: "Well, the ones that aren't will certainly understand after they've had a taste of this." She crossed the grass to the nearest first-year and produced a small tasting cup from her pocket. She poured a little of the solution into the glass and indicated for the girl to swallow. She continued to do the same until each one of us had ingested the vile-tasting draught.

"This potion is a powerful brew from some of our realm's most vision-inducing plants—mandrake root and nightshade, to be exact. Distortive blends are what I was known for in my apprenticeship." The woman beamed. "People say *my* castings enhance them in a way no other Alchemy mage can. You'll begin to feel its effects after the first couple of minutes."

Master Cedric took Ascillia's place in the center of the circle as she stepped to the side. "We administer draughts like these to prisoners of war. They are more effective than traditional methods in questioning. Soldiers are trained to with-

stand many things, but not a mental assault..." He cleared his
throat uncomfortably. "We usually don't use this type of thing
on students as it can induce madness if left untreated for too
lo—"

Sir Piers jumped in beside Master Cedric with a grin. "We
*usually* don't, but good old Barclae has given us the go-ahead
since this year's first-years are more resilient than our usual
batch of half-wits."

Master Cedric cleared his throat. "The dose we gave you
should be enough to induce a nightmare state constructed entirely from your own projections. The hallucinations you experience will seem very, *very* real, and nothing, not even the
knowledge that you are dreaming, will stop you from believing
their effects. Ascillia has worked her castings so that each of
you will have a part of your subconscious reminding you of
this fact and asking you to surrender—"

"—And the moment you do, Cedric and I will administer
the antidote," Ascillia interrupted. "Anything you say in the
casting is spoken aloud. It's how we will be able hear your
submission." She smiled toothily. "The first four of you to forfeit will be cured and sent to pack their bags immediately. The
rest of you..."

As Ascillia continued to talk I leaned in closer to listen,
my head unusually heavy as I strained to catch her words. Her
speech was choppy and quiet, a slow murmur punctuated by
sharp consonants that hurt my ears.

Moments went by, and my eyes started to itch. Sharp,
glistening blades of summer grass became a dull, almost hazy
green. *The beginning of Ascillia's casting?*

I glanced around the circle and saw similar effects occur-
ring for others. Ella's pupils were dilated, so much so that they
almost encompassed her entire retina. She looked more bug-
like than human, and I wondered if it were really her or a vision.

To her left, Alex sat staring intently at nothing, eyes just
as wide, and a cold shiver crept down my spine. Everyone else

seemed equally disturbed, vacant stares quickly filling the remainder of our circle.

Dark tendrils of smoke enveloped my vision. I was blind.

My hand began to twitch, uncontrollably, and I felt unnaturally slaked for thirst.

*Where is everyone?*

✦

*I was alone. No longer on the field, I now stood in a room I
had never seen before. The room was cold as ice. On each side of
me, no matter where I turned, were giant, windowless openings.*

*Just outside, a blood-orange sky was painted with magenta
clouds, sitting bright against the harsh emptiness of my room.*

*A cruel gust of icy wind greeted my bare face.*

*Shivering, I raised my head to look about the room again.
This time there was a long black bench at its center, with three
strangers and Master Barclae seated upon it. The strangers wore
heavy mage's robes in the stark colors of Jerar's three factions of
magic.*

*I hastened to kneel, but my audience was too busy arguing to
notice. I couldn't make out a word.*

*I leaned in closer, but it was still impossible to hear.*

*"They are trying to decide if you are good enough."*

*I spun around but couldn't find the speaker.*

*"I am standing right next to you."*

*I blinked, and Prince Darren appeared. He was no longer
wearing the training attire of the Academy. Instead, he was
dressed like that first day I had passed him in the mountains.*

*"You are not good enough," the non-heir continued. "You
know that, don't you?"*

*I opened my mouth to tell him he was wrong, but no sound
came out. I gasped, clawing at my throat and looking to Darren
with wild eyes. Help me, I mouthed.*

*He threw back his head and laughed.*

*I lunged at the prince, but all I grasped was air, and then cold, hard marble. Knees bruised, palms bloodied, I looked up to see the prince was now on the bench with the others. He winked at me as he whispered something in the Black Mage's ear, and the man laughed hoarsely.*

*"Don't trust him, and you can't get hurt."*

*Ella stood in front of me, dark ringlets billowing as she gazed down at me earnestly.*

*I tried to assure her I never would, but I could only offer silence.*

*Suddenly, the entire room spun, and I found myself outside my parents' house in Dem'shaa. Eagerly, I ran to the door and threw it open.*

*An outpouring of smoke filled my lungs, and I coughed repeatedly, a hand over my nose as I felt along the wall, trying to see through the haze.*

*"Mother, father...?" I choked. "Alex...Derrick?"*

*My voice was back, but it did no good. There was only silence to answer my call. Stumbling, I made my way forward, coughing and shouting as I pounded on the walls.*

*I threw open my parents' bedroom door. The smoke suddenly cleared. In front of me were their bodies—mangled and bruised, spread out across the floor. A pool of blood lay at my parents' feet, and their eyes were glassy, without depth.*

*I sank to the ground.*

*"Ryiah! Help me—please! Ryiah!" My heart dropped. Alex.*

*I raced out of the room in search of my twin. I could hear both his and Derrick's screams coming from across the hall. Pounding on locked doors, ignoring the suffocating smoke, I pleaded for them to answer.*

*Barreling into the final room and finding it empty after the smoke had shifted, I felt hysteria rise within. Where were they? Who was doing this? I slammed my fist against a doorframe.*

*"You are too late, Ryiah. They will be dead too, and there is nothing you can do to stop it."*

Halting, I turned slowly to find myself face-to-face with a stranger. The dim figure was shrouded in a heavy haze of smoke. It was impossible to make out any of her features.

"What did you do?" I gasped.

"You can end it all," the stranger insisted, ignoring my question. Her voice was unsympathetic and yet strangely familiar. "You can end this right now and never lose them."

"I don't know what you are—"

"Call out for Piers. This is a dream."

She was lying. This wasn't a dream…It couldn't be. Could it?

The stranger snapped her fingers, and an image shimmered in the air. I could see myself seated in a giant circle, sobbing quietly, eyes shut, as Sir Piers paced the edge. He held three fingers up, laughing.

The vision ended, and I was back with the stranger.

"Call Piers and surrender, now!" she commanded. A blast of magic hit me, slamming me against the wall.

"No." I struggled to right myself—even if she was telling the truth, I didn't trust her.

"You fool!" the stranger raged. "You would rather lose your family than give up your chance at an apprenticeship!"

"If this is only a dream then I won't lose them." I folded my arms stubbornly.

All at once I found myself hanging across the ledge of an endless pit, suspended mid-air as the shadowy stranger looked down. Her magic was all that kept me from plummeting to its depths.

"Do you think you won't feel death? Do you think you'll be able to tell the difference when every inch of your corpse is screaming out for the pain to stop?" the girl challenged. Still obscure in the shadows, her voice rang with familiarity. "These visions induce madness. You heard your instructor. How many times do you think you can die before you become mad as well? Are you so stubborn that you would rather lose yourself than give up a mage's robes?"

*I remained silent.*

*"This is not a choice, Ryiah. Surrender now, or I will kill you. You have five seconds."*

*"Please—"*

*"One."*

*Why was it so important for me to fail?*

*"Two."*

*"Who are you?"*

*"Three."*

*"Why—"*

*"Four."*

*I couldn't do it. Even though I was going to die, I couldn't call out for Piers. I believed the stranger. I believed when she said I would feel every moment of it, but I couldn't do it.*

*"Five."* *Her cold eyes met mine, and a coursing shock tore through my body.*

*The stranger was me.*

*"Five!" the second Ryiah shrieked.*

*A piercing clap filled the air, and I was falling into a long tunnel of darkness. I clapped my hands over my mouth, knowing I could never surrender.*

*Wind whipped across my face. My limbs twisted and flailed as I continued to plummet into the shadowy abyss. My flesh was being ripped apart by an angry storm, my stomach was lost in my throat, and I was falling, falling, falling.*

*I shut my eyes.*

*So this is what it feels like to die.*

❊

"Make it stop! Make it stop!"

Startled by the clamor, I opened my eyes. I wasn't falling, dying, trapped in some bottomless pit. I was sitting on the grass beside my brother, Ella, and nineteen other first-years.

Across from me a red-haired boy was shaking violently. Like everyone else, his eyes were clouded.

Moments later he cried out again, "Please, just make it end! I yield!"

I watched as Master Cedric came forward and had Sir Piers hold the first-year in place, emptying the contents of a clear vial into the struggling boy's mouth. A second later the boy was alert and hunched over the ground, heaving.

Sir Piers turned to Master Cedric who stood a couple paces away. "Well, that makes number four—five counting that boy at the start. I guess we can administer the antidote to the rest of them now." He paused. "Ascillia, see to the rest."

The mages and Sir Piers began to make their rounds, slowly bringing each student back to consciousness. Ascillia was the first to reach me.

Her eyes widened. "How did you—"

"I don't know."

"Did you even experience a state of delirium?"

I nodded and watched as Master Cedric joined her.

"She woke on her own, fully conscious," Ascillia told the master, still staring. "Her eyes aren't dilated, and she doesn't have any sign of residual effects..."

"That is unusual," the master said softly. "But not impossible."

"How can this happen?"

Master Cedric finished his assessment and glanced at his assistant. "Occasionally, we underestimate the potential of those around us..." He paused. "I believe today is one of those days."

Her jaw dropped. "You mean to say her magic did this?"

The master was silent for a moment, then: "Perhaps."

# CHAPTER NINE

The week before we began our chosen factions was the first time off any of us had received since we entered the Academy.

Of course, it wasn't really free. Now that orientation was over, we were five students down and too anxious to do anything except nervously calculate our odds. In seven days' time we would be selecting a faction. A decision that would dictate the remainder of our year, and nothing had driven that home more than that final day of Combat.

"Do they really think we need a week to choose?" Ella made a face as Alex and I joined her at the table for lunch. It was our second day into the week, and it was obvious everyone had already made up their mind.

"They are probably hoping the nerves will get to us." Alex smiled weakly. "Can't say they'd be wrong."

I squinted at my twin over my second mug of tea. Even though we weren't expected to attend lessons, most of the class, my friends and I included, had continued the normal routine. Which meant I was just as tired as any other day at the Academy. "Do they really think we will resign after that day in the mountains?" I groaned. "If we didn't then, we aren't going to now."

But my brother was right.

By the end of the week seven more students had left. I would have thought that after two months of hard work and resilience, self-resolve would be contagious. But a week of reflection had taken its toll. Several young men and women weighed the price of a robe against their family, friends, and a comfortable career back home. For some, magic lost.

Following my brother and friend, I hurried to the atrium where the rest of our class was waiting. Today was not only the day we would be electing our factions, but also the return of the second through fifth-year apprentices and their faction's leaders. We had seen several new faces in passing the past few days. The possibility of meeting Jerar's future mages was too tempting to ignore. I had so many questions, and an apprentice would know first-hand how arduous year one could be, and maybe, just maybe, they could offer some advice.

Or so I thought.

"Today I have exciting news," Master Barclae announced. "In two months' time we have gotten rid of some of the dead weight that has been holding the rest of you back. As of this evening, two more first-years have decided to pursue opportunities outside of our school, bringing the total to fourteen."

I looked around the room and saw several people doing the same, but I was unable to identify the missing faces from the crowd. There were too many of us as it was.

"I am happy to say Sir Piers and Master Cedric have not disappointed me in their latest endeavor—"

Piers let out a boisterous hoot and toasted the Master of the Academy.

"—And I hope they continue to pull even larger numbers in the months that follow."

I swallowed nervously and glanced at Alex and Ella. They had the same uneasy expressions.

"I understand the majority of you were under the impression that I would be introducing you to the apprentice mages and their instructors...I will be doing no such thing.

The only way you will be receiving an introduction is if you are one of the few to pass our end-of-year trials and become one yourself.

"The training masters and their apprentices will be occupying the eastern wing of the second and third-floor. You are not to disturb them. They will only be here until the solstice, and then they will be setting back out to continue their training in the field. While they are here, they are not to be engaged. *Any of you found fraternizing will be expelled immediately.* The apprenticing mages are the futures of our great institution, and I will not have it squandered by overzealous first-years."

Master Barclae paused and then chuckled: "On a more positive note, I do have the pleasure of introducing the three masters who will be your faction leaders for the remainder of the year...Masters Cedric, Ascillia, and Narhari, please come join me in the center." Our current training master, the eccentric Alchemy mage, and a tall, foreboding man of Eastern descent stepped forward to stand beside the Master of the Academy.

"As you know," Barclae continued, "this week marked the end of your orientation. Tomorrow you start anew with your chosen faction. Masters Eloise and Isaac will continue to lead your sessions on magical theory, but your new faction will dictate what time of the day you report to the library to do so. Sir Piers will still direct your physical conditioning, but again, your sessions with him will depend on the same.

"Master Cedric here will be leading the magical application portion of your studies for Restoration. Due to a recent resignation, Ascillia has been promoted to Master leading the section on Alchemy. And, last but certainly not least, Master Narhari, our returning master for first-year Combat. Between the three of them, I am sure you will be kept more than busy."

The Master of the Academy gave a broad wave of his hand. "Now you are all dismissed. Make sure to report to the constable before curfew with the name of your chosen fac-

tion—without it your time here will be considered a resignation."

⚜

"Are you ready for the biggest mistake of your life?" Ella
nudged me as we trudged up the training hill for our first session with Master Narhari. There were already rumors going
around that the master of Combat sent first-years packing
faster than Sir Piers himself.

"It is the only one worth making," I replied bravely.

"I hope you still feel that way when practice is over."

I was about to respond but found myself speechless. Ella
followed my gaze with her own, and her jaw dropped.

"In the name of the gods," she breathed.

Before us stood the most handsome man either of us had
ever laid eyes on. I hadn't had much time to study Master
Narhari during Master Barclae's introduction the night before,
but now the impression was unmistakable.

Over six feet of sheer, towering muscle greeted my
awestruck stare. The master of Combat had well-oiled black
hair pulled sleekly back behind his ears, smoldering eyes of icy
blue, bronze skin, and a short, rough stubble that lined his upper lip and chin suggestively. He couldn't have been more than
thirty-five years, and there was an unmistakable air of confidence to his stance.

Ella and I stood dumbfounded on the side of the field.
Soon we weren't alone, as more and more girls approached the
dais they seemed to filter off one-by-one in a state of confusion.
I counted the number of students.

There were far less girls than boys to our faction, seventeen amongst the forty or so young men. Most of my gender
had chosen Alchemy or Restoration. They'd been under the
impression that we were disadvantaged for Combat—after all,
most boys had grown-up playing at knights, but few girls had
done the same.

Now, we were proving exactly how foolhardy our sex could be as the seventeen of us stood frozen in place at the commanding presence of ideal masculinity. It was a pleasant surprise.

We soon realized our mistake when the shirtless training master ordered everyone to line up and begin the same casting drills as the week before. Unlike Master Cedric, Narhari did not allow weakness, which became evident the moment we ran out of stamina.

"This is Combat!" the new master of Combat shouted. He paced up and down the lines as we attempted to conjure enough force to distance our targets.

Try as I might, I had no magic left. The barley sack would not budge. The prince's group was still going strong, but the rest of the class was faltering. Badly.

"You chose my faction because you wanted to be pushed, not coddled! Don't tell me you have used up your magical reserve. No one has unless they are face-down on the ground without a spasm left. The *only* way you will build up your force is if you challenge yourself. Easy will *never* be good enough." Master Narhari bent down to meet the darting eyes of a nervous boy to my right. "*Now!*"

The boy fumbled, and we all tried to summon enough magic to make the sacks move. Nothing.

"Harder!" the training master shouted.

I tried again, visualizing the force I needed to cast, and launched the projection with all my might.

"You are fighting for your life. Is this all you can give me?"

My arms were shaking badly and I was light-headed. But I held on, feeling as if I were slipping away in the process.

Several bags, including my own, shuddered and tipped back. A girl to my right fainted.

Straining, I ignored the burning sensation in my lungs and carried on, willing the sack to complete its fall to the ground. It shuddered again, and I threw the mental image with every ounce of energy my body could hold.

I felt myself fall as the bag dropped back, and a second later I too hit the ground. My eyes shut involuntarily, and I was dead to the world until someone splashed cold water on my face.

Sputtering, I sat up while Ella gripped my arm, holding me in place. The moment I tried to stand, my knees gave out, and an unpleasant sensation hit my stomach. Gasping, I quickly turned my head and threw up the contents of my lunch.

Similar sounds were happening all around me, and I realized that there were at least ten others on the ground, retching away. Looking up at my friend, I could see how clammy Ella's skin had become, and there were dark lines under her eyes. Her hands shook as they held onto my shoulder.

"Now you see what it is to push yourself," Master Narhari told our class somberly. "I expect each of you to reach this hard *every* time. If you have a problem with my approach, then you should resign immediately as you will not last long in my faction."

Fifteen minutes later we were dismissed. Ella and I could barely stand, and it was all we could do to hold onto our staffs as we walked down the long training hill for our evening meal.

Between the increased workload of Eloise and Isaac, the new weapons drills with Piers, and practices with Narhari, we were quickly acclimating to a ritual of misery and little else. After the first month of Combat it became a daily joke between us that we would "last the year or die trying."

Alex didn't seem to be faring any better, either. According to my twin, Master Cedric had been holding out on us, and now, despite his old age, had turned his two hours of healing into the "stuff dreamt only in nightmares."

"He tried to have us animate a corpse the other day," James piped up, who was also in Restoration with Alex. "Never seen anything more disturbing in my life."

"How is Alchemy going, Ruth?" I turned my attention to our other friend.

Ruth snorted. "Terrible."

I could barely see the girl. She was buried beneath a stack of manuscripts that took up the entire space in front of her.

"It can't be worse than Master Cedric," Alex said quickly.

Ruth shoved the pile of books and parchment across the table. "You try carrying every herb lore manuscript known to man and then recite it for me."

My twin laughed. " You have Master Ascillia. She used to be one of us a couple years ago."

Ruth rolled her eyes elaborately. "It just means she has more to prove. You know Cedric is an old softy. You're just afraid to admit you're beat."

"You can trade stitching up animal carcasses with me anytime, sweetling," he replied flirtatiously.

Ruth made a face and went back to reading her books while Ella and I quizzed Jordan and Clayton about their own experiences in Combat. We never had an opportunity to catch up in class, so we spent most of our meals critiquing each other's performance.

It wasn't always the easiest conversation, to have someone else point out your flaws, but it was something I had decided was necessary after my run in with Darren weeks back.

Better to hear truth, he'd said, than false flattery. I couldn't believe I was actually following the hypocrite's advice, but it had made sense and stuck with me long after.

I had to admit it was helping, though I'd never be able to pinpoint the exact degree of success it warranted. I still struggled day to day in each and every activity in which I participated, but struggle had become a regular condition. If I weren't struggling, if I weren't keeled over in agony, if my muscles weren't screaming at the end of a long day...then I wasn't trying hard enough.

Master Narhari continued to test our breaking points. At first I had thought his methods cruel and unrelenting, but as the weeks wore on, I realized he was just a man who saw the sky as our limit. Narhari expected the world of his students because he expected the same of himself. He wanted us to succeed, even if his definition included shattering our magical boundaries on a daily basis. It didn't mean I resented him any less for pushing. It was impossible to remain positive during continual rounds of mental and physical torment—but I did recognize what he was trying to do.

It was beginning to pay off.

One month ago I would have been thrilled to see my magic's stamina outlast the previous week by a couple of minutes or an extra block during my jousts with Ella. Now my castings carried on a half-hour most of the time. My reserve wasn't guaranteed, but even if it failed to increase right away, I was usually able to conjure more powerful castings in the weeks that followed.

First-years were beginning to slow down, or quit. By the end of the second month in Combat, eleven more had withdrawn from the Academy. They had left not because they ran out of drive, but because they hadn't improved their castings in weeks.

All my life people had stressed the importance of "potential." *The amount of magical stamina one was capable of building.* We all had a limit. You could have some magic, but did you have enough? Only time would tell which of us did.

The hype was beginning to make sense.

The Academy gave me a year. I hoped it *would* be enough. I'd seen Darren and his close-knit following. Each one of them had yet to falter. They remained at the top of each class and carried on long after the last of us fell.

Some of us were still improving, but we were all fearful how much longer our stamina-building would continue. Sure, I had magic, but eventually I would reach the end of its limits. As long as Darren and his friends were improving, there wasn't much hope for the rest of us.

Fortunately, as the third month of Combat commenced, some of the prince's friends began to falter, though I was loath to admit neither Priscilla nor the non-heir himself was a part of it.

The two burly brothers, Jake and William, had stopped gaining in stamina, and they were beginning to struggle in the increasingly difficult assignments Eloise and Isaac assigned. The only area those two still excelled in was Piers's drills, but it was common knowledge that would not be enough. The brothers hadn't left yet, but Ella and I had a wager going for how much longer they would remain. Neither of us had a fondness for the wealthy brutes.

A week later, our friend Jordan resigned, and a couple days after, one of the lowborn boys from Darren's group of twelve. There was no shortage to the resignations taking place, and I wondered how many more would follow. Master Barclae had warned that half the class would leave by winter holiday. I had a nagging feeling he was going to be proven right.

⁜

On the third week of our fifth month at the Academy, I walked into my session with Master Narhari expecting nothing more than the same routine that had been drilled into us for the past two and a half months.

Instead I found Piers, whose session we had just came from, leaning against the edge of fencing that encompassed the boundary of our training field. Masters Barclae and Narhari stood beside him. The three of them looked particularly formidable.

I shivered and wrapped my arms around my chest, eyeing the masters with apprehension. The three of them together was not a good sign. Considering the last time Sir Piers had teamed up with a master, I feared for today's outcome.

Glancing down the line, I saw Eve smile, albeit uneasily, and Priscilla and Darren exchange knowing looks. They knew something. The rest of the class seemed unsure, but it was clear that the prince had not been kept in the dark.

"Don't they look just lovely?" Ella muttered.

"I feel like they put on those disturbing smiles just to mess with our heads," Clayton whispered back.

I laughed. My friends and I could not be more alike.

Moments later the humor was gone when Master Narhari explained exactly why the visitors were present.

"They've come to check your progress," he announced. "We will be staging a duel between each of you and another student in this class. This will be a chance to demonstrate what you have learned thus far. This is not a test. There are no winners and losers today, and this will in no way influence your trials at the end of the year."

I breathed in a small sigh of relief and heard Ella at my right do the same.

"That said," Narhari noted, "I want each of you to remember today as the day you gained confidence in yourself. I know how hard all of you have been training, and the next two hours should be the culmination of your efforts."

I glanced at Ella, and she at I. We knew who our partner would be. We had sparred so many times in class, as well as after. We knew each other's strengths and weaknesses almost as well as we knew our own. Between the two of us, we could easily impress the masters without embarrassing ourselves.

Several other students seemed to be thinking the same thing. First-years began to pair up almost instinctively.

"Children, children," Sir Piers chuckled loudly, stepping away from his post to stand closer to Narhari. "You are sadly mistaken if you think I will let you pick the same person you have been practicing with all these months."

My stomach dropped.

"I believe Master Narhari and I have a better understanding of your skill set than your pea-sized brains
acknowledge. The two of us will choose the one who is...shall
we say, *best-suited* for your abilities." His words made my skin
crawl, and I was even more wary from the way his eyes had lit
up mischievously during the phrase "best-suited." Something
told me Piers had been looking forward to today for far too
long.

As the sets played out, one-by-one, I came to understood
exactly why. There were only a couple of us left by the time
my name was called, but I already knew exactly who my opponent would be.

Piers had not forgotten that day with the staffs.

"Priscilla."

I took a large swallow as the raven-haired beauty took
her place opposite mine.

"Begin."

The two of us circled one another, slowly.

Priscilla looked like a wolf honing in on a kill. She smiled,
white teeth flashing, and laughed throatily as I stumbled, desperately searching for an opening.

Her muscles gave away nothing, and since we had not
been provided any weapons, I had no idea how she planned to
initiate her assault.

"You can always forfeit now," the girl said, voice carrying across to our entire audience. "Save yourself the humiliation."

I ground my teeth but said nothing. The only way I
would win this match was if Priscilla became too confident and
slipped up. My magic was no match for her own. I'd seen her
often enough in class to know that it would be a mistake to
engage her directly. Maybe someday I would be able to beat
her outright, but not today.

"Go ahead. Play the coward," she taunted. "I have no
problem leading the attack."

Priscilla raised her hand. I recognized the move from training right away. She'd always been a fan of extravagant gestures.

Immediately I cast out a shield, clutching its arm holds with all the strength I could muster.

The air whistled loudly, and her magic slammed my defense, splitting the shield and knocking me to the ground in the same breath. I'd underestimated the force she would use. None of us had ever practiced being at the receiving end of that drill.

I quickly scrambled to my feet, just in time to spot a flying dagger headed for my face. I let myself fall to the ground, hands thrown across my face instinctively. A searing pain shot across my forearm. Warm blood coated my wrists and hair, but I was lucky all the same. The cut had missed any important veins.

Wincing, I pulled myself back up, throwing a crowd of flames at my enemy's feet.

Priscilla cried out as the fire touched her skin, but a second later all that remained was a poof of smoke, an outpouring of sand had drenched what remained of my attack.

"Is that it?" the girl jeered. "Two seconds of flame? How about some lightning?"

Lightning? We hadn't learned weather attacks yet. Let alone the deadliest of them all. That type of magic was reserved for the apprenticeship, not first-years. We weren't supposed to know such complicated castings. Panicked, I glanced up at the sky, only to get the air knocked out of my chest as I was sent sprawling back against the grass.

Priscilla was laughing as I doubled-over, unable to get back up. "Really didn't think you'd fall for that one," she giggled.

I spat, blood and saliva hitting the ground as I tried to stand once more. Again, the pain sent me reeling at the core.

She could have just finished me off then, but I could tell Priscilla wanted to continue to drag out my degradation.

"You have no place here," she said lazily, circling around as she spoke. "*Trying*," she added, looking directly at Sir Piers, "is *not* good enough. The ones that *need* to learn are the ones *I* am least worried about—"

Priscilla's speech was cut short as she was sent flying against the fence. Arms flailing out widely in front of her, she emitted a loud shriek as she hit the wood.

As she fell, I rose up, painfully, using a wooden pole I'd conjured for support.

"You little—"

With my spare hand I waved away the throwing daggers she had sent chasing after me and redirected them at their former owner. A chill crept up my spine. I had never tried the casting before, though I had seen it once or twice in practice.

All at once, a sharp, gnawing sensation surged across my stomach, and I realized uneasily I was fast approaching my limit. Apparently, real battle and adrenaline depleted my magic much faster than two hours of practice.

Then again, I had just used a large span of magical force to knock over a girl easily the weight of four barley sacks at once. And attempted a new casting. So maybe my exhaustion wasn't all that abnormal, in the given context.

With a violent gesture, Priscilla halted my blades and let them fall to the ground harmlessly. She stood, breathing a little unevenly, brushing off splinter fragments and dirt.

"It's time I end this, lowborn," she said, narrowing her eyes.

I braced myself for the attack, envisioning a shield as before, but this time her casting came before I could create a substantial projection.

Her force field slammed my defense. My head spun wildly as I tried to maintain my casting's spectral form, holding the shield for as long as I could. For the longest ten seconds of my life, I held my ground, shaking violently and fighting the sharp, searing pain that was filling my head.

Then, all at once, my shield shattered, splaying into billions of tiny pieces as I was sent staggering backward.

This time when I fell, I did not get up. I did not look to Piers or the masters. I already knew what their expressions would say.

*This girl does not belong here.*

Half of our class had failed, same as I. That was to be expected in a tourney of one-on-one competition. The difference was that my unsuccessful classmates had put up a good fight. I had humiliated myself.

"Will someone please help her back to her seat?" Sir Piers finally asked after I had finished retching onto the grass.

Ella and Clayton rushed forward and grabbed my arm on either side. The two helped me off the ground, and then Clayton ran off to fetch some water while Ella pushed my hair back so that its strands no longer stuck to my sweat-soaked face.

"Thanks," I said quietly when Clayton returned with a flask. I took a long swallow and then glanced up at the masters and Piers. As soon as the commander noticed my gaze, he looked away grimly.

*So much for no consequences,* I thought bitterly. I had just disappointed the one teacher that had been rooting for me. The commander had paired me with Priscilla so that I'd knock the over-confident girl off her high horse. He'd told her that I could be the one to beat her one day, but instead of validating his declaration, I had just made him seem the fool for vouching for me in the first place.

Swallowing the sinking feeling that had set in my throat, I watched the last two matches in a melancholy silence. My friends had already participated in their own rounds.

Ella had won her bout against a boy who usually tagged along after the non-heir's crew though he wasn't a part of it himself. The boy had started strong, but my dark-skinned friend had persevered and delivered a harsh blow at the end when the boy had been foolish enough to engage her in swordplay.

Clayton had lost to a quiet boy Ella and I had hardly spoken to since the first day of class. Their match had been a pretty even exchange, until the boy had conjured a glaive, feigned an attack to the left, and held the curved blade to our friend's throat.

The last pairing to go into duel was none other than Eve and Darren. Watching the two of them engage, I wondered if this was what Ella had meant when she described Combat as a dance…the dark, detached prince and the fragile, almost translucent young girl with violet eyes. Their exchange carried on for fifteen minutes, each serving a series of crippling assaults that the other deflected with startling precision. I had seen the two of them practice often enough in class, and today was no exception.

A shower of flame was greeted by a wall of ice. A powerful exertion of force was met with a large metal-embossed shield that deflected and sent the other's magic crashing into the forest behind. The ground beneath Eve gave way, and she used the same force she attacked Darren with to send herself back upon solid ground. An exchange of blows played out between two spectral blades, until the two ended their castings and held in their hands their personal weapons of choice.

Clutching the hilt in both hands, Eve held a long sword that almost reached the entire length of her frame. We had briefly practiced with that type of sword during our sessions with Piers, but the way she confidently held the weapon now made me believe she'd spent a lot of time with it before the Academy.

In contrast to his partner's double-edged sword, Darren clutched a single-headed battle-axe in each hand.

The two of them circled one another wordlessly. Eventually Darren jumped in, swiping at his opponent to engage. The two continued to feign and parry, metal on metal thundering across the field.

Suddenly, Eve swung out, and Darren hooked her blade with his off-hand axe while his other hand's axe struck out, the barest of inches from her neck.

Eve dropped her blade, and Darren lowered his weapons. The entire class burst into applause. Even the masters.

I kept my hands at my sides, seething with envy. Ella was the only other not to join in.

We were all dismissed then, and as I limped back to the dining commons, I heard snippets of conversation all around me.

"...Definitely not a mistake to let the prince join the Academy..."

"...Might as well announce the apprenticeships already. I think today was indicative enough of who the five for Combat will be..."

"...Probably the best performance I've ever seen between two first-years."

"...That girl, the one with the red hair, I heard her family runs an apothecary."

"Shame she didn't choose Alchemy since Combat clearly is not her calling..."

It was too much.

Fighting back unwanted tears, I broke free of the crowd.

"Ry?"

"Don't follow me." I spoke sharply so Ella wouldn't hear the tremors in my voice.

My friend nodded and turned back with Clayton trailing close behind.

I couldn't face another person after what had happened in class today. I felt as if my entire world had come crashing down, and someone had ripped my dreams away just as fast.

I spotted a thick-trunked oak to the side of the field. Immediately, I sank down to its base, hugging my knees and indulging the wave of self-pity I knew was about to hit.

"You should go back to your friends."

I looked up, recognizing the voice of the person I least wanted to hear from.

"Leave me alone," I snapped, shame-faced. I must have missed the non-heir in my tear-induced rage.

The prince stepped away from the side of the tree.

"Everyone has bad days."

I stared out at the grassy field. "I don't need your rhetoric right now, Darren."

He stood his ground and continued to watch me, an odd light in his eyes.

"Please," I said, conscious that I would not be able to carry on a defense much longer. My eyes were beginning to water again, and I did not want Darren to see me cry. "Please," I croaked, "just go."

I shut my eyes against the tears that were about to break.

There was a pause, then the shuffle of movement, followed by silence.

I opened my eyes and found myself completely alone. The tears fell freely then. I let them.

# CHAPTER TEN

The next morning I woke with the knowledge that yesterday's nightmare had not been "just a dream." I didn't feel any better in the early morning light, and the feeling stayed with me throughout the day.

When I arrived to Master Narhari's session and saw we were two first-years short, I felt an increasing sense of unease. The master confirmed it a moment later when he announced that two of our own had resigned.

"I would have thought you'd join them," Priscilla sneered when she caught up with me after practice that day.

I bit my lip, and Ella shoved her way forward. "Go back to wherever it was you crawled out of, Priscilla!"

Priscilla shot Ella a look of contempt. "I am just advising your friend what she is too stubborn to admit herself."

"Don't you have other first-years to torment?" Ella retorted. "Ryiah hasn't done anything to—"

"Her very presence offends me." The girl looked me over coldly. "I am tired of being surrounded by lowborn scum, and as a daughter of nobility yourself, Ella, I am alarmed you don't share my thoughts. Why not have her leave now? It's not as if she actually stands a chance." Priscilla called out to someone who had been standing off to the side.

"Darren, weren't we just saying how silly it is that the lowborns are here in the first place?"

The non-heir's eyes met mine, and I looked away. He'd had plenty of opportunities to criticize me in the past, so why stop now?

"No."

My head jerked, and I looked back to the prince.

"But you said—" Priscilla began.

"I said that they were foolish," Darren said, dark eyes never leaving mine, "but that does not mean they shouldn't try." He turned and walked away, leaving Priscilla, Ella, and me in his wake.

Seconds later, Priscilla left, chasing after the prince, while Ella regarded me curiously.

"That was strange."

I didn't know how to respond.

"Well," she went on awkwardly, "that may be the first and only time I ever agree with a prince."

※ ※

In the week that followed, three more students withdrew. This time though, Priscilla kept silent.

We were down to thirty-three in Combat, and Alex and Ruth informed me their numbers had dwindled as well. The exact number was revealed during the final day of our fifth month at the Academy.

"Fifty-nine!" Master Barclae announced over the evening meal. "We are now sixty-three less than when we started! I am pleased to announce that the masters and I have met our goal and disposed of half the waste that was taking up our valuable resources!"

*That many?* I glanced at my friends. They exchanged looks. None of us had realized how many had left. Or that we had already completed that much time. We'd been conscious of the truth, but we had not yet acknowledged it.

"In celebration of reaching our goal," the Master of the Academy continued, "the masters and I have decided to include you in our annual winter solstice ball the day before your weeklong reprieve begins. This festivity will be done in conjunction with our apprenticing mages who depart for field training the following day.

"As such, this will be your one and only opportunity to participate in activities with those you would not have the pleasure of speaking to otherwise. Do not waste it." Barclae raised his goblet and roared: "To fifty-nine!"

To fifty-nine indeed.

⚜

"Can you believe it, Ry?" Ella asked me when I returned from the library, much later that night.

"You're still up?" I asked incredulously. The bell had just sounded for the second hour into early morning.

She watched me put away my books. "I Can't sleep."

"I wish I suffered from your affliction," I told her. "I am pretty sure I drifted off for half my study tonight."

She tilted her head. "Well, it's good to see you back at it."

I shrugged. "I don't have much of a choice."

She looked at me earnestly, "Are you feeling alright, Ryiah? You didn't seem too excited by Master Barclae's news today—"

"I guess I'm just ready for this year to end."

"Don't tell me you are thinking of walking away!"

I smiled, somewhat bitterly. "I've made it this far. I'm going to stick it out." I paused. "It's funny. I arrived here knowing full well there was a good chance I would not succeed...I guess I just forgot that."

I looked to my friend and forced a smile. A real one. "It's okay, though, because I remember now, and I don't plan on forgetting it again anytime soon."

Ella shook her head vehemently. "You are too serious, Ry. You never forgot that. You just gained confidence and lost it when Priscilla knocked you down in front of our entire class."

She began to remake the sheets on her bed as she added, "You just need some good weeks to wash away your bad one...and I, for one, think the ball will be perfect for it. We'll have a whole night off to celebrate and feel mortal for once. And then a week to rest up! It's just what you need to get your conviction back."

I crawled into bed, not sharing my friend's enthusiasm. "I hope you're right."

---

The next three weeks passed by in a sea of endless commotion, thanks in large part to the Master of the Academy's announcement. Everyone was looking forward to a break after the grueling progress we had been making the past six months. Spirits were lifted, and despite the increasingly difficult sessions in class, the count remained at fifty-nine for better or for worse.

I had to admit that some of the cheer was contagious. As frost began to cover the field and every inch of the Academy's campus, I started to feel better than I had in weeks. That day with Priscilla had faded away into a distant memory, and as my stamina continued to climb while others' faltered, I grew more and more hopeful that the pattern would continue on into the new year.

---

In no time at all, the evening of festivities had arrived.

Ella and I had just exited our barracks, having changed out of our dirty training clothes into more presentable dress, when we caught sight of Alex running down the snowy path to greet us. It was noticeably dark, but the moon was full and gave enough light for us to cringe at the snow he was kicking up in his tracks.

"You two are never going to believe it!" he declared.

"Alex," Ella scolded, "you just got snow all over us—"

"Just you wait!" He snatched both our arms to drag us over to the Academy doors.

"You big oaf..." Ella paused as she noticed our surroundings.

I stumbled as I took in the same, feeling as dazed and out of place as a girl from the country could.

"I told you," Alex boasted. "I told you that you had to see it!"

All across the dark gray slabs of the Academy walls were hundreds of tiny sparkling lights twinkling down upon us.

Every inch of the school was covered in the tiny glass orbs, and they shone brilliantly across the white velvet landscape. Even the roof and rafters glowed. It was as if the entire world had been shrouded in the crystalline blue of a flame's inner core, and then speckled in violet magenta.

It was the most breathtaking thing I had ever seen in my life.

"How did they...?"

"Alchemy," Ruth answered from behind us.

The three of us jumped, having not noticed our study friend's soft-footed approach.

"Master Ascillia taught us how to make the liquid glow last week. We brewed a whole batch of the stuff and handed it off to the constable's team to bottle and string."

Alex chuckled. "No wonder the servants were in such a foul mood."

"Look at the trees!" Ella exclaimed beside me.

I turned and was once again overwhelmed by the startling display before me.

The trees were shining. Every pine within a hundred feet of the Academy's walls was shrouded in the same blue and purple mist as the Academy. It was surreal.

"It's so beautiful," Ella said softly. She squeezed Alex's hand. "Thank you for showing us."

I watched as my brother turned a deep shade of red. "You would have seen it eventually," he mumbled, averting his eyes from my knowing grin.

Ruth pushed forward, oblivious to the awkward moment between her two friends. "Let's see what it looks like on the inside," she urged.

We were not disappointed.

The servants had lined the sandstone walls with the same combination of lights, and with the absence of torches and the magnification of the black marble floors, I felt as though I was part of a flickering orb myself. The pattern continued all the way through to the grand atrium where the festivities were being held.

Inside the ballroom, long transparent curtains hung almost romantically from pillars at each corner of the room. Twinkling stars glittered out from the many-paned window at the center of the stairs, and the stained glass ceiling shown magnificently against the soft violet lights of scattered globes. There was much less lighting here, and it created an ethereal setting amongst the grandeur of the stairwell and its spiraling rails.

All along the back of the walls were gold-clothed tables with platters of delicacies, cider, and tea.

The entire length of our stay we'd only been offered the barest selection of dishes since first-years were not, as one of the kitchen staff had pointed out, "valuable enough to use the finer stores on." My tongue salivated at the display. With the exception of today, the servants had been on orders to only serve the array of fresh meats and cheeses to the masters and their apprentices in the private dining room on the second floor.

"Oh, it has been far too long!" Ella announced, dragging me with her to one of the tables. There was a long line of students ahead, but it passed quickly enough with Alex, Ruth, and Clayton following shortly behind.

After our plates had been filled, the five of us sat down to eat.

"Is this what it's like at court?" I asked. I was feeling out of place among the grandiose dress of most of the Academy students. Out of the fifty-nine first-years that remained, only a third came from backgrounds similar to my brother's and mine. Ella and Ruth came from outlying regions rather than a full life at the capital, but they were still highborn.

Looking at Alex, I knew I was not alone. My twin was dressed in simple beige trousers with an ill-fitted jacket that was too tight for his burgeoning frame.

My own gown was a simple forest green with a cinched waist of golden thread. It was modest in comparison to the re- vealing corsets of the others, years behind the current trends of billowing sleeves and extravagant skirts.

When my mother had passed the dress down, I'd been overwhelmed with its grandeur. I'd been *thrilled* to have such a fine possession. Now, next to Ella's beautiful violet dress and Priscilla's dramatic silk, my dress was an heirloom.

It was easy to see why someone would want a life at court. The dress Priscilla wore now made her look the part of a duchess. The smooth material cascaded down her sinuous form in rivulets. It shimmered and sparkled as it moved. Delicate lace fell freely from the girl's wrists. Even her hair was elegant- ly coiffed with a single gold chain wrapped gracefully around her forehead.

I sighed, envious.

Ella followed my train of sight and then cleared her throat loudly. "Thank the gods Priscilla will never be queen!"

A couple feet away the highborn turned and glared. The look of abhorrence she shot my friend was enough to melt ice.

I couldn't help but smile. "You didn't have to do that."

Ella grinned. "What are friends for?"

Just then the string quartet by the stair started a new song. It was fast and jovial—something a lowborn could rec- ognize.

My twin wasted no time in asking Ella to dance. She acquiesced most willingly. The two of them carried off onto the floor, spinning and turning in the crowd.

Others joined in too, including Ruth and Ella's shy admirer, James. The couples continued to grow, including some faces that I didn't recognize.

I realized after a moment that the new ones were older than the rest of us.

The apprentices had arrived.

Clayton sidled next to me. "Care to dance?"

I smiled apologetically. "I'm sorry, but I never learned."

"Now is as good a time as any." His eyes were unusually bright. Something in them made me cringe, an unspoken question beneath the nonchalance of his request.

"Maybe after a couple more songs," I said quickly. "I don't think I have the courage to try it just yet."

Clayton smiled. "I'll be saving you a dance," he assured me. A moment later he was gone, and I was left to myself with four half-empty plates of food.

I watched the dance play out in front of me.

"How is it that a beautiful girl finds herself alone with more food than even Sir Piers could eat?"

I started. To my right was a young man not much older than myself. He had short, curly brown hair and hazel-green eyes. They were crinkled with silent laughter.

Whether it was the festivities or my intuition, I liked the stranger immediately.

He wasn't hard to look at either. *Not hard at all.* I felt a wave of gutsiness.

"I find myself alone," I replied shamelessly, "because no one has captivated my interest."

"Yes." The stranger smiled. "I can see that…The question now is whether I have?"

"I wouldn't know. Perhaps you should keep me company, so I can find out."

He laughed. "Fair enough." Taking a seat beside me, he turned to watch the dancers.

After a couple moments of silence I gave up waiting. "Are you one of the apprentice mages?"

His smile was crooked. "Yes, I'm a second-year. Are you going to ask me which faction?"

I studied him, eyeing the scar on his left cheek and the burn marks on both his palms. "Combat."

He laughed easily. "That would make you beautiful and clever. Not too many of those here tonight."

I swatted away his pretty words with the flip of a hand, though it was more a clumsy swipe.

He caught my wrist and leaned closer. "What is your name, girl-of-many-talents?"

I found myself staring into the young man's eyes, unable to look away. There was something about them, something warm and safe that reminded me of flying. Whenever I had looked to Darren, the non-heir had made me feel as though I were falling, plummeting to the depths of a dark, perilous pit. This stranger made me feel reckless too, but in a fun, spirited, *wanted* sort of way. I liked it. I liked him.

"Ryiah," I said.

"Ryiah," the stranger repeated. "Well, Ryiah, I am Ian." He chuckled and let go of my hand to gesture dismissively at our surroundings. "So what do you think of the Academy? Is it everything you hoped it'd be?"

I made a face.

"I thought so." Ian grinned. "Piers and Barclae have that effect on people."

I glanced at him, "Was it so bad for you?"

He shivered dramatically. "It was a terrible time," the apprentice admitted. "It usually is for lowborns. Nobody actually expects us to stay beyond the first month." He laughed loudly. "But I made sure to prove them wrong."

I sighed. "I am still trying."

He grinned. "Surely you are not *that* bad."

I snorted.

"A lot can change in the time you have left."

"I've only got five more months."

"You'd be surprised."

I laughed. "The only way I'll win this thing is by luck."

"May I?"

Before I could react Ian had snatched my palm and brought it to his lips with a mischievous smile. He kissed it lightly. My insides danced.

"I have been told my kiss brings good luck," Ian said wickedly.

I snatched my hand away, albeit regretfully. The boy was clearly the best part of my evening. "You must have kissed a lot of girls to get that kind of reputation."

"Maybe, but that doesn't make the gesture any less sincere."

"I—" I began, flustered. I didn't know whether or not to take the charming flirt seriously.

*"The lady does not welcome your advances!"*

I turned around to find Clayton glaring venomously at my new neighbor.

"Clay, it's okay—" I began.

Clayton's eyes never left the apprentice's face. "You need to leave. Now."

"I will leave when the lady wants me to leave." Ian's eyes met mine. *Who is your crazy friend?*

"Clayton," I tried again, a tinge irritated by my friend's overzealous approach. "I am fine, really. Ian's intentions are harmless…"

Ian gave Clayton a wolfish smirk. "I never play at matters of the heart."

I shot Ian a glare that he missed as Clayton turned a stormy red.

"You'd rather sit here talking to this *charmer* than dance with me?" Clayton sputtered.

"Can you really blame her?" Ian drawled. "She can't help it if you are not that interesting."

Tensions were growing, and I made a fast decision to leave before things became worse. I really wanted to stay and get to know Ian better, but with my overprotective friend and my brother soon to follow, it seemed best to head out before one of the boys did something stupid. Alex was levelheaded in almost everything, but his sister's romances had never been something he took to rationally. Even if he *was* the biggest flirt I knew when it came to women.

Grabbing my cloak, I regarded my audience coolly. "You two can continue your lovely chat. I am going to get some fresh air."

"Are you sure you don't want company?" Ian grinned.

"I'm sure." I wasn't, but it was best not to let him know. I wasn't sure I wanted to get mixed up with a flirt. Had I not watched my brother break heart after heart in Demsh'aa?

Clayton kept silent, staring at the floor.

"Don't forget," Ian said, leaning in to touch my arm as I passed. "You're lucky now, which means this won't be the last time we meet." He paused to chuckle, "Only next time, you'll be an apprentice of Combat."

"How...?" I stepped back dumbfounded. I'd never told him my faction.

"My training master is good friends with Narhari. The entire faction was regaled with tales from the mid-year tourney earlier this month."

I cringed.

"Given that you're the only first-year girl with red hair and blue eyes, I figured I had a pretty good idea of who I was talking to."

I stepped outside the Academy doors and slammed them shut behind me. It was still early in the evening, too soon for anyone else to have left the celebrations behind.

At first, I had only intended on stepping out for a minute. But after hearing how my humiliation had been the entertainment for every apprentice mage in Combat, I'd been overcome with the overwhelming desire to run away and never look back. Realizing, however, that it was not a viable option in the dead of winter, I had figured the next best thing would be to get as far away from the residents as I could.

It was ironic, really, how my moods could change so quickly in the course of an evening. It had taken me all of a month and a half to recover from that day, yet only seconds to bring the emotions crumbling back.

As I plodded through the snow, I was barely conscious of how long I had walked until I found myself at the entrance of the armory. The bottoms of my dress and cloak were drenched in ice and mud, and my hair, which had been pinned neatly back for the ball, was now a wet, curling mess. I should have been upset that I had ruined the one valuable article of clothing in my possession, but at that moment I would have gladly burned a dozen of the same if I'd thought it would bring me any peace.

The Academy was an impressive sight, I refused to look back as I tried the handle on the armory door.

It was unlocked.

Opening the door slowly, I conjured a bit of light in my left hand and entered the building quietly. All around me shadows danced, and my casting's flame reflected off the blades lining the armory walls.

Discarding my cloak, I let it fall to the floor as I approached the back of the room. Near the back wall was another door leading to a second room that I had never bothered to inspect before, but now I did. Pushing the wooden frame open, my breath caught as I came face-to-face with my reflection at every angle.

The room's walls were entirely encased in mirrors. I could see myself everywhere I turned, a wary, red-haired girl with somber gray-blue eyes and a jade green dress.

Going back to the main room, I grabbed a candle and a broadsword off its rack, and returned to the mirrors. Using a sconce to hold my light in place, I turned back to face the glass.

Almost unconsciously, I started the swordsman drills I had practiced so many times in class. One by one, my steps led way to an intricate dance of blades. I slashed and cut in rhythm, never striking the same spot twice, while I watched my form in the mirrors.

It was strangely soothing as I picked up pace and continued the assault. Forward and back, striking left and feigning right, I parried each attack until I became familiar with its replication in the mirrors.

Instinctively, I summoned an opposing blade to deflect my broadsword's assault. I continued the dance, metal and metal meeting at every turn.

Each time I struck, the casting blocked. It happened again and again with increasing intensity until the second blade began an attack of its own.

I wasn't sure exactly how it happened, but as the exchange continued, my magic no longer needed me to direct it when and where to go to parry each blow. It was a mind-numbing revelation, but I forced myself to keep on as shadows continued to play out across the room.

"Very good."

Startled, I dropped my blade, and my casting disappeared. In the mirror, I could see Darren behind me.

The non-heir stood, leaning against the doorway, with the semblance of a smile on his face. He looked particularly disconcerting tonight in a fitted leather vest and dark pants. After seeing him so many days in training breeches and tunics, I had forgotten how morose his attire usually was. Morose, but also easy on the eyes. Possibly too easy.

My pulse quickened.

"What are you doing here?" I wasn't sure whether to be pleased the prince had given me a compliment, or mad that he had interrupted me. I wanted to be angry, but it was hard when the prince didn't have the usual condescension that was always written across his face.

Darren took a step forward, ignoring my question. Instead of answering, he motioned for me to pick up my blade.

Clumsily, I reached down to grab the weapon, and by the time I had pulled myself back up, the non-heir was holding a blade of his own.

"Begin," he said.

I didn't know what to do. I had never gone up against the prince. Priscilla, yes—shamefully—and once Jake, but never Darren. He was the best there was, and he only ever sparred with the top of our class, which I was certainly not.

"Ryiah, I am trying to help you," he said tiredly.

I clutched the sword and widened my stance. *You can do this*, I decided. *You've got nothing to lose at this point.*

Darren began to circle, and I imitated his pattern. The mirrors were distracting, and I forced myself to concentrate solely on the dark-haired boy in front of me. He was almost cat-like in his movements, lunging in and out with a surprising grace that spoke of years of practice in contrast to my own awkward attempts.

Still, it was painfully obvious the non-heir was holding back.

"Just get on with it," I told him, blocking an easy strike and countering with one of my own. "I know you are much better than this."

Darren frowned amidst blows, though he still carried on smoothly as his sword wove in and out of the air before us.

"This is not about me beating you," he replied. "I want you to cast out your magic again, like you were doing before you noticed me. You shouldn't have to think before you use it now. When you fail to defend yourself with the real sword, I want your casting to engage me instead."

I tried calling on the blade again, and it came along easier than the last. I willed it to hold its own defense, as Darren had suggested, and continued to strike and parry with the sword I held in my hands.

Darren began to move faster—so fast, in fact, that I had trouble keeping up.

As his blade struck out unexpectedly, I didn't have time to think. But just as his blade should have cut into my unprotected shoulder, my casting and Darren's handheld blade collided, leaving me untouched.

This continued to happen. Each time Darren's sword struck out, my magic blade deflected what my real one was unable to reach. The prince's cuts, unlike Ella's much slower ones, did not allow me enough time to visualize how my casting should guard. With Ella, I'd always had enough time to realize my mistakes and project the intended defense in time. With Darren, he was too fast for thinking. My magic had to rely on instinct, something it'd never been capable of doing before.

After ten more minutes of sparring, without a single hit on either side, Darren lowered his blade, and I followed. He was breathing a little uneasily, though nothing like the heavy gasping of my own.

"That was incredible," I said, when I finally was able to speak.

Darren produced a bench and took a seat, setting his sword to the side. "You've come a long way."

I continued to stand, awkwardly. There was an odd expression in the non-heir's eyes, as if I was being appraised, and I was immediately conscious of what I must look like.

"Why did you come here?" I asked before I could stop myself, trying to break free from the strange feeling that had formed in the pit of my stomach.

"I followed you."

"What do you mean, you followed me?"

"I mean," Darren said, stretching lazily, "that I was on my way to the barracks when I saw you leave the Academy and stomp off angrily into the snow. I wanted to see why someone would choose to ruin her dress—"

I flushed.

"—and enter the armory, of all places, during the middle of a ball."

*Well, when he said it that way*...Still: "It's not any business of yours, what I choose to do at any point of any day."

Darren regarded me amusedly. "It's not," he admitted, "but given our erratic rapport, forgive me if I was curious to see what my *favorite* classmate was up to."

I glared at him. "You are not exactly my first pick either."

He laughed, loudly, and it caught me off-guard. I'd been expecting him to find offense.

"You know, Ryiah, it might just be the festivities tonight, but I don't find you nearly as grating as usual."

I guffawed. "Well, my impression of you hasn't changed at all."

"I would be aghast if it did." Darren stood up, bench and blade disappearing. He started toward the doorway and then turned back suddenly. He looked annoyed for some reason, and he seemed to be having an internal debate with himself.

I stared, watching the non-heir with interest. I had never seen him at a loss for words, and I had to wonder what had caused the out of character reaction in a person of such close-guarded composure.

"For what it's worth," he said finally, "a shield is not meant to be hit head on—"

*Huh?*

"—it's meant to be held at an angle so that you can deflect or, at the very least, lessen your opponent's blow. If you do it right, it gives you the chance to lead a counterattack, something that most opponents are unprepared for in the heat of the moment." Darren paused to look directly at me, two fevered flames taking hold of my breath. "You should try it next time."

Before I could reply, the non-heir disappeared, leaving me alone with a series of unanswered questions.

❧

It was much later that night, after I had already fallen asleep, that I woke up with a start.

*You should try it next time.*

At first, after the prince had left, I had been irate. His remark was just another insulting critique, one that insinuated I didn't know what I was doing, all in the guise of advice.

But then my nightmare had come and gone. And in it, just as each night before, I relived that horrible day on the battlefield. The day Priscilla had made a fool of me in front of our entire faction.

The day haunted me each time I closed my eyes.

Only this time I noticed something that I had never cared to discern before.

My shield.

Each time Priscilla had led the assault, I'd held my casting directly in front of my body. I had assumed that the best defense was one that left no part of me exposed to her attack...but, by doing so, I had let the full force of her magic hit my shield head on. Not only had her casting destroyed my defense, it had sent me sprawling to the ground.

*What would have happened if I'd held the shield at an angle instead?* According to Darren, it would have deflected and lessened Priscilla's blow. Maybe even have left her open to an attack of my own.

I was so used to fighting with weapons directly, I had never stopped to consider how I used my defense.

And that's when it hit me.

The non-heir had been trying to help me.

Against Priscilla.

# CHAPTER ELEVEN

The next morning I was up long before the morning bell. Rather than lying in bed wide-awake, I headed down to the armory with a renewed sense of vigor. Others might choose to sleep in during their week off, but I fully intended to spend each and every day practicing until my lungs collapsed.

I was afraid of losing the magical *and* physical stamina I had worked so hard to build during my time at the school thus far. But, as it turned out, I needn't have worried. The new routine I was following left me just as exhausted as my sessions with Piers, and like my days in Narhari's class, I kept on until the pain in my head overwhelmed me. It was much harder to push myself on my own, but I managed as best I could.

The room with the mirrors provided a much-needed reprieve from the monotony of my training with Ella, and while she and I still practiced each day, I spent a good portion of my mornings in the armory. There was something intrinsic about being able to watch my reflection as I performed each routine.

Using the casted blade as an opponent, I was able to see how my physical movements gave way to my intended assault. I had become fair enough at discerning my adversary's moves through the usual telltale signs, but I'd never been able to watch for my own until now. It became quickly apparent that I was an open book. It was no wonder Ella and Clayton had always been able to counter my blows. I was horrible at hiding my offense.

My "feigning" had not been fooling anyone, but as I continued to edit my form, it began to become more convincing. My stance no longer gave away lunges until a split-second before I engaged, and while still relaxed, the muscles of my arm remained fluid until the decisive moment I struck. I began to practice the patterned drills we had learned in class with a variation of my own. Eventually, my body's movements and the steps I took no longer revealed an assault. I still slipped up from time to time, but for the most part I was an unreadable opponent. Even my casting had trouble anticipating where to defend.

I struggled at the newness, but I was beginning to feel more confident at the prospect of a free-form exchange. Since my match with Priscilla, I had been worried about the end-of-year trials. I was sure at least one part of them would be a duel or battle of some sort, and what better way to test a student for the faction of Combat than actual combat? In class and with my friends, I had only ever performed a pre-set routine, or drills. Real opponents would not be so obvious. Priscilla hadn't been.

I needed to be prepared. The mirror room was the necessary solution. It gave me the perfect opportunity to hone my skills and practice technique away from the rest of my year. If I wanted to do well in my trials, I needed to be unpredictable. I could not control how much potential I had, but I *could* do everything in my power to ensure my technique was further along than the others in my class.

My discovery the night of the ball had given me a new appreciation for magic. I'd already known my stamina was improving, but what I hadn't realized was that my castings could develop an instinct as well. My magic was learning from me, from experience, from practice.

Despite the new changes taking place however, I still needed to exercise restraint. Swordplay and weapons' casting were well enough, but Darren had warned me to focus on defense as well. And as much as I might regret to admit, his counsel was well warranted. Again.

At first, I tried shield-casting in the armory, but it was too hard to conjure a guard and an assault at the same time. I needed an opponent that wasn't me. So I saved some of my reserve, and made it a point to find my friends to continue the training later on.

⚜

"What is it you want me to do again?" Clayton asked uncertainly.

"I want you to blast me with your magic."

"Are you sure—"

"Yes." Hands on my hips, I met my friends' gawping stares defiantly. "You both saw how badly I performed at the mid-year duels. I'm never going to get better if all I do is practice with weapons. A mage isn't going to come at me with a sword the entire time. You saw Priscilla. She went after me with magic. I need a better *defense*."

"I understand what you are saying, Ry, but we don't want to hurt you either," Clayton pointed out. During Narhari's drills, he was nowhere close to Priscilla or Darren, but Clay was still one of the stronger ones in combative casting. He was my best shot at learning a strong defense.

"I'll be fine," I told him, backing up, so we were about twenty feet apart, the same distance I had been when I dueled Priscilla.

"You ready?"

"Just do it!" I shouted. Immediately, I conjured up a shield similar to the one I had used during the tourney. This time, however, I angled it instead of holding it directly in front of my body.

It felt strange, being exposed. I tucked my left shield arm inward so that my wrist almost brushed my chest. I held my feet a shoulder-width apart: right foot forward, knees slightly bent.

*Wham!*

Clayton's casting hit me at full-force, slamming into the shield with an almost bone-shattering intensity. I stumbled, arms shaking as the impact hit, his force flattening the thick wooden panel against my chest.

The armor cracked, and I was sent flying backward.

I'd failed to hold my defense.

"*Ryiah!*" Clayton cried, dropping his offensive stance to come racing forward. Ella stood back, trusting I was okay and raising a brow at our friend's over-the-top reaction.

Wincing, I brushed off the splintered fragments and waved him away. "Do it again," I choked, mouth full of dust.

"No I won't—" Clayton protested, but Ella cut him off, exasperated.

"*I'll* do it!" She grinned at me. "Ready to be pummeled, Ry?"

I returned to my starting stance. This time I widened my feet a bit more than the last, and I held my new shield at a greater angle, bracing myself.

"Now's as good a time as any."

Ella nodded and cast out her force, using both hands to launch it into the air as if she was thrusting a pile of bricks at my ribs.

I dug in my heels as her magic slammed my defense, gritting my teeth as I struggled to maintain my bearing. My shield arm roared from the sudden blow, but it was a much less terrible ache than the exchange with Priscilla or even Clayton moments before.

A loud, cracking noise rang out behind me, and I turned to see one of the beams in the fence had split open, causing a cloud of splinters to puff out into the air, settling moments later on the frostbitten ground.

*I did it!* I had deflected Ella's magic and sent it careening into the barrier behind me!

"You've got this, Ry!" Ella shouted. Clayton stood beside her, but said nothing, his disapproval obvious.

"Let's try another." I told her.

So she cast out her magic again. And again. And about ten more times until I was on the ground, vomiting the contents of my breakfast into the freshly fallen snow.

About a quarter of the time, I gripped my shield at just the right angle, and my defense held. The rest of Ella's castings, I missed completely, and her force sent me staggering back with the broken fragments of a shield along the snow.

I now had a splitting pain in my head, and I knew with certainty it was not subsiding anytime soon. Every inch of me smarted, and I willingly sat out the rest of the practice to watch Clayton and Ella try their hand at defense.

Clayton grasped it easily, having a much better knowledge of technique than both of us. Ella struggled a bit more, but she wasn't far off either.

By the time they had finished their own session, my friends were just as exhausted as myself.

"What made you decide to try this approach?" Ella asked abruptly, the three of us leaning against the frame of the fence, trying to catch our breath.

I laughed, despite the pain in my ribs. "You'd never guess."

Clayton eyed me curiously. "Did someone tell you? It *is* a little out of the blue for you to come forward with the idea almost two months after your duel. It's not as if it hasn't been done before. It's just strange for you to realize it now—"

At just that moment I noticed a pack of first-years approaching the field. Among them was Darren, dark eyes averted and mouth pressed in a permanent frown of contempt. He looked like a stark, black wolf against the white, snow-pressed landscape.

I swallowed as I watched him pass, not knowing what to say. I felt as if I needed to thank him, only I couldn't get the words to form in my mouth. Last night he had been approach-

able, almost friendly even, not a prince or a non-heir but a
teasing rival I could find camaraderie with. Now, he was as
aloof as ever, a dark prince unreachable in all but the most ca-
pricious of mood swings.

My gaze trailed after Darren as he and his group continued their trek to the top of the hill.

"Ryiah?"

I glanced at my friends, startled. Ella had a strange expression on her face. "What?" I demanded.

"You never answered Clay's question."

"Oh." I reddened as they continued to stare. "I'm not
sure...I guess it just came to me. You know how these things
happen."

The expression on both their faces said they didn't. But
my friends had no reason to doubt, so they did not press further. We continued our trek back to the barracks in silence,
but it was much later that day that I finally acknowledged the
unspoken question.

*Why had I lied?*

⚜

The week of winter solstice came and went in the blink of
an eye. Before I even realized it, the final day of our break had
arrived. Perhaps it was because there really was no "break" to
the days at hand, but I felt as if it had only just begun.

As I sat next to my friends in the dining hall that evening, I couldn't help but return to the same question I had been
asking myself all week. Why keep Darren's help a secret? Was
it because I didn't trust him, or was it the judgment I would
face if I did?

Ella had made it pretty clear how she felt about the non-
heir, and all of my friends had at one point or another been at
the receiving end of the prince's malice. Darren had made my
stay difficult too. I couldn't forget all the times he had insulted
me, or how he had deliberately jeopardized Alex's and my

chances during that final week of Combat orientation in the mountains.

But he had also helped me more times than I cared to admit.

I set my glass down with a bit too much force. Water sprayed across the table, and my friends guffawed.

"Watch yourself, Ryiah!" Ruth snapped, pulling her books off the table and attempting to dry their covers with the sleeve of her tunic.

"Everything okay?" Ella asked, eyeing my water suspiciously.

I avoided her gaze. "I'm fine," I lied.

"You haven't eaten," Alex observed.

"I have a lot on my mind." I stood hastily. "I'm going to retire for the night."

Before they could protest, I left the dining hall and started for the barracks.

I was about halfway to my destination when I spotted the source of my frustration. He was in the midst of conversation with Jake and William, the two burly brothers that always seemed to be everywhere he went. They were debating the merits of the crossbow when I arrived.

All three of them turned to stare when I stayed instead of moving on to the door behind them. Jake had a sour expression on his face, and I silently returned the sentiment, having not forgotten that day during Piers's obstacle course. After Priscilla, Jake was my least favorite of the group.

"Yes?" Darren asked, amusement in his eyes.

"Can I talk to you?" I asked, conscious of the audience we had present.

"Go right on ahead," Darren said.

"Alone," I said through my teeth.

"What business do you have talking to a prince, lowborn?" Jake growled.

"Whatever business I have is none of yours," I snapped.

Jake and William exchanged speculative glances. Darren motioned for them to leave, unable to contain a grin as his friends parted, and the two of us were left standing alone in the dark hall.

"What is it this time, Ryiah?"

I stared at the wall, and then forced myself to meet the non-heir's eyes.

"I want to apologize—"

His jaw dropped.

"—I've been doing a lot of thinking lately, and I have come to the realization that I've been making the same mistakes I accused you of."

Darren's eyes widened, and I made myself continue. "You're not a very nice person," I admonished, "but you aren't the horrible one I make you out to be either. And for that, I'm sorry. You've helped me when you had no reason to, so *thank you*."

Silence greeted my admission. I felt foolish, standing there, when it was clear he had nothing to say. *It doesn't matter*, I told myself, *you've made your peace. You're conscious is clear now.* Rather than stick around in awkward silence, I gave a curt nod and made way to leave.

"Ryiah, wait—"

I turned abruptly, just as Darren's hand shot out to grab my wrist. I barely caught a glimpse of the strange expression on his face before a series of sparks shot out all across my body. It was as if someone had lit fire to my veins. All at once I felt too hot and cold and could feel nothing else.

My gaze inadvertently fell to Darren, who looked as if someone had stuck him with a red-hot poker. He was staring at my hand with a look stuck somewhere between wonder and abhorrence.

He dropped my wrist at once, but my skin still tingled in the spot where we had touched.

I waited for him to speak, but he seemed unable to in the silence that followed.

"I think I am going to head back—" I started to say, but the prince cut me off.

"I helped you because you have potential."

I looked up to see Darren watching me with an odd light to his eyes. There was nothing hostile, nothing condescending in the way he was looking at me now.

"You *are* meant to be here, Ryiah," he continued, looking unusually out of sorts, as if he wasn't sure why he was saying the things that he was saying. "You are..." He sighed and then forced himself to meet my eyes. "You are possibly the one good thing about this place."

I didn't know how to respond. All I knew, during that moment, was that his eyes were the most interesting shade of garnet I had ever seen. I had always thought they were so dark they were almost brown, but now I realized they were ebony, somewhere between the pitch-black of night and the mahogany of a rich wood.

The longer I stared, the more I realized I had never really noticed *Darren* before. Sure, I'd seen an arrogant young prince that had grown up with the world at his feet, but never a human being. Not someone like me, capable of mistakes and feelings, *someone vulnerable.*

I felt a chill run through me as I became conscious of the fact that he was staring right back. There was that odd light in his eyes, and it was burning right through me...but I was incapable of looking away.

"T-thank you," I mumbled. "For what you just said, even if you didn't mean—"

"I meant every word..."

Darren took a step forward. And then another. And then when there was no more space to cross, he looked down at me, shadows dancing across his face. "I am going to do something against my better judgment," he said softly. His eyes were like two embers melting my flesh as he reached down to put one hand against my waist and the other underneath my chin. "You can scream obscenities at me after."

And then he kissed me.

It was a long, slow kiss. One that sent shivers from the stem of my neck to the very bottoms of my toes. It burned hot and cold, making me dizzy as my knees buckled and collapsed beneath.

Darren chuckled softly as his hand steadied me in place, pressing the two of us against the rough sandstone walls.

I started to pull away, but the non-heir increased the intensity of his kiss... and I lost all will to move.

After a minute or so, the flood of emotions receded just long enough for me to react with a startling fervor of my own. I found myself kissing Darren back, wrapping my arms around his neck and letting myself fall into the moment.

The prince jerked back, sooty lashes shading his eyes as he regarded me in surprise.

At just that moment, the sound of a door slamming open and the chatter of excited voices came echoing down the hall.

Darren released me, taking a step back to take inventory of his surroundings while I steadied myself.

"Ryiah! What are you doing out here?" Alex exclaimed, as he and the rest of our study group came clamoring around the corridor.

I flushed and looked back to Darren, but he was gone, the door to the Academy closing softly behind.

"Yes, what *were* you doing out here?" Ella said, eyeing my red face suspiciously.

I shook my head, not trusting myself to speak. My friends continued to prod me with questions, but I hurriedly made excuses and rushed away to the barracks while they continued on to their nightly practice.

⚓

Arriving at the barracks, any sense of elation I had was immediately drained as I spotted a familiar face across the room.

Priscilla.

It shouldn't have caught me off guard, but the memory of what had just happened in the hallway minutes before was still very vivid in my mind. Seeing Priscilla, the girl who everyone believed was intended for the prince, left a bitter taste in my mouth.

*What did he see in her?*

"I see you still haven't left," Priscilla declared, loudly enough to make the two girls who were helping her dress glance up as well.

"I'm not going anywhere," I told her flatly.

"What a shame." She held up an elaborately designed dress to her chest and looked at her friends. "What do you think? My cousin's seamstress had this made for me. It's perfect for the post-trials ceremony...Do you think Darren will like it?"

The girls assured her it would make her more beautiful than any lady of the realm, and that the prince would surely propose upon seeing their friend in it.

My jaw clenched.

Priscilla turned to smirk at me. "Don't worry, Ryiah. No one will see you wearing another ratty hand-me-down like the one you did for solstice. Only the apprentices will be noticed...and since you are attempting Combat, you won't have to worry."

"Or maybe I can just borrow yours," I told her tightly.

"We both know you are just ornamental. The masters would never be daft enough to give an apprenticeship to a convent girl like you."

One of her friends laughed unexpectedly, only to quickly cover it up with a cough as Priscilla glared at both of us.

"For a commoner you certainly think highly of yourself. Don't get any delusions, Ryiah. You are nowhere close to the prince and me. Sir Piers may have believed in you once, but that was before mid-year. You'd be a fool to still think you had a chance now."

Her words had a truth that bled, and I was momentarily tempted to tell her what her precious prince had done. She already hated me, so what was stopping me?

*Don't be a fool, Ryiah. You know perfectly well that would be a mistake. Alex always tells you to control your temper. Right now is that time.*

Rather than continue the unpleasant exchange, I headed to the baths to soak away the bitterness and frustration that were threatening to take over.

By the time I had returned, Priscilla and her friends were long gone, leaving me alone to the silence of an empty barracks.

*Good.* The last thing I needed was more time alone with that witch.

Everyone else was still out, studying, dining, or enjoying one last night of freedom with friends. I should have been doing the same, but I wasn't ready to face the interrogation that would undoubtedly follow from my brother, from Ella, from myself.

I didn't know how to feel about what had transpired in that dark hallway, and until I knew, it was best to keep the secret untold.

I'd been kissed before. Many times, actually.

In Demsh'aa there had been a boy...but there had been no spark, no sense of worlds colliding when his lips had brushed up against mine.

Darren's kiss tonight had been everything Jason's had lacked.

It had made my legs weak, my lungs burst.

It had been an assault of everything wrong and right, right and wrong, wrong and right.

I'd seen fire when he touched me, and he had made me want to burn.

Jason had held me gently, as if I was a doll he hadn't wanted to break. Darren had grabbed me—roughly, impulsively—like he couldn't stop if he wanted to. He hadn't asked permission. He'd taken it, and for some inexplicable reason I had let him.

*And then I had kissed him back.*

The mere fact that I had liked Darren's kiss was upsetting enough. That my body had betrayed me and acted on its own accord was unfathomable.

There were a thousand reasons why kissing the non-heir, or letting him kiss me, was a mistake. He was a prince. He was fickle. He was rude. He was arrogant. I knew better. I was lowborn. He was *wrong*.

I didn't even like him.

And what about Priscilla? Most everyone in the Academy, including myself, assumed she and the prince were set to be betrothed and that it was only a matter of time before the engagement was announced.

What was Darren thinking now?

Did he think he'd made a mistake?

Was I just another conquest he had hoped to win over a lonely night?

Had he been testing me?

I'd seen the look in his eyes when he had realized I was kissing him back: *shock.*

What if the kiss was a joke? A horrible, cruel, sadistic joke?

I slammed my fist into my pillow. Blast the prince for being so unreadable. I never knew when to take him at his word, let alone his actions.

*Don't trust them, and you can't get hurt.* That was what Ella had told me that day after she saw me arguing with Priscilla and Darren. She'd never told me what had happened back at court, and now I was unable to think of anything else.

*It doesn't matter what Darren meant by it,* I told myself after an hour of restless turning, *you are here for one reason. That reason is not him. You are here for your magic, and that alone. So get some sleep.*

The next morning I woke up with dark lines under my eyes. Much to my dismay, I had barely slept. I'd continued to relive that kiss and its sequential doubt all night long. The only time I had slept I'd been back to my familiar nightmare on the hill, losing the mid-year duel to Priscilla for all the world to see.

It was by far the worst night's sleep I'd ever received.

"You look like death," Ella greeted me as I opened my eyes.

"Thanks," I told her dryly.

"I would have thought you'd be the most rested, considering you went to bed just as the sun was setting," Ruth pointed out from the bed next to us.

I glanced at the two of them. "Is there something you want to ask me?"

"Just making an observation," Ruth said shrugging.

We headed out to the dining hall to meet up with the rest of our group. As I piled my bowl high with porridge, I tried to avoid looking across the room to see how the non-heir was faring across the way.

"I hope you tell me what's bothering you," Ella whispered as I passed her the jam.

"There's nothing bothering me," I said quietly.

Alex shot me a raised brow. My brother didn't believe me either.

"You two can pester me all you like—"

"*Attention, first-years.*"

Everyone was immediately silenced as Master Barclae entered the room looking formidable and intimidating in his black silks. He stood near the front of the room, almost adjacent to where the prince and his friends were seated. My eyes darted to Darren, and I saw that, unlike me, there was nothing disheveled to the non-heir's appearance. I could also see

Priscilla running a hand through his hair, and my stomach clenched.

"Today marks your halfway progress to the end-of-year trials," the Master of the Academy began. "From here on out, expect your training to become much more intense. You may think that you are already giving your studies everything you have to give, but trust me when I say the next five months will prove that theory wrong.

"At this point your masters have pushed you to your limits. They have shattered your will and built you back up into the resilient warriors that remain. Now, it is not your masters, but your peers who will challenge your stay.

"You already know what it is to break. You also know what it means to survive. You didn't last this long by chance. The masters did everything they could to encourage you to leave. The first-years that remain now will not shy away from a challenge. They will not leave willingly.

"You will become your own worst enemies. You will push yourselves further than your masters require. You will not sleep, eat, or breathe without the apprenticeship in mind. Not a day will go by that you won't compare yourself with others of your same faction, and this will spur an inevitable competition.

"By now I am sure all of you are aware that the best way to increase your probable success is by reducing the count among your own factions. In the past, students have encouraged one another's departure by any means necessary.

"While I believe competition is a healthy and necessary part of your schooling, I am here to remind you that during this time the rules of conduct still apply. Hazing is not permitted, and any student caught participating in such will be sent home immediately. I do not condone such actions as have occurred in the past, and I have already advised the constable that he has full authority should inappropriate proceedings arise."

Master Barclae scanned the audience with a furrowed brow and then gave a wolfish smile. "That said, I am pleased to announce two more students have departed from your ranks. It appears a week of respite was too much temptation. I can only hope this trend continues in the months that follow." He chuckled and then gave a cursory gesture with his right hand. "Now, continue on with your meal. I wouldn't want to ruin your morning completely."

The Master of the Academy exited the room, black silks billowing, as the rest of us picked at our plates in silence. From what he had just told us, we were in for the worst five months of our lives.

I could hardly wait.

# CHAPTER TWELVE

It wasn't even a full week into the second half of our year before the Master of the Academy's predictions began to play out. For better or for worse, every first-year had increased the intensity of their studies, and no one, *no one*, was ever seen at a meal or break without a book in hand. Training had become a nightmare, and first-years were sent to the healing ward on a daily basis. Narhari's expectations became nothing compared to the limits we had set for ourselves.

Students had stopped sharing in each other's progress, and friendships were becoming strained. People were guarded, secretive, and tempers flared.

Each of us had an apprenticeship in mind, and Master Barclae's warning had forced us to acknowledge the reality that everyone, even friends, threatened that progress.

Unfortunately, there had been two parts to the Master of the Academy's warning, and the latter had taken effect as well. Hazing had begun, though it was seldom referred to as such, and while it was forbidden, no one was bothering to halt it.

Most of the class secretly supported its purpose, though they were afraid to be at its receiving end. Even the masters seemed unusually oblivious to its presence, and I suspected Master Barclae's public condemnation had been just that: a public cover and nothing more. After all, wasn't he one of the ones that wanted to "cut our waste?"

The first time I witnessed the hazing was during Piers's drills three days after the announcement.

Ella and I had just started our fourth mile when the burly brothers Jake and William had sprinted past, laughing a little too loudly for comfort. She and I had looked behind, just in time to see one of the younger boys of our faction pitch forward into a giant trench that had suddenly appeared in the middle of his track.

The boy broke both legs and spent the rest of the day being treated by the healing mages of the Academy. A day later, he resigned.

Master Barclae interrogated our class, but no one gave up the names of the boy's tormentors. I had wanted to at first, but Ella hastily pointed out that if we did, we would find ourselves first in line for the next hazing.

"The boy could have come forward himself, if he had wanted justice," she said. "If you tell, you'll be considered a snitch. Whether you want to admit it or not, this is just another test. Most people believe the masters already know who did it—they just don't care. Combat mages don't ask others to solve their problems. Hazing is just another way for them to tell us that we are not cut out for our faction. Don't give them a reason, Ry."

I hated to admit it, but she had a point.

So now we were into our second week, with two more unfortunate incidents under our belts. Another boy in Combat had woken up screaming to a hoard of snakes hiding out in his bed. One of Priscilla's friends, the girl who had laughed at her expense a week before, found all her belongings drenched in what I could only assume was a slimy mass of fish guts.

One by one, everyone who had ever criticized a member of the prince's inner circle was becoming victim to the notorious hazing. And while no one had been hurt in a manner past healing, I grew increasingly upset that the non-heir and his counterparts were leading the assault.

Sure, Darren's friends were reducing the odds, but they were also increasing their own. No one was foolhardy enough to haze his following, and so the group's actions just promoted their own standing, making it that much harder for others to move up.

I was tired of sleeping with one eye open, and after my encounters with Priscilla and Jake, I knew it was only a matter of time before I was next.

I hadn't been alone with the prince since that moment in the halls, but I swore that if I had the opportunity, I would give Darren a piece or two of my mind. I wasn't sure whether I was more upset by the kiss or the hazing, though I told myself it was the latter.

"You know it's going to be us soon," Ella said, eyeing Priscilla as we sat down for the evening meal. Two more weeks had passed, and Combat was running out of first-years who had openly feuded with the non-heir's crowd. Only one of their victims had left, but it didn't mean the hazings were any more pleasant.

"We've only had two hazings in Alchemy," Ruth pointed out.

"No one has attempted Restoration yet," shy James admitted, attempting to sit between my brother and Ella until Alex gave him a sharp look.

As soon as James returned to his seat at the edge of our table, my brother spoke up: "It's probably because we've only got ten left, as is."

Ella sighed. "I wish we had ten. Those are much better odds than the five in thirty-three for Combat."

I elbowed my friend. "That's the thinking that brought on the hazing in the first place, Ella!"

My friend swallowed uncomfortably.

"Why do you think you two are next?" Alex asked.

"Because they *are*. Priscilla hates them," Ruth said matter-of-factly. She stared at my brother. "*How* have you not noticed that?"

Alex shrugged his shoulders good-naturedly. "I try to keep out of girlish drama."

"Well, Ry's got bad relations with the prince too," Ella said before I could stop her. "Didn't Darren go after the two of you during orientation week for Combat?"

"Oh, yeah," Alex admitted ruefully.

"Right, Ryiah?" Ella pressed.

I stared at my plate, using my fork to stab small indents into a slice of roasted potato.

"Ryiah?"

I glanced up at her. "Right."

I excused myself, promising to meet up with Ella and Clayton for our nightly practice outside the armory: "I need to stop by the barracks first. I think I left one of my books there." It was a lie, but I needed to get some space, alone, before I faced my friends again.

The last thing I wanted to do was discuss the prince. Even the mention of his name brought back memories of that night, and the last thing I wanted was to remember it.

Yes, I'd enjoyed that kiss. But so would have any hot-blooded female. It wasn't a crime, just a lack of judgment on my part.

"Ryiah?"

I almost jumped out of my skin. Standing in the shadows of the hall just beyond was Darren.

My heart began to beat wildly, and blood rushed my face. I tried to appear uncaring as I asked shortly, "What?"

"Can I have a word with you—outside?"

"No." I was proud of my resolve. I did not bat an eye.

"Ryiah, please." Darren walked over to where I stood, frozen, and reached down to take my hand.

The second our skin touched, I was hit with a rush of fire and ice, the same tingling sensation as before.

I looked up involuntarily. A flash of recognition—and guilt—flared up in those fathomless eyes. He dropped my wrist immediately.

"You should go back to your friends," the prince said abruptly, turning.

I was furious. Darren couldn't even apologize now that we were five feet apart.

"You coward," I snapped, racing out in front of him so that the non-heir was forced to meet my angry gaze. "First you assault me, then you try and send me on my way like I'm some lovesick fool? And don't think for a moment that I am not aware that you are the one behind the hazing. You really have some nerve—"

"You think I *assaulted* you?" Darren had stopped his retreat to stare at me in blatant disbelief. I was sure he was remembering my body's traitorous reaction to that kiss.

His doubt only enraged me more. How *dare* he assume I had liked it! Even if I had.

"Believe it or not, not every girl welcomes the advance of a weakling prince that has no chance at a throne, even one so lowborn as me." It was cold and untrue, but I knew it would hurt someone as prideful as Darren. And I wanted to hurt him in any way that I could. The non-heir's earlier dismissal stung more than I cared to let on.

"Well, I am sorry I offended you," Darren said shortly. "I assure you I will not make the same mistake twice." His eyes darkened. They were now as unflinching and barren as stone.

"You had better!" My breath caught, and I was dismayed to find my vision was becoming blurry. *What was wrong with me?* I needed to get away before he saw me cry.

Something flickered in the prince's eyes, and I realized it was too late.

There was an unbearable silence, and then I spotted the Academy door a couple paces away. I reached for its handle, intent on escape.

Darren paled. "Wait, Ryiah, *don't*—"

A sea of red greeted me as soon as I stepped outside. Buckets of sticky, foul-smelling gore covered every inch of my frame. I was drenched, rivulets of scarlet raindrops dripping from my hair, my face...not a part of my skin untouched.

"Go back to where you came from, lowborn."

It took me a moment to wipe enough blood away to see the person who had addressed me, though I had recognized his voice immediately.

A few steps forward Jake, the speaker, William, and Priscilla stood watching with malignant smiles plastered to their faces.

I was right: the hazings *were* personal.

"Save yourself anymore humiliation," William suggested.

Priscilla snickered. "Go home, Ryiah. This school was never meant for commoners."

My skin burned beneath the plaster of repugnant red. They were just trying to get under my skin, trying to break me.

Hadn't Ella and I suspected something like this would happen? I was irate, and rightfully so. But that didn't explain the shattering, the tearing at my chest.

I felt betrayed. I felt used. I was angry. Fire was filling my veins, and a dark loathing was met with unbidden tears.

Darren stepped out from behind me, eyes averted, to stand beside his friends. His clothes were immaculate.

And then I knew for certain.

"I have to say," Priscilla remarked, "the pig's blood was a nice touch." She turned to me, savoring my reaction as she spoke the next words slowly: "When the prince first proposed the idea, I was reluctant. Seeing you now however, I am pleased we went forward with the plan." The highborn beauty smirked. "I never would have guessed it would take this effect. Darren did a good job, did he not?"

I could not control the shaking of my hands. There was a loud pounding in my head that was threatening to explode. Magic was filling my senses, and I was seconds away from flinging the traitorous prince as far as my limits would go.

"Don't be a fool, Ryiah," Darren said.

Fighting back tears of rage, I met the eyes of my enemy. In that moment I didn't care that he was a prince or the most powerful first-year in the school. All I knew was that he was a boy who had hurt me, tricked me, kissed me, betrayed me, and somehow won my trust against every instinct and piece of advice I had ever received.

"I might not beat you," I snarled at the non-heir, "but it will sure feel good to try!"

"Give the wench a lesson!" Jake urged.

Flames enveloped my vision.

"No."

The fire subsided just enough for me to catch Priscilla frowning at the prince. "Why not?"

"She's not worth it." The words cut like a knife.

The four of them began to take their leave.

"I am worth a thousand of you!" I shrieked, casting out as much magic as I could summon. I launched the force forward, sending it barreling towards the prince's unguarded back.

Darren spun around. With the flick of his wrist, my casting was sent staggering into the forest behind. He dark eyes met mine, unreadable.

"It looks like you never needed that apology after all," I spat, ignoring the baffled expressions of the three that stood beside him.

*Let them think what they will.*

"It turns out I was wrong," I continued, "I never made a mistake. You are *exactly* who I expected."

---

Twenty minutes later Ella found me in the barracks, furiously scrubbing the stain of pig's blood from my skin.

"Oh Ryiah," she began, as soon as she saw me.

I didn't respond. I just kept washing.

"Are you going to say anything to Master Barclae?" She grabbed a cloth to help rinse the red from my tangled hair.

I stayed silent.

"I wouldn't fault you if you did," she said quietly. "Was it Priscilla?"

"Darren."

"The prince?" she gasped. "How did he—what happened?"

I watched the crimson haze twist and curl around the tub's drain. "I should have listened to you," was all I meant to say, but instead I found myself spilling the secret I had been holding onto for the last month. I told her everything.

"I think it's time I told you what really happened in Devon," Ella said, once I had finished. "There's something I think you should know…" She looked at me, eyes clouding. "I would have told you sooner, but I was ashamed."

That night I stared up at the ceiling, long after Ella and the rest of our barracks had fallen asleep.

*How had I been so naïve?*

For some unknown reason, I had really thought there was something genuine to Darren, something likable and kind, something that could justify the reckless attraction I had felt in the midst of all his sarcasm and condescending talk.

Now I knew with certainty there was not. Ella's tale haunted me, and while she had clearly moved on, I couldn't help but feel righteous anger on her account. Darren had hurt me, but what he had done to my friend was despicable.

Ella and her family had lived in the capital for years, in one of the palace's many rooms for visiting nobility. She'd grown up playing with the children of various courtiers, though the two princes had usually not been a part of that group.

*Blayne and Darren were too important to mingle with any but the most important residents' children...It was only as they got older that they started paying attention to the intrigues of court.*

*Darren was private and aloof, much like he is now. He spent most of his time with the knights. I hardly ever saw him.*

*Blayne was the older, more sociable, of the two. He was handsome, popular, self-aware. He was also charming, and he could do no wrong.*

Ella had only been twelve when the crown prince had lured her away under the guise of amity and attempted to rape her. She had tried to fight him off, but Blayne had muffled her screams.

*But Darren heard me anyway.*

*When he came to investigate the shouting, he found his older brother on top of me. He could see there'd been a scuffle. It was obvious from the rips in my dress and the long scratches on Blayne's neck.*

*Darren looked me right in the eyes, Ryiah. He knew exactly what was happening. I felt hope. I knew if anyone could stop the prince it was his brother.*

But Darren had just walked away.

*At first, I thought maybe he had gone for help...but no one ever came.*

The only reason Blayne had not succeeded in his mission that day was by accident. In the heat of their struggle, the boy had slammed Ella's head against the wall.

*Like your first time, the pain released my magic. Until that day I hadn't even known I'd had it.*

Her powers had knocked the crown prince unconscious, and she'd been able to escape. Her family had left court the very next day.

Ella had warned me repeatedly. She'd said it since day one. Don't trust Darren. Don't trust the non-heir. Don't trust a prince.

The overwhelming hostility had never made sense.

Now it did.

Darren had willingly stood by as his sixteen year-old brother had attempted to rape my best friend.

Prince Darren, second son to King Lucius III, was the most base, amoral, cold-hearted person I had ever met.

He wanted to try and send me home by pig's blood?

Well, he had just guaranteed my stay.

I was not going anywhere. Someone like that would not win.

⁎⁎

"He did *what?*" Alex roared over breakfast the next morning.

I grabbed my brother's wrist in an attempt to quiet him. "Please Alex," I begged. "Don't make a scene."

Much to my dismay, Ella had told the rest of our group about my encounter with Darren and his friends the night before. Ruth, Clayton, and James had taken the news in stride. They had been disturbed, but each one of them understood that reporting the incident was not an option.

Alex, however, had refused to see reason. He was the level-headed twin, the pacifist…except when it came to me. Then brotherly instinct took over, and no one, not even me, could calm him down.

The last time I'd seen him this upset was when his best friend Jason had called an end to our courtship. It had been amicable. But that still had not stopped my brother from ending a ten-year friendship and swearing that he would gut the trader's son, should he ever come calling again.

Alex had broken many hearts in his wake, but the gods should fear if anyone ever hurt his sister. I had tried to point out as much last time, but it hadn't gone over well.

My brother broke free of my hold and took off toward the front of the room.

"Ryiah!" Ella cried.

The two of us raced after my brother, calling his name, but he had already shoved his way past Jake and William and grabbed the non-heir by the neck of his tunic.

The entire room went silent, all eyes following Alex as he sent a fist flying into the prince's face.

Alex had only a split-second of advantage. Moments later my brother was airborne, plummeting into the table behind, as Darren stood brushing himself off angrily.

"You spineless predator!" Alex roared as Jake and William held him down. "All you do is prey on the weak!" He coughed blood as Jake's fist collided with his nose.

"You think you are the next Black Mage," Alex continued, as William kicked him hard. "All I see is someone too insecure to let anyone with potential try! You think you can bully everyone into leaving. Well, guess what, my sister Ryiah—"

Darren's eyes shot to me, startled.

"—is staying and so will anyone else you victimize, if I have anything to do with it!" Alex stared defiantly ahead as Jake prepared to land another punch.

"*Stop!*"

Jake lowered his hand to glance at the prince.

"That's enough," Darren said, walking over to where Alex kneeled, spewing blood across the floor while he tried to balance himself. Darren offered him his hand. Alex spat at it.

Ella thrust herself in front of the prince to help my brother up, glaring at the non-heir and his friends. "Will you hit me too?" she demanded.

I joined my friend, lifting Alex's other arm.

Darren stared at the three of us for a long moment, anger burning in the dark shadows of his eyes.

Then he turned and left the room, Priscilla, Jake, and William following in his wake.

⁂

After that morning, my brother became a bit of a hero.

The hazing had come to a halt. In the weeks that followed, there were no new incidents to report. And while no one had offered up an explanation, none of us had any doubt in our minds who was responsible for the change.

Darren's group had become altogether complacent, though that didn't extend to the looks of loathing Priscilla still shot me whenever she had the chance. *That* would have been expecting too much.

We gained a few new faces to our study group, others who had been upset by the hazing—only they, like the rest of us, had not had the courage to speak out against it. Alex had also acquired a fan base, and unlike his exchanges with Ella, his present flirtations were met with success.

Ella seemed unusually irritable. I couldn't help but notice. At first she'd been happy that we were no longer the outcasts of our class, but after two weeks she sang a different tune.

"Just look at them fawning over him," she complained, sawing away at a defenseless piece of cabbage. "They are treating him like he's a god...They wouldn't look twice at him a month ago!"

"You sound jealous," I told her, grinning.

She glowered at me through a mouthful of stew. "I am *not* jealous. I am *disgusted*." She eyed my promiscuous brother, who was now seated a good five spaces ahead, having been crowded out by his newfound admirers.

"It'll pass," I told her. "You'll get your friend back."

Ella didn't answer. She was too busy watching Alex to hear me.

I smiled to myself the second she looked away and he glanced our way. Alex hadn't forgotten Ella. He was just enjoying the chance to make her squirm. Not that I could fault him. She hadn't given my brother the time of day until he had stopped trying to charm her. Then again, I couldn't blame her either. She knew his reputation, and the last thing I wanted to do was lose a friend.

It was funny how our minds worked.

# CHAPTER THIRTEEN

Before I knew it, two months had come and gone since the winter break. With the absence of hazing, all focus had returned to study.

Five more had resigned from Combat: two during the period prior to hazing, and three after they had reached the limits of their potential.

There were others whose development had ceased as well, but they refused to acknowledge it. For most of us, we had gone too far to quit.

I was lucky. Even as others' stamina was fading, my magic was continuing to build. Ella's too. It could be argued that those of us with the least training had the most opportunity to grow, but I knew that was not the only factor. While I had yet to outdo the more talented first-years of Combat, I was passing others whose limits had started to stall.

I still had a long road ahead, but I was fast approaching the top third of my faction.

Unfortunately, Darren, Priscilla, and Eve were still at the head of our class, alongside Ray, one of the lowborn boys their group had adopted early on. It was frustrating, but none of them had finished building their magical stamina either.

It seemed that no matter how hard I tried, the prince would always be one step ahead.

I'd started waking up and training two hours before the morning bell to improve my weapons skills for Piers. I practiced an extra hour of casting with Ella each evening in hopes of impressing Narhari. I was still up long after the midnight hour studying for Eloise and Cedric...but none of it changed my standing.

I was still behind *him*.

I wanted to be rewarded for my efforts, and I couldn't help feeling as if the gods had jilted me. Would it never be enough? After everything I had been through, everything the non-heir had done to make my life a misery, it would have been nice to stand a fighting chance. Because I knew. If I was paired up with Darren, or any of his friends during our end-of-year trials, I would lose.

Well, I wasn't giving up now. I'd made it this far, the next three months couldn't get much worse. And if they did, well, I'd already taken part in several nightmares.

⁜

"I'm sure all of you have been wondering what the trials are going to be like," Master Eloise declared loudly as she entered the giant library, bearing a mountain of papers in her wake.

Everyone stopped talking at once. The woman had addressed the very thing we'd been anxiously awaiting for weeks.

The large woman took her place at the podium beside a fidgeting Isaac. "As of this morning, you have officially crossed the two-month threshold..."

I bit my lip apprehensively. Someone was nervously tapping a quill to my right.

"Yes, my dears, two *short* months remain, and then your lives forever change." Master Eloise regarded the class grimly: "Some of you might already be familiar with how the process works—perhaps through family or friends who attended our school in the past—but I can assure you that it is a completely different experience when you are the one undergoing the exams instead. Given the proximity of your impending trials, we have decided to enlighten you as to what role your academic learning will play."

Master Isaac joined his counterpart: "To a contender of Combat, brute strength is everything. I can hardly deny this. You have spent countless hours learning how to fight, and to cast. It is a very hard, very grueling feat to have endured as much as you have. Please keep in mind, however, potential and training are not all that makes up the great faction of Combat, and they will not be all the judges look for in your trials.

"The judges want to see a warrior, not a soldier. Soldiers follow other soldiers into battle—they obey orders, fight valiantly. A warrior can do the same, but he is also a commander, an independent mercenary, and a strategist. The warrior fills many roles, and the capacity to do so requires an intelligence that ordinary soldiers are not trained to possess.

"In the course of your study thus far, Master Eloise and I have been attempting to impart the groundwork that would behoove a warrior's learned wisdom. You have been introduced to the principles of climate, Crown and Council law, geography, strategic planning, diplomacy…and, most importantly, the history of Jerar.

"Each one of these disciplines will play a pivotal role in an apprenticeship, should you be so fortunate. Because of this there will be two trials for each first-year. The first test will focus on your magical prowess. The second, the application of your studies in this classroom."

Eloise cleared her throat. "Every student will be given a twenty-minute audience alone with the judges. The panel will be asking questions directly related to your strategies in Combat. They *expect* to hear citations from Academy lectures, but what they *want* is to understand how you would make those facts a part of your own approach. The tactics of warfare are ever changing—the more creative your technique is, the more

they will take notice. The worst disservice you can possibly do
for yourself is quote a plan that is factually-challenged or has
been proven flawed by history."

A couple of students groaned, and I thanked the gods I
had made it a point to carry out my nightly studies.

Master Eloise narrowed her eyes at the class. "I take it
you feel unprepared. Well, fortunately for you, the next two
months will be spent reviewing everything we have covered.
*Unfortunately,* that will not be enough to make a difference for
the ones that need it most. Still, I advise you to try because
being able to tie *everything* in, and think in terms of strategy
rather than relying on brute force...*that* will be what separates
a novice from an apprentice in your studies here at the Academy."

⚜

After four hours of magical theory, Ella, Clayton, and I
left class with more apprehension than when it had started.
We'd already heard rumors that there were two parts to the
trials, and Eloise's announcement had just confirmed it.

I was relieved, in a sense. I was in very good standing
compared to most of my faction. The downside was that now
everyone else was going to be attempting to catch up. Until
today, most of the students had been focusing solely on casting. Now that they knew half of our trials would be devoted to
military tactic and strategy, derived entirely from Eloise and
Isaac's course, there was bound to a plentitude of sleepless
nights ahead.

"So I think the both of us will be joining your late-night
library runs," Ella told me, as she and Clayton sat down beside
me for lunch. The rest of our study group was still missing. No
doubt Ruth was running late from her lessons with Master
Ascillia, and I could see Alex at the end of the room flirting
outrageously with a pretty girl from Restoration.

"Just make sure no one notices you when Barrius comes round to do the final dismissal," I warned. The last thing I needed was to get caught because half the class had suddenly decided to take up late-night study.

"Does Darren still go there?" Ella asked abruptly.

My face burned. "Not since that kiss."

Clayton's goblet fell to the floor with a loud clatter. He ducked under the table to retrieve it.

Ella raised a brow, grinning, and I scowled in return. I knew what she was thinking, and I did not care to comment.

Clay had been going out of his way, recently, to try and make me laugh. He was thoughtful, kind, good-looking...but it didn't matter one bit.

There was only one person I felt anything for, and *he* was the last one I ever wanted to see.

⚜

The next month slipped by far too quickly for comfort. If a student wasn't in the library, they were on the field, practicing drills or conjuring spells out by the armory. Most of us weren't even aware of the passing of days. We were far too consumed with our studies to take notice.

The trials were to be a weeklong affair. The masters had since broken down the exact schedule, and now that everyone knew what they would entail, we were frantically preparing for the worst.

For Combat, the structure would be almost identical to our mid-year tourney. Each one of us would be taking part in a duel, and the competitions would span out across a day. This time our matches were expected to play out between fifteen minutes to an hour—however long it took for one person to concede. The main difference was that our opponent would be random, decided entirely by chance. Each student would draw from a bag of tokens, and whoever had the matching statuette would be the person we went up against.

I wasn't sure if I was excited or alarmed by the change. I might not fight Priscilla, but I could end up sparring with someone far worse. Eve and Darren were the true contenders to beat, and it would be even harder to go up against a friend. There could be no victory to the latter.

Restoration's first trial would be a healing demonstration of sorts. Students would be taking turns curing one another of projected ailments. It had sounded well enough, until Alex pointed out an unpleasant factor: the more he restored, the more complaints his or her partner would be forced to endure. "In other words," my brother had noted, cringing, "you better hope you go up against someone who doesn't know what they are doing because if they do, Master Cedric will be inflicting increasingly painful conditions for your partner to 'cure' you of."

Ruth told us Alchemy would be the first trial to take place. Her faction's section would consist of two parts: the brewing and application of various potions. The first half of the day, her class would be mixing their draughts according to the judges' request. The final hours would be spent experiencing the resulting effects.

After the initial trials concluded, there would be two days in which every student was called before the judges for a private oral exam in the west tower of the Academy. That was the portion Masters Eloise and Isaac had warned us about.

On the seventh day, the judges would make their choice. They'd spend a good portion of the day before weighing one student's performance against the next, and then, after the evening meal, they would call everyone to the atrium for the results.

It was bound to be the most nerve-wrecking week of our lives.

⚜

"I don't think I am ready for this," Ella confided over the course of a late evening in the library long after everyone else had gone to bed. She and I were pouring over a mountain of scrolls for the hundredth time while Clayton snored loudly on the study's couch behind us.

"I don't think we'll ever be 'ready,'" I told my friend, trying to stifle a yawn and failing. "If they wanted us to be ready, they would give us more than a year."

Ella sighed. "Well, let us hope the time was not in vain."

"Agreed." Despite my calm response, I was terrified. I knew I had done everything I could but self-doubt was a hard habit to break.

Throughout my entire stay, I'd been able to tell myself the trials were months away. That I had plenty of time to become the greatest Combat mage the school had ever seen. Now ten months had come and gone, and I had no more room to pretend.

I was as good as I was going to get. I only hoped it would be enough.

※ ※

"Welcome proud families, friends, visiting mages and nobility. Today marks the beginning of our first-year trials. I am Master Barclae, the current Master of the Academy, and I will be your guide to all that encompasses the competition for the next seven days..."

Master Barclae continued on as I scanned the rows of high-rising benches across the training field. I knew my family was somewhere in the audience, but with the sheer magnitude of people and the dramatic costume of the spectating nobility in front, I could not make out their faces.

Right now, all forty-three of the remaining first-years, myself included, were lined up facing the stands so that the audience could get a good look at the surviving applicants. It was a bit degrading to be introduced by each of our faction's

training master while the first couple of rows whispered
amongst one another.

I had no idea who most of the spectators were, yet they
all had opinions about me and the rest of my class. Which one
of us looked the strongest. Who was the weakest. Who would
be apprenticed. And who would fail.

Barclae had gathered all of us that morning before the
visitors had started to arrive. He and the rest of the staff had
explained exactly what we could expect to see in the next few
days. Our families would not be the only ones arriving, he had
noted. Graduated mages would also be returning to catch a
glimpse of the newest faces, and so would the Crown and its
ensuing nobility.

It was true that King Lucius and Prince Blayne had family participating this year, but what I had not realized was
that the king and his court came *every* year. Since the Crown
was funding the Academy, the trials were "an opportunity to
check on the progress of its efforts." They also made for entertainment—nobility contributed donations in exchange for the
privilege to attend. They made sport of the event, taking bets
and wagers on the rest of us.

The Academy allowed the practice because the extra coin
helped fund its continued enrollment. First-year study was
financed by the Crown, but the training of apprentice mages
and the salaries of the Academy's prestigious staff—*those* were
financed by the trials.

Another advantage to spectatorship was that the entire
village of Sjeka made more than half of its yearly earnings
from a week's worth of board. The township raised the rent on
all of its housing, which the nobility and visiting mages easily
afforded. The king and his family, apparently, had rooms in
the Academy—which was interesting to consider, since Darren
had spent the entire course of his study in the barracks. Further south was cheaper board, much less accommodating and
nearly a two-hour walk from the Academy, but that was where

many of the visiting lowborn families, including my own, were
expected to stay during the trials.

So now here we were: forty-three fumbling first-years for
all the world to see. Fifteen of us would become mages. The
rest would be a courtier's joke for a month or two until the
shame was finally forgotten.

I was standing before a sea of hungry faces, and at their
own private bench, just beyond my row and facing the audience, were the Three. In glistening, many-layered silk robes
edged in gold, the Black Mage of Combat, the Red Mage of
Restoration, and the Green Mage of Alchemy sat patiently
awaiting the end of the ceremony. Our reigning Council of
Magic, the three Colored Robes, was to serve on the panel of
judges for our first-year trials alongside the Master of the
Academy.

When they had first been introduced, the stands had
gone wild with excitement. Many of the nobility had brought
flowers, and their intentions had become clear as soon as the
Three arrived. Elated shrieks and flying petals had greeted the
three most important mages of Jerar while they had taken
their seats. I'd barely caught a glimpse. The glittering ceremo-
nial robes and jewel-studded hoods had left little for me to see.

When Barclae was done giving his speech, the crowd had
still not gotten over its initial excitement. Half the stands
rushed after the departing Three, while the rest of the mass,
undoubtedly the visiting families, stumbled across the field,
attempting to greet the students they had come to see.

Amidst the commotion and cries of delight, I stood,
squinting in the brightness of the late afternoon sun, trying to
spot a familiar face. It had been so long, I had started to forget
what they looked—

"*Ryiah!*" a high-pitched squeal to my right alerted me
my younger brother was near.

I barely had time to turn around before a flurry of blond
curls came crashing into me. I nearly fell as Derrick hugged
me, squeezing me so tight I could barely breathe.

"It's nice to see you too!" I choked, laughing.

"I can't believe you and Alex are still here!" Derrick told me, his shout muffled by my tunic.

"Nei-ther can I," I said between deep gasps of air.

"Ryiah." I glanced up from my brother's curls to spot my father and mother shortly behind, patiently awaiting their turn.

"Get off me, you lump!" I pried my little brother off me and then turned to my parents.

"Mom, Dad!" I hugged them fiercely and then stepped back, so I could remember exactly how they looked. It had been so long...My vision started to blur, and I realized I was crying.

"Has it been that terrible?" my father asked, concerned.

"No," I stammered, "it's just...I missed all of you so much!"

"Well, you and Alex will make sure it was worth it!" Derrick circled me, taking in the changes to his older sister's appearance. "You're so fit now!" he crowed.

I snorted. "Not even close. Wait until you see Sir Piers. Or my Master of Combat, Narhari! He's like—"

"You chose Combat? I *knew* you would!"

"Not Alchemy?" My mother was puzzled. "I would have thought you and Alex would take after your father. You two are so well-versed in herb lore and tonic making..."

I grinned. "Alex chose Restoration, Mom."

My father didn't look surprised. "You and your brother have always been stubborn. You two are fans of the long road." He sighed. "Choosing the easiest path has never been a part of your destiny."

I smiled, wiping the tears away. "Remind me to listen to my father next time around."

He grinned. "You wouldn't be my daughter if you did."

As I led my parents off the field, I caught sight of some of my friends exchanging tearful reunions like my own. My twin was nowhere to be found.

Ruth's and Ella's families were much more refined. Each had come from nobility, though their attire was much less decorated than some of the other highborn families' I had seen today. Ella's father had the looks of a retired knight, a shade past his prime. Ruth's parents gave me the impression they might faint under the direct light of sun. Ruth was a stark contrast to the timidity of her parents. She had no siblings who had come to visit.

Ella, on the other hand, had her older brother Jeffrey, and was in the throes of a huge, spinning embrace. Jeff was five years her senior, with short-cropped hair and the same amber eyes as his sister. Though Ella had once told me her older brother was a bit of a gambler, and a lazy one at that, it was clear she and her parents still loved him very much.

I was about to bring my family over to introduce them when an excited voice broke out behind me.

"This is her! This is the girl I was telling you about!"

I recognized the voice and turned to find Clayton, his parents, and a younger sister trailing behind. Clayton raced forward to grab my arm and drag me over until he caught sight of my own family.

"You must be Ryiah's parents," the boy said, addressing both my mother and father with a hand outstretched. My dad shook it with a raised brow as my mother smiled.

Derrick stared at the first-year pointedly. "And you are?"

"Ryiah hasn't told you about me?" Clayton glanced at me and then shrugged, still smiling. "I'm Clay. Ry and I are in Combat together."

"Ryiah, you never told us you made a *friend!*" My mother said, placing a special emphasis on that last word.

I cringed.

"So, this is the mysterious *Ryiah*, the girl we have heard so much about."

I blushed and wondered exactly what Clayton had told them. Clearly they were under the same impression as my mom.

"I hope the stories are not all bad," I said.

His mother smiled at me, a little too fondly for my liking. "Most definitely not."

I fell silent, not knowing what else to say.

"Are you going to introduce me?"

I whirled around to find Ella and her family grinning broadly behind us. I immediately brought her over to my family, sidestepping Clayton.

"This is Ella," I told them eagerly. "She is the reason I am still here!"

Ella's brother chuckled. "She seemed to imply it was the other way around."

Our families exchanged greetings, and once they had finished listening to some of our shared stories, I noticed Ella looking for Alex. He was still out there in the center of the field but he was surrounded by several girls from Restoration.

"Alex hasn't changed at all," Derrick remarked.

"Is that the boy you were talking about?" Jeff asked Ella.

My friend looked away, embarrassed, and her brother grinned. "He's not the type you usually go after, that one."

I laughed, and Ella shot me a glare. "He wasn't until it was too late," I told Jeff.

"Now that makes more sense."

With our families in stride, Ella and I headed to the backdoors of the Academy. We noticed Constable Barrius and Frederick giving tours of the stables to a party of interested nobility, but we did not join in. It was getting late, and my parents still had a two-hour walk back to their inn.

We had just reached the atrium when we came across some of the visiting mages and a cluster of highborn families that was listening to their every word. The mages were explaining their own experience at the Academy years ago, and it seemed pleasant enough, until I noticed Priscilla and her family at the center of the audience.

I recoiled by instinct.

"Is that who I think it is?" Ella's brother asked, wide eyed as he stared at the raven-haired beauty.

Ella elbowed him, hard. "Don't even look her way, Jeff. She hasn't changed from court."

"Priscilla is not half so beautiful as your lovely sister here." My twin had arrived.

Ella flushed.

"Alex!" my father chastised my brother. "How nice of you to finally join us after you finished flirting with half the school."

Derrick was not distracted by the commotion. "Who is Priscilla?"

Alex ruffled our younger brother's hair. "The meanest girl you will ever meet."

Derrick turned back to study the girl curiously, and then his jaw dropped. "Is that the king?"

I glanced back to see who my younger brother was watching, and sure enough, coming down the spiraling stair was Darren, another boy of similar features, and an older man with stark white hair and a permanent frown who I could only assume was their father, King Lucius III.

The king of the realm held himself much the way his sons did, composed and almost disconcertingly aloof. Like his heir, the man wore his hair short, but with a meticulously trimmed beard that was his alone. Both father and eldest bore the same piercing blue eyes, and I wasn't sure what was worse, the sharp cobalt of ice or the bottomless shading of Darren's garnet brown.

Each member of the royal family was dressed in the same stiff, fitted brocade robe that was associated with the Crown. It was an elaborate, heavy material that gave off the impression of unrelenting force. While the king and his heir wore their robes with thick golden-laced embroidery and chain adornments, Darren wore his simply, though he did still wear the hematite stone pendant around his neck.

Even if they had not been the Crown, the kings and his sons were easily the most ominous family in Jerar. I shivered as Prince Blayne caught sight of Ella, and when the crown prince smiled the small, cruel smile of their shared secret, I instantly hated him more than the non-heir himself.

Prince Blayne whispered something in Darren's ear, and the non-heir glanced over at Ella. Darren looked upset, and as soon as he spotted me watching, the frown turned into a glare.

"What was that?" Derrick asked, noting the look that had passed between the non-heir and me.

"It's complicated."

My mother looked shocked. "How did you get on a prince's bad side?"

Alex clenched his fists but said nothing. I just shook my head and let Ella finish for me, "Oh, Darren? Don't worry too much about him. He hates everyone on sight."

"Oh." My mother seemed convinced, but I could tell Derrick was still suspicious.

We continued to make our way down the halls to the entrance of the Academy. Ella's family had already gone ahead of us, and my parents and Derrick hurried to follow their trail while Alex, Ella, and I waved our goodbyes.

After our families had retired from view, the three of us headed back down the corridor in the direction of our barracks. We had only just crossed the atrium when we found ourselves face-to-face with the crown prince. While I couldn't be sure, I had the distinct impression he had been waiting. A second later my thoughts were confirmed when Prince Blayne stepped out directly in front of us, cutting off our path.

"Lady Ella," Blayne said, ignoring my brother and me. "It's been too long." He reached out and snatched my friend's hand.

Ella instantly paled, and I could see fear written all over her face.

An awkward silence passed. Ella was suddenly incapable of speaking. She was usually so outspoken, but now she was as silent as a rock.

I took Ella's other arm, seeing as how Blayne still hadn't let go of her first.

"Let's return to the barracks," I said very loudly. I curtsied the barest inch that a crown prince would afford and pulled at my friend's arm. "We need to get back."

The crown prince faced me with a sneer. "Ella will leave when she's ready." His grip hadn't lessened, and I could see white marks on my friend's arm.

Alex put himself directly in front of the prince. "She needs to get back."

"Just who do you think you are speaking to, lowborns?" Prince Blayne spat at the both of us.

Alex opened his mouth to reply with some chosen words—and I wasn't far behind—when Darren appeared, seemingly out of nowhere.

"Let them be, Blayne," he told his brother.

"Darren—"

"I said let her go!"

Prince Blayne fixed Darren with a stare to rival his brother's own. After a minute however, the heir looked away, releasing my friend's arm.

"We will catch up some other time, my sweet," the crown prince told Ella.

Darren turned on the three of us. "Now leave," he snapped, "and next time you had best address my brother with the respect his title deserves!"

Ella turned to me as soon as we entered the barracks. "I don't know why I let him affect me like that." She had refused to discuss Blayne in front of my brother. I was the only one who knew about her past. "It was like I hadn't aged at all, and I was that twelve year old girl all over again."

I put my hand on her shoulder. "Alex and I won't let him come near you again, I promise."

She gave me a grateful smile. "I am lucky to have the two of you as friends."

"I think you and I would have found each other, one way or another," I said grinning. "How else would we have survived a full year of Piers and Narhari?"

She laughed, and the two of us relaxed into a comfortable silence.

"Do you think Alex still cares for me?" Ella asked abruptly. It was the first time I had ever heard her acknowledge any sort of tension between them.

I sighed, not sure I wanted to encourage my friend, or my twin. Things were complicated enough as it was. "Let's just survive the trials first," I told her. "We can figure out my dolt-headed brother's intentions later."

She sighed. "Fine...It's probably better not to know anyway." She paused, "Did you see Ruth earlier? Thank the gods Combat doesn't go first. Poor thing, I don't think she'll be sleeping at all tonight."

"Our turn will come soon enough," I pointed out.

*Too soon*, I added silently, pulling my covers as far as they would reach. Tucked in a cocoon of blankets, I tried to ease my racing mind. There was no point in studying late this evening. I was too nervous.

Bidding Ella goodnight, I willed myself to dream.

# CHAPTER FOURTEEN

My family arrived early the next morning looking much better rested than any of my class. Since the first four hours of the Alchemy trials were not for public viewing we took a tour of the village instead. Most visiting families did the same, and this time Alex and I were able to tell our parents and Derrick a bit more about our experiences at the Academy. When we returned to the school around noon, a quarter of the nobility, including the Crown, was noticeably absent.

Derrick, of all people, was the one to offer up an explanation. He had overheard conversations the day before, and he explained that the first half of the Alchemy trials actually *was* viewable—for a price.

Usually first-year trials were held in the training field to accommodate a large audience. For the brewing stages of Alchemy, however, students needed certain accommodations. As a result, seating in the upstairs laboratory was awarded to the highest bidder. Nobility paid handsomely for the inevitable advantage an experience like that bought.

After the afternoon meal, I followed my family to the raised seating bordering the Academy field. Anyone who wasn't participating was allowed to watch. I probably should have been preparing for my own trial two days away, but the appeal of watching the culmination of everyone's efforts was too tempting to ignore. The rest of the factions shared the same opinion. Not one of us was absent.

A loud span of clapping erupted, and I looked back to the grass. Master Barclae and the twelve students of Alchemy had arrived. Each first-year carried a small wooden crate filled with flasks of differing colors and sizes. Some liquids were translucent and bubbling. Others were thicker and more mysterious in nature. I spotted Ruth near the end of the row, looking as pale as a ghost with bloodshot eyes and dark circles beneath. Everyone in her faction looked equally distraught.

*Did they realize how hard everyone had worked to be here today?* Whether any of us won an apprenticeship or not, the forty-three students left had beaten impossible odds to last this long. We had carried on at all costs. A wager was a cruel way to measure that sacrifice.

"My dearest friends," Barclae spoke, his voice resonating across the field. "We will now commence the second half of the Alchemy trials. For the next four hours, Master Ascillia will be naming one desired casting every thirty minutes. Students' potions will be judged on their ability to produce a desired outcome. The judges and I will evaluate each first-year's draught, apply the necessary remedies, and then continue on to the next. No scores or remarks will be given aloud for any of the trials. Only on the seventh day will our decisions be made public during the official naming ceremony."

Barclae took a couple steps forward so that he could join the Three on their bench in front of the first row adjacent the king and his two sons. They had a small table in front of their bench with rolls of parchment and writing ink.

Master Ascillia stepped forward. "Paralysis." Her voice boomed and crackled across the rows of seating so that everyone could hear.

Twelve nervous first-years reached down into the crates they had carried in and pulled out a small vial no bigger than my palm. I saw Ruth shudder as she swallowed her own concoction, and then watched as everyone else did the same. Each one of them seemed nervous. I wondered if it was because they wanted their results to be the most effective or the least.

Minutes ticked by. The students stood underneath the bright sunlight, sweating and nervously eyeing one another's progress. Nothing happened at first, but then some of the audience began to murmur amongst themselves.

A loud thud sounded. And then another. And another. Slowly, in the course of five minutes, each first-year of Alchemy dropped to the grass, shaking spastically, almost uncontrollably, while their eyes stared blankly up at the sky.

I watched in horror as the bodies continued to twitch, and then held my breath as the spasms stopped completely.

Twelve motionless bodies were sprawled out across the field.

Excitement rose in the audience. The first two rows began to point and shout, naming the students they had placed bets after.

Ten minutes later one of the first-year bodies began to shake violently. The boy coughed, and his tremors abruptly ceased.

Slowly, the boy rose. Tears fell silently as he took in the immobile first-years around him.

Two nobles in the second row violently tossed their wine skins to the ground.

The boy had placed last in the first round of the Alchemy trials. That much was clear.

The final ten minutes of the round commenced. Five more students rose unhappily before time had ended. When the judges came forward to examine the remaining young men and women, Ruth was one of the six that had stayed the effects of her potion's enchantment.

The green-and-red-robed judges administered healing magic in their own faction's manner. The Green Mage, leader of Alchemy, tipped a small flask of discernible clear liquid down the throats of four first-years nearest. The Red Mage, leader of Restoration, knelt down to touch the throats of the two remaining students.

Immediately, the four students that had been cured by potion sat up coughing and spewing blood and the remnants of their brews. The two first-years cured by touch began to tremble, pouring pools of sweat as their body emptied itself of poisonous toxin.

Ruth, I noticed, took the longest to stand. Some of the audience were whispering excitedly, and I wondered if my friend had won. Maybe she had, but without the judges' commentary, seven more rounds to go, and then the oral exams later on, I had no way of knowing whether Ruth would be one of the five to earn an apprenticeship. Only time would tell.

The Alchemy trials continued for the next three and a half hours. There were two more self-inflicted draughts, one for aging and another for sleep. The aging potion's effects were unnerving to watch: twelve first-years took on sagging skin and hair loss, taut arms became feeble and weak, and everyone was instantly shorter in stature. The sleeping draught was uneventful. All I heard were snores. The peaceful look on the participants' faces left many in the audience yawning inadvertently.

The last five concoctions were intended for battle. Five potions were summoned, one by one: liquid fire, fortify metal—they were given blades for the demonstration—toxic sludge, exploding earth, and choking gas. The judges stood close by to rectify the results as first-years occasionally collapsed from their own doing.

At times it was hard to watch the students throw down their bottles, knowing that something dreadful awaited them once the fumes were released. The only casting I was left with questions after was the oil they had used to reinforce their swords. They didn't test the blades, though the metal had seemed to shine and grow heavier upon contact. The judges had collected the weaponry for further examination later on, and so the audience was unable to ascertain who had succeeded in that particular act.

Overall, most of the students did very well. Ruth had stood out in five of the eight tests. I wondered how she was feeling. Master Ascillia came forward to escort the twelve first-years off the field. The class had looked terrible when they started, but now after the completion of their first trial, they looked like walking death. It left a sinking feeling in the pit of my stomach, and I wondered how I would feel in two days when it was my turn instead.

⊰⊱

The following day, I watched the nine remaining first-years of Restoration live out eight hours that were, if possible, worse than the previous days' castings. Alex, James, and the others had drawn from the same marble statuettes that Ella and I would be using to decide the pairings for our faction's trial. The first-year that did not have a matching figurine was given Master Cedric as a partner, which was a good thing because the man would not be participating and, therefore, not need to cure his associate's ailments.

Alex had warned us what would happen if you were paired with the best, and unfortunately, my brother appeared to be living his worst nightmare out there on the field. He'd done well during his turn casting. He'd cured increasingly difficult maladies, ranging from swelling to deep, gashing wounds that were horrific to watch. He'd stumbled a bit, during the healing of black frost burn, and his session had ended with his performance putting him on par with the three pairs of students that had come before.

His partner, a quiet boy of dark, black braids and almond eyes, proved to be my brother's undoing. Alex had been good, but the boy was better—*much* better. The boy's turn had barely begun, and within twenty minutes Alex had already suffered severe cuts, blackening frost, intense burns, a concussion, and a heightened state of paralysis. His partner continued to cure as fast as the ailments were cast by the judges. The dark-haired boy never faltered, and he was cut off at the end of his forty-five minutes without so much as a blunder the entire act. Certainly, the boy looked as out of breath and exhausted as the students that had gone prior, but he had also doubled the outcome of everyone else's casting.

Half the audience stood after Alex's partner had finished, and the air was found with enthusiastic shouts and the thundering of clapping. "Ronan!" The audience kept repeating the dark-haired boy's name.

Poor Alex looked miserable beside the new champion of Restoration. While I pitied my twin, I silently acknowledged that Alex was lucky still. He had a one in two chance that he would make his faction's cut.

The final pair to present was James and Master Cedric. Sadly, Ella's shy admirer did not fare so well. While he was clearly trying, James could not cure beyond the fourth ailment. It was a surprise the boy had lasted as long as he had, and I wondered how much of that had to do with my dark-skinned friend. If he hadn't been so infatuated with Ella, would James—who was clearly not cut out for a lifetime of hardship—would he really have stayed the course?

The Restoration trials ended. Same as the day before, the retiring first-years looked incredibly ill as they followed Master Cedric off the field to the Academy.

"Tomorrow is you, right?" Derrick asked me, staring after our brother.

"Yes." My stomach curdled at the prospect. I felt faint and dizzy, and apprehension was in every breath that I took.

Ella and I said farewell to our families shortly after, and when we returned to our barracks, we both glanced at each other wordlessly.

We had done everything we could to prepare ourselves for what lie ahead. It was a hard truth to admit, but there was nothing more we could do.

"Good luck, Ryiah," Ella said, eyes unusually bright.

I swallowed. "You too."

"It'll all be over soon," she promised, voice catching.

I nodded, and then lay down in bed, preparing for a night of restless sleep.

—✦—

All twenty-two of us stood in the grand atrium of the Academy. Each of us held in our hands the small marble figurine that would be deciding our fate. Master Barclae and the Three Colored Robes were explaining which statuette would indicate first, and which would end the final round of our tourney. We made eleven pairs.

I glanced around the room, wondering if anyone else had gotten any sleep. All of our families, the king and his visiting court, and even the realm's mages were waiting outside to watch us duel for the chance at an apprenticeship.

In the palm of my hand was the tiny carving of a fox.

Master Barclae called each token's name forward, starting with the rabbit and ending with the wolf. Ella and Jake were both first, having each selected a rabbit. Eve and William were next, the serpent. Ray, the talented lowborn boy from Darren's following, and I had the fox. Next went the fish, the lion, the bird—Priscilla and one of her friends, Jade, a tall girl with dark blue eyes and endless lashes—the boar, the dog, the buck, the horse, and, finally, the wolf: Darren and Clayton.

We lined up in pairs and followed Master Barclae and the rest of his panel down the long corridors and beaten path that led onto the Academy field. As we took our place at the far end of the grass, Master Barclae came forward, leading Jake and Ella to the center of the field so that the audience could see with whom the first match would take place.

The crowd began to chant. "COMBAT! COMBAT!" And then shrieks and hollers filled the air. This was what everyone

had been waiting for: the most prestigious faction, the mages
of the black robe.

—╫—

I watched, helplessly, as my best friend twisted and
dodged a giant, spinning whirlwind of flame.

Jake held a devious smile as he lodged another at my
friend. This time Ella wasn't quite so fast, and part of her tunic
caught fire as she scrambled to get out of the way. She barely
managed to put out the flames when Jake sent a third fire careening her way.

Ella threw out a blast so strong it knocked the flames
aside. She sent the fire spiraling back, and without hesitation,
Ella cast out a storm of blades, launching them with all her
might.

Jake only just managed to throw up his shield. A second
later and he would have been mauled.

The two had been exchanging crippling blows for the
past thirty minutes. With every second I was growing more
and more anxious. Any of my own anxiety had been displaced
in the onslaught of my friend's duel.

It was exhilarating to see all that Ella had learned in a
year. At the mid-year tourney Ella had not used half the castings she was using now. She was faring well, and even though
she was quickly reaching the end of her stamina, she was still
putting up a fight that Jake was struggling to put out.

BOOM! A blast of Ella's magic split open the ground beneath the boy, effectively doing to Jake what he and William
had done to that poor boy during hazing. Jake fell.

There was a sickening crunch, and then I saw my friend
run forward, holding a bow and arrow in hand as she circled
the hole, ready to shoot should Jake try anything at her approach.

But he didn't. With a broken leg and no magic left, Ella had effectively expended the boy's limits and left him with no defense.

The look Jake shot her was worse than any Priscilla or Darren had ever given me.

"I yield."

The crowd went hysterical. And above the madness of it all, I could hear Alex screaming her name louder than anyone else.

"ELLA! ELLA! ELLA!"

She had won.

✢ ✢

Next up were Eve and William. The match wasn't even a fair fight. Within twenty minutes Eve had exhausted her rival's stamina and become the second champion of the day.

The crowd was even more hysterical than before. Eve's victory had been astoundingly quick.

As the pale, seemingly fragile first-year and her bulky opponent exited the field, I saw Darren catch Eve's arm and congratulate her on the match. William's eyes flashed dangerously, but the prince didn't seem to care.

Before the match had even begun, it had been obvious who would win. Anyone who had ever paid attention in practice would know that Eve was second only to Darren in casting.

William hadn't stood a chance.

"Ryiah."

I turned to see Master Narhari waiting for me. Ray was already walking onto the field in anticipation of our match. My stomach sank.

*It was time.*

I followed my training master, trailing behind Ray until I was in my starting position, two hundred yards across from my opponent.

The sun was bright in the sky, not a cloud to help ease my vision as I squinted at Ray across the way.

I had never had any qualms with the boy standing before me. One year my junior, he had fast become a member of Darren's following early on because of his potential. Ray had come into this place like me: a lowborn, untrained, uneducated first-year with a dream and ten months to prove it. Ray had never taken part in the hazing, never tried to act as though he was better than me. He was just a tall boy with olive skin, dark wavy curls, and serious amber eyes.

And right now, he was the only person standing between me and an apprenticeship.

"Annnnnnnd begin!" Master Barclae roared.

All I saw was red.

Before I even knew I was doing it, I had cast two tunneling trails of flame. I watched as the twin fires bit across the landscape. In moments they had reached my opponent and cut him off from escape at either side. He was trapped.

As Ray attempted to quench the fires with an outpouring of sand, I threw all the force I could muster at Ray's feet, willing the earth to crack open just as it had done for Ella. The ground moaned loudly and collapsed, but I was too slow. Ray was gone.

Suddenly, I couldn't see anything. A thick cloud of smoke had appeared out of nowhere, and now I was surrounded by thick, gray fog anywhere that I turned.

Coughing, I tried to summon enough wind to rid me of the heavy vapor, but before I could blow it far enough away, the sharp "zzzzzing" of metal slicing through the air alerted me seconds before Ray's sword came slashing through the haze.

I had the barest instant to throw up a shield to block the overhead blow, and then Ray's sword slammed my defense. My arms buckled and quaked, but I held on. As soon as Ray withdrew his blade to try a different cut, I blindly slammed my shield into his chest. I threw myself into the blow, effectively cutting off my opponent's windpipe as the impact knocked the both of us backward and out of the blinding smoke.

The two of us fell expertly. Both had spent months practicing how to land correctly. I tucked in my chin and knees, letting the impact hit my bottom, rolling until the impact faded. Then I pulled myself up at the same time as Ray.

We faced each other warily.

I braced myself, keeping my stance limber as I awaited Ray's next attack. I had used up a lot of my magic in that first—and now useless—attempt to entrap him. I had to be careful to conserve the rest for my defense.

Ray had always done well in our class but I had never paid much attention to his training. I'd been so consumed with watching Darren and Priscilla that I had never stopped to think about the others in their group.

Now I wished I had.

A minute passed, and then I saw it in the way Ray was holding his arms. I threw up my shield, widening my stance and angling my guard arm so that I would not receive the full impact of his casting.

His magic hit me much harder than Ella or Clayton's had ever done in practice. I had to dig in my heels to keep the magic from taking over my defense.

There was a shattering vibration and then Ray's magic rebounded. Magic shot off the shield and into the woods behind me. A moment later there was a loud crack as a pine split in two.

I swallowed, realizing how close I had come to losing the match. That shield trick had just saved me from an instant defeat. I never would have been able to block a casting like that head on.

Ray's mouth fell open in shock. He recovered quickly, but it was just enough for me to realize that while I had not noticed him in practice, he had clearly paid attention to my duel with Priscilla. That attack had been no accident. He had been planning to capitalize on my weakness. Thankfully, it was a weakness I no longer had.

Ray narrowed his eyes, and I readied myself for another casting. When nothing happened immediately, I squinted, trying to see what could possibly be delaying his attack. A second later I noticed the glint of steel and the strange curve of metal in my opponent's hand. It was similar to the battleaxes we had practiced with in class, only this new weapon was much smaller, and the haft was not even two feet in length.

*Why did he pick such a small weapon?*

The answer came moments later when he hurled the object at me with staggering force. I threw up a shield and took off at a run, sprinting as fast as my legs could carry me.

If Ray had been a knight I would have been able to dodge the axe easily. But we were mages, and Ray was using his magic to steer the weapon. It crashed down upon my shield.

The blade was heavier than I had expected. The impact sent me stumbling to my knees as the shield splintered in two. The axe's thick iron-tipped edge dug into my right shoulder, cutting a deep gash that was felt all the way down my arm.

I bit my lip, hard, and forced myself to stand. Blood was pouring from the wound and it was costing me everything not to cry out in pain. I glanced to Ray and saw another throwing axe had appeared in his hand. My heart stopped.

If he kept throwing those axes, he would be able to wear out my stamina much sooner than he did his own. Normal long-range weapons couldn't break a shield. An axe could, but up until now I had foolishly assumed that it would not be a problem in distance encounters.

The second axe came hurtling toward me. I made a swift decision to change tactics. Instead of running away, I ran toward the axe. I threw my shield as hard as I could, sending the two items tottering off harmlessly to the left of the field.

I hadn't wanted to engage Ray directly. He was tall and stocky, and I knew he would be able to outlast me in any weighted exchange. *Especially with an open wound.* But as long as he kept throwing those axes at me, I had no choice...unless I used my magic for something big, and I wasn't sure I wanted to do that again, seeing as how my last two attacks had done little else than drain my magic.

Summoning two blades, a hefty broadsword for myself, and a spectral blade for an additional attack, I lunged at Ray with everything I had.

It was a mistake. As soon as I engaged him I realized how reckless the decision was. Ray only needed to wait for me to bleed out and make a mistake. I shouldn't have rushed him.

It was too late though, and I tried my best to ameliorate the situation. As predicted, Ray made no attempt to expend himself. I felt like a fool as we continued to exchange blows. Piers had spent  months lecturing us about the realities of injury in battle. *"Nine times out of ten a knight dies not because of a direct wound, but minor ones that amass over time. The blood loss ultimately makes him dizzy and weak, which will cause him to make more mistakes than usual. This is what the enemy will wait for. The smart ones don't strike to kill. They just wait for you to do the work for them."*

This can't be how it ends.

I continued to lead the assault. Ignoring the throbbing of my right arm, I clutched the sword in both hands and delivered blow after blow with endless vigor. I tried to will my second casting to do the same, but Ray was prepared with a spectral blade of his own.

Our match transformed into a flurry of swordplay.

I knew I would lose if I kept the contest going, but I was out of ideas. We were thirty minutes into our match, and Ray still looked as composed as when we had started. Meanwhile sweat was stinging my eyes, my limbs were aching all over, and my shoulder smarted terribly whenever I shifted weight.

My spectral blade faltered. Just as it deflected Ray's oncoming blow, I felt the casting shudder. I slammed the broadsword I was holding as hard as I could into Ray's left side. He

blocked easily, as I had known he would, but the impact gave
me just enough time to jump back before my second casting
vanished completely.

I began to run toward the armory.

All I had left was the sword in my hand. My magic
hadn't been able to hold onto both. It had exhausted most of
its limits trying to float the spectral blade and wield it on its
own. I was beginning to feel light-headed, and the searing pain
in my forehead had begun. It was only a matter of minutes
before my magic expired completely, and then I'd be defenseless.

I had to get my hands on a real weapon.

Mid-sprint I released the broadsword casting and used
the last bit of magic I had to summon a shield at my back. I
was too open to attack, racing across the grassy field.

Not even a second later there was the sharp whistle of arrows and then the repetitive thuds as they lodged themselves
harmlessly into my shield.

The ground beneath my feet began to tremble. I dove to
my right. Glancing back, I saw a fissure where I had been
headed just moments before.

I was close to the armory door now. Just another minute
and I would be safely inside. It was off limits, I knew, but I
didn't have a choice. I couldn't just let Ray win. I had to put
up a fight any way that I could.

We were supposed to rely on our own magic, our own
prowess. Well, I had, but now there was a resource I couldn't
ignore, one that might somehow give me a chance in this after
all. It was either forfeit now or bend the rules and hope the
judges overlooked my decision. I chose the latter.

I grabbed the wrought iron handle, ready to throw open
the door...

Ray's hand shot out behind me, snatching my injured
shoulder and yanking me backward so that I was sent sprawling into the grass behind. This time when I fell I didn't land
the way I was supposed to.

I fell on my outstretched arm. There was a sickening snap.

Turning my head, I saw the odd angle of my left wrist. I didn't need a knowledge of Restoration to understand that it was broken.

"You know you're not supposed to enter the armory," Ray panted. He was shaking. The last couple of castings had cost him dearly. I wasn't the only one running out of stamina.

"Surrender, Ryiah. You've got nothing left." His eyes held pity. "Don't make this any worse than it already is."

He was giving me a chance, I realized. Ray didn't want to hurt me more than he had to, but he would should I continue to stand between him and an apprenticeship.

Using my right arm to push myself off the ground, I gritted my teeth and stood. The shoulder pain was excruciating, and my surroundings were becoming blurred.

Ray let me stand, but after a couple seconds of silence he became impatient. Drawing his sword, he regarded me grimly. "Surrender *now*, Ryiah, or I'll have no choice but to make you." He took a step forward, pressing the blade of his sword just above my collarbone, into the deep wound on my right shoulder.

The pressure of metal against swollen flesh and bone was so overpowering that tears streamed down my face involuntarily. My stomach roared in anguish.

I tried furiously to conjure a sword, a shield, any sort of defense to put between myself and the blade at my shoulder, but I came up empty-handed.

Ray pushed down with his blade.

The agony in my head was so terrible that I could no longer discern anything except the pain and the heavy breathing of my opponent.

This was it. This was how I would be remembered: just another first-year that had tried. I'd done well, but not well enough.

*No!*

The thought came raging through me as Ray increased the weight of his cut. There was nothing I could do about the pain. He had me there. He had me trapped, defenseless...the perfect ending to a perfect victory.

But there was one thing Ray could not plan for, one glimpse at hope he might not have suspected in his careful approach. It was dangerous, and until today I had never bothered to consider it...but now...I had nothing left to lose.

I threw myself onto Ray's sword, letting its metal pierce my wound as the blade severed and cut, tearing down, down, *deep* into flesh. My vision went black, and I fell forward, shrieking and dragging Ray down with me as I threw out my magic in earnest.

Somewhere in the midst of my shouting and Ray's own startled cry, the harsh booming of what sounded like thunder entered my awareness. I was barely able to register the bone-shattering blast before something heavy collided with my skull, and I lost all semblance of consciousness.

⁎

*"Do you think she'll wake?"*

*"I don't know, she's been through a lot..."*

*"I can't believe Ryiah! She almost killed the both of them!"*

*"Master Barclae and the judges are furious..."*

*"Did you see the look on the king's face? She just cost the Academy thousands with that stunt!"*

Slowly, I became aware of the voices surrounding me, and I opened my eyes to find Ella, Alex, and the rest of my family standing next to my bedside in what appeared to be the healing ward. Two mages in the red robes of Restoration were frowning. I was immediately filled with a hundred questions.

I tried to sit up, only to gasp and clutch my ribs as the immediate pain sent me doubling over in agony.

"She's awake!" Derrick cried, and suddenly all eyes turned to me.

I tried to shift more comfortably and groaned. There was an almost unbearable throbbing in my shoulder. Every muscle ached. My left arm stung as if someone had hammered it repeatedly with a red-hot mallet.

"W-what happened?" I croaked. My mouth was like sand.

My mother handed me a glass brimming with water and motioned for me to drink.

"Ryiah, dear, when you impaled yourself on that boy's sword, your casting collapsed the entire structure you two were struggling beneath."

Derrick bounced from one foot to the next. "You destroyed the armory!"

"You sent the entire building crumbling when you lunged at Ray, Ryiah. The whole structure fell, toppling both of you," Ella told me.

"You almost killed yourself!" Alex interrupted, eyes flashing dangerously. "All so that you could take Ray down with you!"

"Barclae is beside himself." Ella paused. "So is everyone else. That area was off limits, but you knew that, didn't you?"

I bit my lip, avoiding everyone's furious gaze. "I was going to lose," I said softly. "I had no stamina left...I–I knew pain was an unpredictable way to call on magic, but I thought maybe its casting would be enough to disarm him. I didn't realize it would bring down the entire armory..."

"I don't know whether you are a genius or the biggest fool I've ever known." That was Alex.

I started to laugh, and then quickly stopped as my ribs shook painfully. "At least I won," I choked.

Silence.

And then: "But you didn't."

I glanced up at my friend, but Ella refused to meet my eyes.

"Ryiah, you lost," my mother said, brushing a strand of hair from my face.

My heart stopped. "How?" I rasped.

"The entire building fell. All of us thought you were dead." Ella swallowed. "But right as the judges and Master Barclae reached the scene, Ray appeared, dragging you out of the rubble..." She swallowed, "He managed to survive your attack using some sort of defensive sphere. He saved you too...if it weren't for Ray, Ryiah, I don't think you would be alive right now. Even Restoration has its limits."

And that was it.

My world came crashing down around me as I realized what my friend was saying. Not only had I broken the tourney rules and destroyed a valuable building, I had almost killed the both of us. The pain had made my magic spiral out of control. If I had succeeded, the two of us would have died from its impact. But, my opponent, *my noble opponent*, had saved the both of us.

Ray had won.

I had lost.

And I had managed to do so in such appalling fashion that nobility would be talking about it for years to come. The Colored Robes and Master Barclae would remember me. That was for certain. Not as an apprentice, a girl of much talent, but as a first-year that almost killed herself and her opponent in the world's most foolhardy attempt. Why couldn't I have just lost with dignity?

Ray had given me an out. I should have taken it.

While a lost match wasn't ground for disqualification, the last first-year to secure an apprenticeship with one had attended the school more than a decade ago. And in my case, with the stunts that I had pulled, it was pretty clear what my outcome would be.

❖

Later that same evening, after the rest of my family had retired, Ella told me the results for the rest of the Combat tri-

als. Ray and I had lasted the longest—fifty minutes while everyone else had barely used up a half-hour. Priscilla had won
her match with the same strategy she'd used to beat me in the
mid-year duels, and Clayton had lost tragically to Darren within the first fifteen minutes. "Clay didn't have a chance," she
noted dryly, "and when Darren won...Well, let's just say that
the judges themselves took to a standing ovation."

A sinking feeling formed in the pit of my stomach as I
picked at the food Ella had brought in from the dining hall. I
was on orders to spend the entire night in the infirmary, and
while I wasn't happy, there wasn't much I could do about it.
The one time I had tried to stand, I had spent the next hour
puking into a bucket. I was not ready to repeat the experience.

I had only myself to thank for the pain I was in right
now.

"Master Barclae announced the order of the second trials," Ella began. I continued to push peas around my plate,
listening. "Ryiah...you and Clayton and half the others will be
going tomorrow."

My grip on the fork tightened, creating red indents in my
palm. I stared up at my friend in horror. "Tomorrow?
Shouldn't Alchemy and Restoration go first? They've had
more days to rest!"

"It was a random drawing." Ella's expression was sympathetic. "Combat has the most students so some *had* to go
tomorrow."

I set my plate to the side. "I should just leave." I said abruptly. "It doesn't matter how I fare tomorrow. They will never let someone like me get a robe after what happened today."

She looked away, patting my arm.

"You can't tell me I've got a chance," I added.

Ella forced herself to meet my eyes. "There has never
been a doctrine stating you had to win the tourney to earn a
place."

"How many have been apprenticed after losing a
match?" I challenged bitterly.

She didn't answer. We both knew the truth.

✦ ✦

The next morning I awoke feeling resigned as I slowly lowered myself from the cot and dressed for the day's events. My body had healed miraculously overnight, thanks to the potent draughts and restorative touch of Restoration. Those healers knew what they were doing. I might be miserable inside, but on the outside it was as if I had never been injured at all.

I could have left the Academy that day. I could have packed my bags and waited out the rest of my twin's trials as a spectator.

I could have, but I was too proud. Ella was right. Whether I was willing to admit it or not, I had given my life for the chance to be a part of this place. Every waking dream of childhood, every hope I had ever held—they had all centered on becoming a mage. I could not leave my dream behind without completing this one final test.

I would stay for the ceremony, too. I would watch as Darren, Eve, and the others received something I had not been fit to earn. I would stay so that I could close this final chapter and leave my foolish aspirations behind.

There was always the Cavalry.

Pulling on my ragged tunic, I was grateful that the others would be forced to wear the same. I had already stood out enough this week. I didn't need anything drawing more attention to how ill-prepared I felt.

Rather than heading to the library to spend the next six hours studying until my eyes bled, I followed the training field to the hill to where I had sulked so many months ago after my mid-year duel with Priscilla.

The exams were held in a tower to the west of the Academy, just overlooking the cliffs. I had never been. No one other than the judges would be allowed to hear our responses there.

The building was disconnected from the rest of the castle's structure, and it stood a good hundred feet taller than any of the roofs surrounding it. There was an ominous staircase inside, but it did not intimidate me in the least.

Each toll of the Academy bell to the east and another first-year was summoned. We had been given our individual count. I was to be one of the last for the day. I stayed on the hilltop, watching the small green specks of nervous first-years enter and exit the doors at the edge of the grounds.

Once the late afternoon sun had set my turn was fast approaching. I left my post and started the descent. By the time I had reached the tower's base my count had rung. It was time to begin my ascent.

For ten minutes, I climbed the stairs with increasing apprehension. The inside of the passage was dark and I had to be careful where I stepped. A small flicker of light from the wall sconces was all I had to guide me in the prevalent darkness.

After five more minutes, I heard the shutting of a door above and moved to the side to let the returning first-year pass. It was only after the halting of footsteps that I looked up and realized who it was I had come across.

Darren stood, two steps above me, shadows covering all but the barest fragments of his face. He seemed just as shocked as I, though he was much quicker to recover. But not so fast that I missed the flash of guilt that shot across his face.

My pulse quickened, albeit unwillingly. The non-heir and I had not been alone together once since that day weeks before, and as much as I might loathe him in mind, my traitorous body was slow to follow.

"Excuse me," Darren said, making way as if to leave.

I started to step aside, but then I stopped myself. I would probably never cross paths with the non-heir again, and trials were almost over. This was my one chance to ask.

"Why did you do it?"

After everything Darren had done, it shouldn't have mattered. It didn't, really, but I needed to hear the words regardless. Because as long as we kept this distance, as long as he avoided me, there would always be some small part of me trying to explain away his actions. Because of that kiss. That stupid, irresponsible kiss, and the way I had felt because of it.

Darren narrowed his gaze. "You were always so eager to think the worst of me. Would it really make a difference what I told you now?"

No. It wouldn't. "I suppose not." I glanced away, furious that I wanted his answer anyway. *Let it go, Ryiah.* I clenched my fists, wishing I could make myself as cold and unfeeling as the prince.

The movement did not go unnoticed.

Darren studied me in the shadowy passage, head cocked to the side as if I was an experiment he wasn't quite sure of.

The warning bell chimed.

"You should go," Darren said abruptly. "The judges won't take kindly to you being late, especially after yesterday's trial."

I shot him an incredulous look. "It's a bit of a formality, isn't it? You and I both know my fate has already been sealed."

The non-heir frowned. "You shouldn't discount yourself, Ryiah."

I stiffened. "You are truly something," I told him, "still playing at your mind games even after all you've done—"

"Mind games?" Darren looked outraged, even though he had no right to be. "Are you *really* so daft?"

"Not enough to fall for false flattery twice."

"For the love of—" Darren slammed his fist against the wall and glared down at me. "I guess I should congratulate myself," he declared, "on helping the world's biggest idiot!"

"Helping?" I spat. "*Helping*? What part of your actions was 'helping?'" I climbed the remaining steps so that he could not escape. Fury was keeping my senseless attraction in check.

"Was it when you were sabotaging me in the mountains? Insulting me at every turn? *Or when you kissed me and then dumped an entire vat full of pig's blood on me the next time we talked?*" I grabbed the non-heir's sleeve, forcing him to meet my cold, angry eyes. "Really, Darren, which one of those should I be thanking you for?"

Our faces were inches apart, and Darren's livid gaze was burning me alive. "You really want the truth, Ryiah?" he demanded.

I refused to cower.

"Priscilla was going to go after you whether I led the hazing or not." He watched the full impact of his words hit me like a ton of bricks. "She had something far worse in mind, something that might have *actually* made you resign. She *hates* you. And after she found out that I'd...that you and I..."

I released Darren's arm and dropped his gaze immediately, suddenly aware that I had been holding onto both for far too long. There was a heavy pounding in my chest.

"Jake saw us that night," Darren continued, unfazed. "Eve warned me what they were planning. I thought maybe if I avoided you, Priscilla would drop the vendetta, but she didn't..." Darren exhaled loudly. "I am sorry I didn't warn you, Ryiah, but Priscilla would never have listened to me if I'd asked her to stop. It would have just complicated things...so I told her I wanted to help. I figured it was better that way. I could halt the worst of her plan without anyone being the wiser. She was much more willing when she thought you were a mistake."

"You call that 'helping?'" I choked. "You still let her haze me...and it was *you*, not Priscilla, who led me straight into it."

Darren raised a brow. "I *was* helping you. It was much better than her original idea, and everyone knows hazing is a tradition—"

"So *that's* your argument."

"I knew you could take care of yourself," Darren countered. "Plenty of Jerar's mages have gone through the same."

"You weren't hazed."

Darren rolled his eyes dramatically. "If you must know, Ryiah. I still almost stopped you, only you opened that door anyway, and by then it was too late..."

A long silence followed his confession.

He had to be lying. *He is just trying to manipulate me again.*

What had he said right before I went outside that night? *"Wait, Ryiah, don't—"*

And then to Priscilla when she was about to attack me: *"She's not worth it."*

Had he been protecting me? He couldn't have... But then why had he only deflected my casting when I had tried to attack him? And why had he ceased brawling with my brother the second Alex had mentioned my name? And stopped his own brother that first day of trials?

Millions of thoughts were racing through my head, and none of them were making any sense. Or rather they were. I just wasn't sure I wanted to trust them.

"Still can't make up your mind about me, can you, Ryiah?"

I glanced up, startled.

Darren's garnet eyes met mine. He seemed tired, and I wondered if it was because of me, or the trial he had just come from.

"You are probably wondering why I went through the trouble."

*Yes.*

"I've asked myself the same question many times," the prince continued, "and I have come to the conclusion that somewhere along the lines of this year I went mad." He gave me a wry smile. "Luckily for me, it seems to only pertain to things that involve you."

"But..." I couldn't think, and my heart was beating impossibly fast. I wanted to believe him, wanted to believe that my irrational feelings were justified...but there was still something missing, something pressing at the back of my mind that

I was forgetting. Something important that could void all the explanations he had just put forward.

Darren was looking down at me, waiting for my response to his long-awaited explanation. Were we friends, or enemies? After all he had done, it would seem the former.

*Friends? But what about Ella?*

Immediately I remembered what I had been forgetting. "What about Ella and your brother?" I burst out. "What was your excuse then?" I was thankful not all sense had left me.

Darren stopped smiling. "*What* in the name of the gods are you talking about, Ryiah?"

"When she was twelve, you left her all alone with your brother. You saw what he was doing and just left—"

Darren's expression darkened. "Is that what she's been thinking all these years?" He glowered. "Why don't you try asking your friend if she's sure it was *her* magic that saved her?"

"But she said—"

Darren made a frustrated sound and started to push past me.

"Darren, wait!" I didn't know what to think, but I did know that I didn't want him to leave again, not with all these unanswered questions between us. If it was true and he had been helping me all this time, if he had helped Ella too...

Darren turned to face me. His eyes were clouded and unreadable. "You need to decide whether I am the evil tyrant in your head, or a friend, Ryiah. I cannot make that decision for you, and I am done trying to earn your trust."

I looked away. Trust and Darren? The two were opposite ends of a spectrum.

The bell tolled loudly, and I jumped as I realized I was now late to my second trial.

I felt myself go numb. *What did trust matter? I would not be around long enough to find out anyway...*I reached out for Darren's arm before he could start his descent.

Immediately a heady rush of hot and cold was met with an overwhelming sense of home. I felt my breath catch. I had been prepared for the fire, but not the startling refuge that came with it. It took a moment for me to settle my emotions enough to speak.

"If we were friends..." I hesitated. "What would you say to me right now?"

Darren's eyes met mine. "I would tell you that you could still win this, Ryiah."

"Thank you." I released his arm and took a step back.

Something odd flashed across the non-heir's face. "Good luck, Ryiah."

I felt the corners of my lips twitch, and for the first time I realized I was smiling. I gave Darren the barest of nods, and then proceeded up the stairs. Even though I would probably never earn my robes, there was a startling elation that came from thinking that maybe *he* thought I could.

# CHAPTER FIFTEEN

"First-year, you are late."

I reddened and bowed my head quickly, peeking out from under my bangs at the panel of disgruntled judges before me.

There, just as in my dream, sat Master Barclae and the Three Colored Robes. This was the first time I was really able to get a good look at the three mages who ruled the Council of Magic. Each of them looked almost unearthly in their magnificent robes. The gold trim seemed to shimmer brilliantly against the rays of the fading sun.

The Black Mage of Combat had been the one to address me. His head was shaved, and there were two golden hoops dangling from his right ear. He had dark skin and piercing green eyes, the kind that seemed as though they could see straight through to your soul. He was younger than I had expected, no more than thirty-five years at most.

"What is your name, child?"

The second person to speak was the wearer of the red robe, a beautiful blonde woman with violet eyes and full red lips. She was older than the Black Mage, but not by much.

"Ryiah."

"Ryiah," said the third, a formidable older man, with long brown locks and startling yellow eyes. The Green Mage of Alchemy. "You are the one who has given all those fancy highborns a reason to talk. Never in the history of the first-year trials has a student caused so much grief—or damage—to our sacred Academy."

I swallowed uncomfortably.

"What do you have to say for yourself?" Master Barclae asked, watching me carefully.

All eyes narrowed, and I willed myself to speak, despite the wave of nausea that was fast approaching. This would be my one chance to explain, in my own words.

"I never meant to destroy that building," I said, eyes on the ground. "I had only been trying to disarm Ray, the other student that I was up against... Someone once told me that I could use pain to call on my magic. He'd warned me that it was unstable, and I wouldn't be able to control it if I tried..."

I forced myself to continue: "But I had nothing left. No stamina, no magic, *nothing*. If I didn't try, I would have had to admit defeat and...and I couldn't do that knowing there was still something I could use. I knew the armory was off-limits, and I know it went terribly wrong, but I had to try." I glanced at the Colored Robes, desperation in my eyes. "If you want something as badly as I do, you can't give up. I'm sure each of you had a moment like that, where you had to make a choice, and you chose your robe, no matter the consequences—"

"You impaled yourself on a sword," Master Barclae said dryly.

"I would do it again, a thousand times over if I thought it would help." I couldn't help feeling less confident than my words. "It was the only way I could access my magic." I thought of Darren's warning so many months before. "Better to lose a limb than a battle."

"You are a fool," the Red Mage told me shortly. "It wasn't a limb you almost lost. It was your life, and the life of that boy you were with. All for a trial."

"A *powerful* fool," the Black Mage corrected, smiling behind the palm of his hand. "She could rival the prince in that outburst."

The Green Mage chuckled, "Until she kills herself in the process."

"True," the Black Mage acknowledged.

The Three glanced to Master Barclae, and he cleared his throat. "We shall now begin the second portion of your trials, Ryiah. You will have twenty minutes to address three questions, all concerning the art of strategy in Combat..."

⊹⊹

I returned to my barracks much later that evening feeling confident, confused, half sick and half mad. The trial had only lasted a half hour, but the questions the judges had asked left me reeling in self-doubt. *Had my answers been good enough?* I thought they had. I'd cited several battles for each scenario they had given me. I'd weighed the resources, the weather, the landscape, and the politics of each situation to the one approach I thought would best suit their needs. I'd considered all the right questions: Was it a full-scale invasion, or was it better just to send a small regiment to conduct the mission? Was it on our homeland, or in a neighboring country?

For each question they had asked, I'd had a million queries of my own. I'd been desperate to show the product of my endless nights in the library, and even more frantic to prove I was more than the reckless first-year they had seen during the first half of my trials.

*You could still win this.*

Could I?

⊹⊹

The next two days were the longest of my life. I spent the time in restless wonder, following my friends around the small town of Sjeka and trying not to think about what lie ahead.

"It's in the hands of the gods now," Alex declared, as Ella and I followed him into the town's bakery. Ella bought us each a sticky bun, and we exited the fragrant shop licking the honeyed sugar off our fingers.

We had five more hours before the naming ceremony. All of us were trying to pretend the trepidation did not bother us as much as it did.

"I'm surprised your adoring fans haven't stolen you away from us today," Ella told my brother. She'd intended for her comment to come off lightly, but the slight resentment in her tone had destroyed any pretense of indifference.

"I told them to find a new hero," he said easily. "It was off-putting to have so many beautiful ladies returning my favor."

Ella scowled. "Well, I hope you don't regret that later, when you are alone with your jokes and no one to listen—"

"Oh, I won't be alone," he said, winking at me.

I rolled my eyes and walked ahead, letting the two of them return to their silly banter. I wasn't sure how I would feel if Alex started to court my best friend, but I had finally decided the decided it wasn't my decision to make.

Entering the town's apothecary I found my parents discussing the merits of witch hazel with the frazzled shop owner while my younger brother raced over to greet me.

"Ryiah!" Derrick's eyes were as big as saucers. "We didn't see you at all yesterday! Ella said you locked yourself in the barracks!"

I gave a small smile. "I was wallowing in self-pity, but I am done now."

He beamed. "Good. Because today you are going to get a black robe!"

I raised a brow. "Apprentices don't get robes until they graduate."

"Ah-ha, so you do think you'll be apprenticed!"

I shook my head. "I don't want you to get your hopes too high, brother. I lost my first trial, in case you have already forgotten."

Derrick didn't bat an eye. "Just because you didn't win doesn't mean you're disqualified."

I ruffled his hair. "You always were my biggest fan."

"Ryiah."

I turned and saw Clayton standing in the middle of the doorway. He looked nervous. My stomach fell. I had been evading Clay ever since he'd introduced me to his parents.

I didn't know how to let him down nicely, and so while it was petty, I had figured the best way was to avoid him as much as possible. After all, we only had one more day at the Academy. One day and then we'd never have to have the awkward conversation to begin with.

*Too late.*

My brother snickered. I slammed the ball of my heel into his foot. Derrick yelped and then hopped away to join our parents at the back of the store, shooting me a mean look.

"How are you, Clayton?" I quickly busied myself with one of the charms on the counter.

"Better now."

I cringed and fiddled with the locket until his big hand closed softly around my own. I looked up to meet Clayton's gaze., An uncomfortable silence passed between us.

"Ryiah, I like you."

"Well, isn't that just precious," a sneering female voice drawled behind us.

Jumping, I saw Darren and Priscilla standing in the doorway. My pulse stopped.

"Oh, please don't stop on our account," the venomous girl continued, one arm wrapped tightly around the prince's waist. "This will be our last chance to see two lowborns before we go on to our apprenticeship. Darren and I need a good laugh, don't we, my sweet?"

Darren's eyes fell to Clayton's and my interlocked hands. They were unfathomable. "Yes, I believe we do."

My throat became unbearably dry.

"Just because you don't know happiness is no reason to spoil ours!" Clayton told Priscilla irritably.

She laughed loudly. "Come, Darren. We've got to return to the castle in time for me to dress." She her hand lightly to his chest and whispered loudly: "I have something *special* to wear. I had it especially picked out for tonight's occasion." Her eyes fell to me, and she smiled, saying the next words carefully: "It will be the perfect opportunity to announce our betrothal."

My eyes flew to Darren. He was a stone, not one emotion flickering across his face as the world came crashing down before mine.

The prince and Priscilla left the store. I stared after the spot they had stood long after they had disappeared.

"Ryiah, is something wrong?"

I felt as if someone had ripped my lungs right out of my chest. I was sad, angry, confused...and I had no right to be.

"I am sorry, Clay." I swallowed. " I can't return your favor."

Clayton's face burned red. He dropped my hand with a sneer. "You are a fool if you think Darren will ever notice you!"

The boy didn't wait for a response. He stalked out of the shop indignantly.

Alex and Ella observed the boy's dramatic exit from the street and then came running to find out what had happened.

"What did you say to him?" Alex stared after his friend, confused.

"You finally told Clay you didn't return his sentiment," Ella said. It wasn't a question.

Derrick returned from the back of the shop, grinning. "Ryiah said it right after that mean girl told her she was engaged to the prince."

"What does that halfwit's engagement have to do with anything?" Alex demanded.

Ella's eyes shot to my own, and I looked away, unwilling to acknowledge her unspoken question. I'd told her about my

tower encounter days before, and while she was not yet convinced Darren's magic had saved her years ago, she had
acknowledged the possibility that the prince was not as horrible as we had initially assumed. While Darren claimed to have
helped me in friendship, she knew I had hoped there was more
to it.

Clearly there wasn't.

⚜

Much later that evening, Ella and I were standing before
our reflection in the looking glass of our barrack's quarters. She
had lent me one of her many dresses for the occasion, a deep
blue gown that would "capture the gray-blue of my eyes." It
was even more spectacular than her dress at solstice. I tried to
tell her that it didn't matter what I wore, but she was of a different opinion.

"This is a night to be proud," Ella declared brazenly, as
she helped brush out my scarlet red locks. "Whether our names
are called or not, we completed a year where others have failed.
That is not something anyone can take away from us."

We finished dressing, and I linked my arm in Ella's as we
exited the barracks. Outside Alex was waiting for us, looking
handsome in the same clothes he had worn for the solstice.

"Ready?" His eyes shown unusually bright as he took
my friend's arm.

"There's no going back now."

The three of us began our slow march down the path to
the Academy. We greeted our families at the door, and continued ahead of them as we made our way to the grand atrium.
The place was packed from the hundreds of faces standing all
around, and as one of the last groups to arrive, we were forced
to wait at the back of the room.

At every pillar of the atrium, giant torches of crystalline
blue flame flickered magnificently. At the center loomed the
enormous stairwell and its many-paned window with the stun-

ning view of the Sjeka sea. Standing right before it were Master
Barclae, the Three, Sir Piers, Masters Eloise, Isaac, Cedric,
Ascillia and Narhari.

At the base of the stairs, King Lucius and his two sons
stood expectantly, all dressed in their choice colors and fitted
cloaks. Priscilla stood close beside them, looking resplendent in
a red and gold dress fitted in rubies that flared dramatically at
its base. She and Darren's arms were linked, much like mine
had been moments before with Ella and Alex.

I swallowed at the sour taste in my mouth and forced my
gaze to remain at the top of the stair.

Minutes later, Constable Barrius squeezed his way
through the crowd and up the well to stoop beside the Master
of the Academy. He whispered something, and the man cleared
his throat expectantly.

A hushed silence fell over the room.

"I have waited a very long time for this moment," Master Barclae announced. "Ten months ago, one hundred and
twenty-two naïve, young faces stood in this very room. I told
them that half would not make it past the first few months. I
told them that they would make no friends. I told them that
they were wasting my time."

He scanned the audience, letting the effect of his words
sink in. "I did everything I could to encourage them to pack
their bags and leave the very next day. When that did not
work, I had Sir Piers and Master Cedric take them out to the
mountains with the sole purpose that they were not to return
until we had lost the first five. I celebrated with a ball when we
half the class resigned. And I have continued to parade their
loss until we were left with the forty-three standing in front of
us now.

"The forty-three first-years in this room are the culmination of everything a true mage should be. While they may not
have the potential necessary to continue their studies, these
young men and women represent the effort and dedication I
strive to maintain during my reign at this Academy. With

that, I'd like to call forward the fifteen who will be continuing on to the exalted apprenticeships that the Council and Crown are so proud to bestow..."

Master Barclae pulled a tightly rolled scroll from his robes, and Barrius held his torch close so that the formidable man could read from his list.

"For Alchemy, I call forward Piper, Julian, Thomas, Ruth, and Damien."

The five first-years rushed forward. I barely caught a glimpse of my spritely friend as she raced up the stairwell and shook the hand of Barclae and the masters, one by one. When the commotion had finished and the clapping had ceased, Master Barclae had the five new apprentices of Alchemy stand across the right rail of the ascending staircase.

"In the faction of Restoration, I would like to invite Ronan, Alexander—"

My twin turned ghastly white. If Ella hadn't been there to steady him, I am sure he would have fainted. When she finally released him he was looking up at the stairs with the biggest eyes I had ever seen. Ella had to gently nudge him forward before he actually began to move.

"—Kiera, Muriel, and Kaylein to the stand." Barclae watched as the five fumbling first-years found their way up the steps to shake hands and then stand at the left spiral of the stairs.

"And finally, for the faction of Combat, among the twenty-two young men and women that beat out all odds... I welcome Prince Darren..."

The young man with eyes as dark as night itself stepped forward.

"Eve."

The small girl pushed her way through the crowd to join the non-heir at the top of the steps.

"Ella."

My friend screamed and ran forward. There were a couple of laughs among the audience.

"Ray."

My opponent from the first trial nodded solemnly and found his way to the center of the dais.

"And finally, for the last apprenticeship of the evening..."

My heart stopped.

I knew it was foolish to hope, especially when Master Barclae still hadn't called *her* name, but I still held on. More than anything, I wanted the Master of the Academy to say mine.

"Lady Priscilla of Langli."

I watched as she ascended the steps. I watched as her dress glistened along the dais. I even watched as she accepted Master Barclae's outstretched hand.

The girl smiled prettily, shaking the hands of the masters to her right, and that was when the piercing jealousy tore its way across my chest. It continued to bury itself as Priscilla took her place beside the prince.

I could feel hot tears starting to pour down my face, but I was powerless to stop them.

The final five apprentices stood just below Master Barclae, facing their audience on the center stair.

A slow clapping started. It continued, on and on until the room was a thundering storm of applause.

A hand slid in to grip my own and I looked down to see my younger brother. Derrick said nothing. He just held my hand tightly, letting me grieve amongst the clamor of excited voices.

I would be happy for my friends, for my twin, but this moment was too soon. Alex, Ruth, and Ella were somewhere up there with the other twelve apprentices, living out their wildest dreams.

I was not.

And it hurt more than words could tell.

Master Barclae motioned for everyone to settle down so that he could start a speech. "Let us all congratulate our newest order of apprentices—"

I could not stay any longer. It was too much. I turned to leave, letting go of Derrick's hand to exit the crowd.

"Master Barclae." The voice of the Black Mage was urgent.

The Master of the Academy sounded irate. "Yes, what is it Marius?"

"My colleagues and I would like to invite one more to take the stand."

I froze, slowly turning to see the Master of the Academy give the Black Mage a strange look.

"We already have our fifteen."

"Yes," the man agreed, "but I am enacting my right as a member of the Council to include another apprentice in today's ceremony."

"But it has always been fifteen!"

"In the beginning it was more." The Black Mage stepped forward to face the crowd and address his startled audience. "But it was too many. Too little magic. We lost more lives than we gained... Yet, it has always been acknowledged that the number could change, should others arise with the potential we require." He pulled back his hood so that everyone could hear his next words clearly: "And I believe today to be that day."

I couldn't breathe. It was too much to hope. I'd never considered the possibility...

"My dearest Ryiah." The Black Mage found me in the audience with a grin. "Will you please join me, as the *final* apprentice of Combat?"

My heartbeat fell to the floor. I stood motionless, afraid that if I moved for even a second the dream would end.

"Ryiah." Derrick was tugging on my arm. "Ryiah, you've got to get up there."

*This is real.*

The audience fell silent as I walked forward, and the sea of people slowly parted to let me approach the steps. As I drew forward I caught sight of Alex's grin. Ella was beaming.

I could also see the loathing in Priscilla's eyes.

As I passed the prince, Darren gave the slightest nod, the barest semblance of a smile on his lips. His eyes danced as they met mine, and I realized suddenly that the answer to his earlier question was yes. Yes, the non-heir was a friend. It didn't matter that he was betrothed. My feelings didn't matter one bit. Because there had been no shock in his eyes when I had climbed the stair just now—Darren, Prince Darren, the sometimes-bane-of-my-existence, had put faith in a future that even I had never bothered to foresee.

Trembling, I took the hand of the Black Mage and then continued across the line. Eventually, I finished shaking the masters' hands and returned to my spot at the end of the row, right beside Ella.

Master Barclae strode forward to address the audience, again: "Ladies and gentleman, I give you the fif—the sixteen apprentices of our Academy. Please give them the applause they deserve."

This time when the clapping and shouting started, it never stopped.

# ABOUT THE AUTHOR

**Rachel E. Carter** is a young adult author who hoards coffee and books. She has a weakness for villain and bad boy love interests. When not writing, she is usually reading, and when not reading she is usually asleep. To her, the real world is Hogwarts and everything else is a lie.

*The Black Mage* is Rachel's first YA fantasy series, with many more to come. She loves to interact with fellow readers & aspiring writers, and here is a list of places you can find her online:

**Official Site:** www.rachelecarter.com
**Facebook:** www.facebook.com/theblackmageauthor
**Instagram:** https://instagram.com/rachelcarterauthor
**Twitter:** https://twitter.com/recarterauthor
**Pinterest:**www.pinterest.com/recarterauthor
**Tumblr:** http://rachelcarterauthor.tumblr.com
**Goodreads:** www.goodreads.com/rachelcarterauthor
**Email:** rachelcarterauthor@gmail.com

CPSIA information can be obtained at www.ICGtesting.com
Printed in the USA
LVOW11s2327300116

473030LV00003B/61/P